# KEAHI'S LEGACY

## THE EMERALD SCALE

# KEAHI'S LEGACY

## THE EMERALD SCALE

\* \* \* \*

BY

DOMINICK RUSSO

\* \* \* \*

ILLUSTRATIONS BY E. YUDA WAHYUDIANGGA

FILM CHOPS PUBLISHING

MOVIES OF THE MIND

FOR MY PARENTS

AND ANYONE ELSE THAT WILL LIKE MY WRITING

AS MUCH AS THEY DO.

✳ ✳ ✳ ✳

Russo, Dominick

Keahi's Legacy the Emerald Scale / by Dominick Russo

p.    cm.

Summary: A young boy learns of his destiny, that to his surprise

is not playing football, but to save a world unknown to him by

returning the Elemental Scales.

ISBN 978-1-7328110-0-3

Printed in the U.S.A.

First American edition, September 2018

# CONTENTS

# CONTENTS

# CONTENTS

# KEAHI'S LEGACY

## THE EMERALD SCALE

# 1

## ROASTED

**F**reakin' rituals. My ideal situation would have been to never overhear Chad "Steps" Taylor (the senior quarterback that was known for his legs more than his arm) talking with a couple of his cronies about it. There would be absolutely no easy way out of this and I would have to get creative to avoid the madness.

I sat at my desk, my bag halfway slung over my shoulder, my foot tapping at every second of the ticking clock. Everyone else wasted time socializing, and while no one else talked to me anyways, I had a plan to get out before it all started. That is until Mr. Walker, my history teacher, had to do the most teacher thing he could do.

"Mr. Anderson, put your bag down. Class isn't over yet."

We weren't doing anything. It was the last period of my first day of high school, homework was assigned, Mr. Walker had completely checked out for the day, and rituals were planned. I didn't have time to stick around.

"Finn."

Hank, one of the other freshman that would be inevitably doomed, attempted to get my attention away from the clock as it ticked away the last 2 minutes of the day.

"Finn."

Reluctantly, I turned around.

"What are you doing tonight? A few of us are going to Cane's house to have a Halo tournament."

Dang it, that did sound awesome. It was the only thing I actually did after school, but never with anyone else.

"What do you think? I heard you're insane at Halo."

The clock kept ticking down; I really didn't have time to talk. There was no way that he was going to make it to play Halo if Steps got to him first. More importantly, if I didn't high tail it out of there, I was going to get it too.

The bell rang, school was over, and I was screwed.

"That sounds good," I told him, "but I overheard one of the seniors talking about some senior ritual that's gonna go down in about 5 minutes. If I don't get out of here.... Well look at me. I don't survive that kind of thing."

I was one of those skinny nerds. Not blessed with height either. I was the one that got shoved into lockers, not the type that got their lunch stolen away because I brought a buffet of pudding snacks with me to lunch everyday.

2

"No big deal, I've got a way out. My brother showed me a back way to the school he always snuck in at when he was late. Let's go."

Hank jumped out of his chair as we all shuffled into the hallway. We snaked through the flow of kids shuffling to the front doors to the awaiting seniors, as we made our way to the back.

Hank pulled me through the cafeteria, running right passed the lone janitor, which cleaned like a robot through the tables, who was oblivious to the escape.

We leaped over the pay counter through the kitchen and the sinks until we reached the back door to freedom. Hank stopped, "These doors are always open because the cafeteria ladies smoke like chimneys. But keep this place a secret, we don't need the entire school ruining this for us."

"No problem."

Hank took off down the street, "Meet at Cane's place at 8, it's on the corner of 5th and Chestnut. You'll see us there."

I gave him a thumbs up with a sigh of relief it wasn't a set up. I made my way to the front edge of the school and peaked around. Buses began filling up and kids shuffled around saying bye to their friends. It all seemed normal; did they not go through with the ritual? This was high school, what else did the seniors have to look forward to every start of school?

I heard a screech and almost jumped out of my cover. Behind me a small red bird was perched on top of the school. Its head craned around to look at me below as it hopped closer, revealing its chest that looked as if it was glowing red. I backed all the way to the sidewalk trying to get a better look. It was tantalizing. I had never seen a bird that looked like that and couldn't take my eyes off of it, my mouth agape, until I heard a squeal coming from the opposite direction.

A recognizable white, old style Corvette with the top down whipped out of the parking lot. What was even more recognizable was Steps in the driver seat. I ran for it, whether or not he was coming after me I didn't want him to recognize me. However, as I ran, the bird swooped off the top of the building, stopping me in awe. The birds wingspan had to have been at least 6 feet! It circled around gracefully, but in an instant, I ducked as it swooped back towards me and hit me with a warm gust of wind before flying off into the trees.

The bird was the least of my worries at that point. At least it had flown off in the opposite direction, Steps was racing up on me and unfortunately noticed me walking. I bolted towards the forest, down and across the parking lot a little ways as Steps eased off the pedal, turning into the empty parking lot and cruising behind me, honking his horn and laughing. I swerved around trying to shake him but he followed right behind me, getting dangerously close to my backside.

Moments before I was worm food, I hopped over the fence that ran alongside the parking lot, and ran for my life, thankfully he whipped his Corvette around, "Don't worry, I'll get you next time!" He yelled and laughed before squealing his tires again out of the back parking lot.

I kept running for my life. He targeted me, which had to mean he knew I overheard him talking about the ritual and dodged it. Could this be worse than getting the ritual out of the way on the first day of school? I was now in Steps' crosshairs and was poised to be bullied for the rest of the school year. I just wanted to get home.

\* \* \* \*

I spent the first few hours after school finishing up my homework and freshening up my videogame skills (as if I needed it) until my mom finally came home from work. I had already made myself dinner and sat on the couch since we never really were all together at this time to use the dining table.

She quietly walked passed me which was our normal interaction. That shouldn't be misconstrued as she was a lousy mother, she just worked a lot at Keller's Grocery Store, not because she had to but because she always had since high school while my Dad worked on his business at home and was only ever free on Sundays. We still had a good relationship I guess, distant, but they were always there for me if I needed them.

I would usually let her break the silence. If I tried to talk to her too much right when she got home her mind was too scatter brained from work to hold a conversation.

"First day of school went alright?" She finally asked.

"Yea, pretty typical I guess." I kept my head down, replaying being chased down by a Corvette and a bird trying to attack me. Of course once her mind was off work she picked up on my demeanor.

"Anything unusual happen?"

I thought about it for a minute, "Yea," I didn't want her to worry about the Steps situation, "I was invited over to a friend's house to play videogames."

Her eyes widened, even I wasn't as surprised as she was. I'm not that terrible to be around, I was just quiet.

"That's great!" She exclaimed, "When is that happening?"

"Actually right now, I better get going."

"Alright, well have fun." She grabbed me and gave me a hug before I had a chance to run off.

"I will," I said. My Dad began shuffling out of his office as I ran out the front door and could hear my name being thrown around as I closed the door behind me.

It was a 15-minute walk from my house, however I stopped on the corner of 4th and Chestnut when I saw Cane's house. Streetlights were just beginning to turn on, keeping my area lit, as I paced the corner. I took a few deep breaths and reassured myself, "they invited you, they wanted you here."

I could see some commotion through the living room window. Everyone else must have already been there which just made it worse. I shook it off, they invited me to play video games, which happened to be my forte, I was in the perfect position to show off and maybe they would invite me over again.

I watched the sun setting at the peak of the trees. I knew it must be getting late and Hank and Cane had to have been wondering where I was. However, as the sun finally disappeared behind the trees, I saw the peaks of the trees illuminate in near perfect sync. The same bird from after school came soaring out from behind the trees, wings wholly outstretched, glowing red. It flew towards me, staying high in the air.

I stopped pacing, looking around to see if anyone was nearby, a strong sense of interest washed over me, I scanned the area to see if anyone else could see this bird, but the street was a ghost town. It was as if the Loch Ness monster just swam up to me; I was positive, this wasn't just an average house sparrow. I looked around again, it was eerily a ghost town. A sharp screech, pierced my ears, forcing me to look back up, the bird was now circling me.

My feeling of interest quickly faded; the Loch Ness monster was no longer swimming near me, it was targeting me, and my heart started fluttering. "But this was not the Loch Ness monster," I told myself, "the Loch Ness monster is a giant sea serpent from Hell, this was a bird... that was closing in on me.... with a beak as sharp as a razor blade... and glowing red.... From Hell." My heart felt like it dropped into my

6

stomach, I looked around for shelter as if the bird was going to dive for the kill.

A light turned on at the house on the corner I was standing at, so I ran off, trying to not look suspicious and went up to Cane's house and rang the doorbell frantically. I quickly heard some shuffling and what sounded like Cane and Hank fighting, before Hank reached the door laughing.

"I thought you were gonna stand us up!"

I smiled and shook my head no, pushing my way in to get out of the scope of the bird.

"Come on in, we got the game set up, you can play the winner."

"Cool."

As I walked into the living room, I noticed a couple other kids from the Wands and Wizards Club at school. It was actually a pretty cool club. They usually spent the beginning of the year making their wands with some awesome LEDs and electronics to make them look like they would cast real spells.

I sat down on the couch next to a few of Cane and Hank's other friends from the baseball team. I peaked out the window and tried to convince myself the glowing red of the sky was just from the sunset. I struggled to make conversation with them; even Hank seemed distant when he got around his other friends.

I noticed him looking out of the window every few minutes as well. The kids from the Wands and Wizards Club were zoned into the game and another was too busy showing off his wand to an uninterested Cane.

A cars light came into the living room for just a moment and Cane stood up.

"My parents just got home, I'm gonna see if they brought us any drinks."

Hank jumped up with him and said to me in passing, "yea, just wait here, we'll be back. You like Coke?"

I nodded, still silent, but as they left the living room I went to the window and saw the all too familiar white shine of the Corvette that chased me down earlier. I didn't care that someone had finally invited me to play videogames; there wasn't a shred of desire to hang out with Steps. So I turned around to sneak out while every one was fixated on the TV, but as I did, Hank and Cane's friends were blocking both entrances to the living room.

All hope was lost. I was doomed. Whichever way you want to look at it, I knew I had fallen right into the ritual. They didn't want to get busted at school so they lured the freshmen losers into groups outside of school. They were smarter than I thought.

Steps and his cronies busted in through the front door. The Wands and Wizards Club was completely caught off guard as they grabbed them and forced them outside. Steps obviously came for me.

I jumped over the couch, trying to make a break for it, however Steps tackled me, throwing me into the table lamp as it crashed onto the ground. I kicked my feet, connecting with the side of Steps' head. He grunted and backed off for a moment, giving me just enough time to jump up and try to make another escape, but one of Hank's friends blocked my way and sent a fist into my gut. As I keeled over in pain, Steps grabbed me, picking me up as I struggled to get away.

He carried me out of the house and threw me onto the front yard with the other nerds. I tried to scramble away, but there was a reason he was nicknamed Steps. He was fast. He grabbed me by the shirt, lifting me off the ground to see Hank and his friends with their phones up as I felt the premier bully act. It was a staple in every bullies diet. A wedgie.

As my feet hovered just inches above the ground, my face scrounged up in pain, Steps and his cronies (also giving wedgies to the other nerds) lined up for a group photo.

Hank snapped the picture. That was it. Before my second day of high school, my picture was plastered on the Internet along with the rest of the lower level freshman, from my year and every year before. It was like an online yearbook for all the freshman nerds. My high school existence was officially marked as a nerd, a loser, a geek, anyway you put it, I was now the target of every bully at school.

For that night, though, the ritual was over. Steps roughed me up a little bit more, rubbing my face in the dirt and throwing me into a pudding snack nerd that fell on top of me, crushing me with all 250 pounds of blubber, before the seniors took off in their cars while Hank and the rest of the freshman that dodged the ritual, ran back inside to act like nothing happened, obviously not inviting the rest of us geeks back in to play.

I dusted myself off and picked the wedgie out, the other nerds, didn't even stick around for that long. They ran off home, wedgies still at full fledge. Lesson learned.

I followed suit, running home without looking back. If I was going to avoid an interrogation from my Mom I was going to have to pull it together and just go to bed immediately.

When I reached my front door, I wiped my eyes and walked in. The house was dark, I could see my Mom dozing on the couch and assumed my Dad had already gone off to sleep. She only perked up when she heard me come in.

"How did it go?"

"It was fine, pretty much how I could've expected it to go," I said as I hurried up the stairs to my room.

"Wait, is everything ok?" She said in an attempt to get me to eleaborate. I guess I didn't hide the dirt on my face or the dried blood on my lip very well.

I still ignored her, closing my bedroom door quickly behind me. I closed my window in an irrational fear that Steps might come crawling through for round two. I wiped my the sweat off my face on a dirty white t-shirt before throwing it back onto the ground and crawling into bed.

I didn't want to be a wake anymore, sometimes to get over a bad day you just need to start another one. I was exhausted from everything that happened and easily closed my eyes, dozing off into sleep.

Until.

Click...

Click, click....

Click...

I woke up. My eyes still closed, I listened for a moment but too tired to care, I started to doze again.

Click....

My eyes shot open when I realized the clicking noise sounded like a razor-sharp beak beating the glass on my window. I slowly swung my legs off the bed, trying to step around the mess on the floor. I stood in front of my window, looking carefully for scratch marks. I gazed out the window, but there was nothing, I looked out the other window, and the neighborhood was quiet, the leaves on the trees even stood still, and the dark was fading, before you could even see the sun.

I had a feeling that bird was around, every time I replayed the "click" in my head, a jolt would go through my heart, and I could still feel it. I was awake for the night.

\* \* \* \*

I finished up my morning routine, still bummed from the night before but in high hopes that day 2 of high school would be better than day 1. At least I had the weekend to look forward to after today. My Mom drove me to the school in the mornings, however left it up to me to find a way home after school since she would be at work. She dropped me off at the front doors and I blended in with the other kids, quietly making my way to my locker like a school of fish, weaving our way through the halls.

My homeroom was unfortunately with Mr. Walker again. He would sip on his coffee and not even so much as give me a nod in the morning when I walked in. I was always the first kid in class, as the others would rush in at the last second before the bell rang.

I saw Hank making his way in as the bell rang the moment he stepped in, a newfound pride in his step. He was officially a cool kid in high school. As he strutted passed me he lightly punched me in the arm.

"How's the crack feeling today?" He laughed

My head sunk lower towards my desk.

He sat behind me and leaned in, "Don't worry about it Finn, Steps only has a year left, then there will be a new wave of kids for next years seniors and you'll be forgotten. It's just a part of high school."

"It's a bit different being on the other side of the ritual, though, isn't it?"

Hank paused for a minute, "Well just think, in a few years we'll both be seniors and you can be a part of giving the wedgies with us."

It didn't make me feel any better. If I had any luck I could stop the madness. If I had any more luck remaining after that I wouldn't still be getting bullied as a senior.

For once I was relieved to hear Mr. Walker start our history lesson, as he asked everyone to quiet down and got Hank to finally back off my neck and stop talking to me.

I spent very little time in the hallway during my 2nd day of high school and kept my head as low as I could through class without being accused of sleeping.

Other than Steps trying to hunt me down a couple times between classes, things seemed to be getting back to normal after lunch. Like I said before, I was not the target during lunchtime.

Even though there weren't any crazy rituals that were planned today, at least that I knew of, I still sat on the edge of my chair, watching the clock tick down before I was released. Hank wasn't bothering me anymore, he picked up on my vibes and I was able to rush out as soon as the bell rang. Getting a head start on the other schools of fish cascading out of the classrooms. I actually did use the back door of the school through the cafeteria again to avoid any unnecessary confrontation. It worked. I was on my way home ahead of anyone else that would care to bother me.

I just wanted to get home and start my weekend relaxing, watching a lot of cartoons and playing video games, alone of course. I was already dreading going back to school and didn't want to think about it the entire weekend. At this point, I would rather do anything other than go back to school Monday. I wouldn't be able to avoid Steps for the entire school year and another confrontation with him was imminent.

I strolled along the sidewalk in my neighborhood, my head down, completely spaced out. As I thought about it, I couldn't remember the entire walk from school to where I am now. A wave of heat blew past me. Usually I could make it home without breaking a sweat, but it was hot today. Another gust of hot air blew my hair to the side, and I looked around. Another blood-curdling screech sent a chill up my spine. I frantically scanned my surroundings; I knew that freakin' bird was back, but why?

I walked further down the street, my house coming into view. I still kept an eye out for the bird; I would get a glimpse every now and again, a blur of red disappearing into a tree, a bush, behind a house. There might have been more than one this time or was there even one at all. I felt paranoid, I've never felt

like this before, I never had a reason too, but was I seriously seeing a bird at all?

As I reached the end of my driveway, something
didn't feel right. The neighborhood, my house, it
seemed quieter than usual. I didn't feel like I was
home. The one place you're supposed to feel safe at, I
wanted to run away from; ignoring the feeling I
walked up the slope and into my front door.

I closed the door behind me, and it echoed
throughout the house. I took a moment and looked
around cautiously. I saw the office door, where my
Dad spent most of his time, creaked open. I walked
over and peered my head in, slowly opening the door.

The computer was on, with a Word document
open on it. A wave of heat covered my face as I peeked
farther in. My Dad's chair was empty, the entire room
was empty, but the fireplace was on. The heat in the
office was almost unbearable; there was no sense for it
to be lit. I went to take a step forward to turn it off.

"Something I can help you with, sport?"

I turned around to see my Dad standing curiously, a plate with a sandwich in one hand and a beer
in the other.

"No," I said, "I didn't know if anyone was
home."

"Just me," he replied, "Mom's not home, so I
had to leave the dungeon to get myself something to
eat."

I stood in front of the door, unsure what else to
say.

"Well I have just a little bit more I have to get
done today."

I forgot I was blocking the doorway to the office, "Oh right, sure, I'm just gonna be in my room."

He nodded, "Your mother said you've been acting strangely; I'm starting to see it. What's been going
on?"

I rolled my eyes, "Nothing, honestly, I'm fine ."
I tried to make up the best excuse I could, when in fact

between this stupid bird and having to watch my back in the halls, I was starting to stress.

"I was the same way when I started high school, you'll get used to it, find a good friend you like to hang around with, and it'll just seem normal after that. Choose wisely, though, going through high school is a hell of a lot easier with a good friend."

"I know, I'll be fine."

He stepped into his office, "Man it's hot in here."

He reminded me the fireplace was on, and I peeked in. Of course, it was off now. He walked over to the window and opened it up.

"Try to let in some fresh air, is the AC on?" He asked me.

"I think so; it feels ok out here."

He walked over to the vent and made sure it was open and tried to feel if there was air coming out. "Feels like it's on. That's strange."

My dad faced me, thinking to hisself. Once again I saw red. Sitting on the windowsill was the bird, it looked me in the eyes this time as if it was human, and then it flew away, a warm breeze coming in through the window.

"I'm going to my room now," I turned for the stairs.

"I'll let you know when dinner is ready," he called his voice fading as I ran up the stairs.

At the top of the stairs, I heard the screech again, from inside the house. I looked back and saw my dad sitting in his chair, he rolled forward, the chair squeaking every time it leaned back. Now I felt paranoid; something wasn't right.

I ran into my room and sat down on my bed, my face buried in my hands.

Click...

I immediately looked up at my window; the bird was perched on the windowsill, staring in. I stood up and threw my pillow at the window. The bird took off, extending its long wings, to full length. I paced my room, the temperature quickly rising, sweat beading up on my forehead.

The floor began to get hot; dark brown spots started appearing on the hardwood floors. I jumped up onto my bed, feeling like I was playing a game of "the floor is lava!" But it was much more severe than that. I saw smoke rising from outside of my window and ran over. Smoke was barreling out the first-floor windows, I looked for my dad outside, or fire trucks, or a neighbor but there was nothing, it was surreal. I ran for my door, fire slowly eating away at my floor. I swung it open and became blanketed by a dark cloud.

I immediately fell to my knees, coughing uncontrollably; I tried to crawl through the house.

"DAD!" I screamed, knowing if he hadn't found me yet there was something horribly wrong.

"DAD!" I yelled again, waiting for a response, but still nothing. The smoke and the heat were unbearable; my hands were a beat red, sweat dripping off my face with every move. I tried to yell again, but the smoke was too much, the room started to spin and distort, I began coughing uncontrollably; I wondered where my parents were. I needed help.

I fell on my back; I knew that bird had something to do with this. The fire came on so quickly. I began to feel sick until I felt a weight on my chest. I struggled to look up, and regain my vision. I could faintly make out a small red bird, sitting there, looking at me. I didn't have the strength to move, so I let it sit there, maybe it was here to help me.

Warmth crawled up my legs, and I looked down. There was nothing but fire. Strangely enough, it didn't hurt; it just felt warm, like crawling into a bath. The warmth continued onto my back. The bird hopped around on my chest. As my vision nearly faded entirely, I saw the bird leap off into flight, straight into the fire as the fire grew around my body like a blanket. My vision was gone, I began sinking into the floor, further and further, my conscious slowly slipping until one last screech, I began to fall faster my conscious now completely gone.

# 2

# D'HANIN

In my unconscious state, I could feel myself flying through the air. There was nothing visual for me to know that I was flying but I could feel the wind blowing past me, nothing was holding me up, and I wasn't holding onto anything. I couldn't even tell if I had a body anymore, it was just my soul flying through the unknown.

A light finally broke the darkness; I couldn't tell where it was coming from though. As I continued through the unknown, breaks of light would appear and disappear in moments. I couldn't even look around to find it until I didn't have to look for it anymore. The light was sticking around, growing brighter, and brighter until I

17

could see a flame once again, and the all too familiar crackling of fire breaking the silence.

I remembered the way I died at that point, consumed by fire, and I was about to face it once again. Out of all the times I had been to church, I knew what fire meant, I just didn't know why.

As I passed through the growing flames, the world began to come back to me. I could feel my body again, my heart beating, my lungs lifting my chest, and my breath on my lips. I could now feel the ground pressed on my back, the sun beating on my skin, and suddenly a massive splash of water covering my entire body. My eyes opened, wincing at the brightness, before being able to see. I looked at the dirt I was sitting in, I thought I might be in Florida, if Florida hadn't seen rain in five years. At first glance, it all looked strangely familiar, but there was something about this place that didn't feel like home.

"Ay, bakin' in tha sun -- like that you are gonna start ta s--smell like a freshly cooked meal."

I looked around to see a gleaming smile shown down on me. In a slow, deep voice, "What are you doin' lyin' there like that?"

I couldn't find the words to reply, he just towered over me, smiling down. He seemed a little slow, shorter than I was but rugged. He had a leather bag thrown over his shoulder that was brimming to the top with what looked to be animals. He had an under bite and seemed to speak with his tongue.

"Not much fer words I s--s'pose?" He reached a hand down, grabbing the back of my shirt and lifted me up. I struggled to gain my balance, falling back down to my knees, trying to stop everything from spinning.

"Ay, you all right? What is yer business here?" He said starting to sound more concerned.

If I were dead, wouldn't he know it? I looked around again at this world, and this man trying to keep me up, I was sure I couldn't be dead.

18

I attempted to let out a few words, trying to ask where I was, but the moment I opened my mouth to speak, it felt like knives were ripping through my throat.

The man stood up straight, looking puzzled, "Come on, let's get ya back ta town," he reached his hand out again, for me to grab onto this time, "tha name's Leibo Naihue, Lib fer short."

I grabbed onto his hand, and he helped me up. My knees wobbled but I was able to get everything to stop spinning when I was directly upright. His arm swung around my shoulder, dragging me along.

"I'll take ya -- fer a drink maybe ya just need somethin' in your stomach."

I tried to pull myself away from him a little bit. I had no idea who this guy was or where he was taking me, but he had a grip on me a python would be proud of.

"I'll be fine," I managed to say.

"Tha's tha s--spirit, just remain positive," he exclaimed, apparently missing what I was trying to tell him.

I looked up as he dragged me towards a giant entryway to the city. Guards lined the front of the wall as well as the top. I couldn't imagine what kind of kingdom would lay behind these gates.

I didn't know where I was, how I got there, or who this man was. For the first time in my life, I was utterly lost. I'd been lost before, like when I was six and wandered into the toy store in the mall without my parents noticing, but this was much worse. In the mall, I knew I could go to the counter for help from an employee, or I could've flagged down a police officer. I still cried my eyes out, but I knew I had help. I was entirely on my own now, lost, with no idea where to go or who to talk to. I didn't know what I was going to do, I didn't know who I was going to trust.

We reached the entrance, without missing a step, the doors immediately started opening, the guards stood perfectly still. They apparently knew who this man was, and he knew it. He didn't even look at the guards or slow down, the doors opened correctly at his pace. It made me fear him even more.

Before I could see what was behind the giant doors Lib spoke with a smirk, "Relax, it ain't anythin' special." He was right. Behind these enormous, extravagant doors with guards ready to take down an intruder, was a one way, dirt road town with collapsing buildings. With the doors completely open he said, "It's jus' K--Kautun... of D'Hanin."

We walked down the dirt road, his arm still wrapped around me, I did my best to look around, but his gigantic arm blocked most of my view. The buildings were pretty small, only one had a second story at the very end of the street. We continued walking passed a short field, it was completely dried up; an old man walked along the rows and poured water over them almost mechanically, with no expression.

There were four houses that all shared the same backyard in the very middle of the street, they were all identical, but the extreme wear on them made them each unique. There weren't very many people roaming the streets either, it was a quiet town.

I still didn't know where I was, but somehow this village made me a little less frightened, and I finally got my voice back, "Where are we? What are you going to do to me?"

"And 'e speaks!" Lib shouted, "I was beginnin' to feel a bit uncomftable."

"I just want to know what's going on," I said a bit panicky.

"Whaddya -- mean what is going on? I just thought I'd take ya fer a drink. I should be askin' you why you were layin' outside tha gates."

I looked up at him, trying to pull away from his grip, "I don't know why I was, I don't even know, how I got here. One moment my house was burning down, the next moment I woke up out there."

"Ah," he nodded, "so you was affected by tha Obsidian Scale as well, I ran into a bit o' trouble with it as well on a s--scavenging trip. My campfire took over my entire camp before I was able ta get it out. Great idea them Elemental Scales were, wish it had been k-- kept in his head though. "

"No, I don't know anything about a scale," I said getting irritated, "I'm not from this place."

"Not from this place? Then where are you from?"

I didn't know how to explain it. At the risk of sounding like an alien or something, "I'm from Earth."

"Earth? Never heard of it, must be on the northern curve. Still surprises me ya never heard o' tha Four Scales."

I rolled my eyes; I apparently wasn't explaining myself very well.

Rolling his eyes, "I will s'plain about them after we get a couple b--brews."

We were in front of the two-story building, which I now recognized as the Unicorn's Nest. There was a rustic sign hanging above the doors, swinging back and forth looking about ready to fall off the chain.

I looked to my right and saw D'Hanin was much bigger than I thought, well, compared to how small I initially thought it was. The road curved down going about twice the distance we had walked from the gates. It was all the same, little run down buildings except for one. It was about the size of all the build- ings in D'Hanin put together and looked nice, well kept.

Lib shoved me into the Unicorn's Nest, and I fi- nally got excited to see something in this world, but first I had to figure out what I was here for.

The place was full of people, drinking, and eat- ing. One waitress strolled around talking to everyone and filling their drinks. But as the farmer watered his crops mechanically the patrons all ate and drank mechanically. Giant Venus Flytraps were scattered throughout the tavern, almost as tall as me, slowly swaying until they would catch sight of a fly and quickly snap out and grab it. It was nothing like the ones I knew but then again, what in this world was?

The waitress was the only one who seemed to have any life. She seemed young to be a waitress, with short brown hair and a naturally alluring look. She carried a knife that went all the way down her thigh. She definitely didn't look mean, but she definitely looked as if she had been in a few battles of her own.

We sat down at a table, as she waved at us, letting us know she would be over in just a minute. We sat in awkward silence for a moment, as I watched everyone else, feeling out of place. I had to speak up.

"Can you please help me, I need you to understand, I am not from this world. I remember being burned alive when my home caught on fire. Is this Heaven or purgatory, or a form of the afterlife I'm in?"

I could tell Lib was trying really hard to understand, "Whaddya mean yer not from this world?"

"Like I said, I thought I had died, anyone in my world probably believes the same." I thought about my parents, at that point. I thought to myself, *"Did my Dad make it out? What was my Mom going through right now?"* It sent my heart tumbling into my stomach; I had to focus on getting back if I could so I could see them again and make sure they're okay.

I continued, "I have never seen anything like this place. I'm used to big buildings, and cars, buses, towns without gates or guards, and videogames."

He was processing this at a languid pace, "You said you were -- dead by fire and then ya ended up in D'Hanin?"

"Yes," I exclaimed almost getting out of my chair for joy that he understood.

"Tha's not usual, are you a wizard or somethin' from where ya came from?"

"No, that type of stuff doesn't exist, the closest we can get is electronics and illusionists."

Lib took another moment to absorb the information, "As I told you -- before D'Hanin is in a dark time wit tha Four Scales gone. I don't think that you showin' up here was a mistake. How do you know about fire?"

"We have fire, and water, earth, wind, we have elements like what you were saying about those Scales."

"Wind?" He questioned and thought about it, "I never thought 'bout tha' as an element alone. Isn't w--wind created from -- tha elements bein' in motion?" A glazed look went across his face as he stared off into space, starting to go off on another tangent, I tried to reel him back in.

"So what are you trying to say about me showing up here wasn't a mistake?"

He looked back at me, "I think you're here to help us fight, tha Fade told me 'bout somethin' like this. We will have to alert him tha' you have come!"

About that time, the waitress showed up at our table setting the drinks down, "Lib! You have to keep calm, I don't need this place all riled up."

"Sorry Aliner, but this 'ere boy came from another world. B--By Fire."

"I know, I heard you discussing, but just keep it down, you'll need to get him to the Fade, let him handle it." She turned to me, "I'm sorry, I don't mean to be rude, my name is Alina, Aliner if you're Lib, "She smiled at him, but he had his mug up to his face, slurping down a black drink with a milkshake-like texture. I reached out to shake her hand, as I noticed her forearms were scarred, all the way up to her elbows. I tried to keep eye contact, as she shook my hand gently, "I'm Finn," after a brief pause I decided to add in, "Anderson," like it mattered. There was just something about her that made me nervous. I guess all girls did that but in a different way this time.

23

An obese man, yelled across the room at Alina, demanding more service. She raised a hand to him and before walking over to help said, "I hope you are here to help us, we need someone to give us even a sliver of hope."

I watched her as she left to help the patron, and then looked down at my drink.

"It's Spider Ale if you didn' know."

"I didn't," I said as I picked it up, feeling the iciness of the drink and rolling it around in the glass, "Is it alcohol?"

"What's alcohol? It's ta drink," he said, tipping it back once again, seeming a bit more airheaded the more he drank.

"So what am I doing here? What is going on?"

He set his drink down, "Righ,' so we need to get the Four Scales back. A hundred an' twen'y seven years ago a Light Summoner, Keahi, created the Four Scales ta protect D'Hanin. There was the Sapphire Scale of Karma, meant ta keep all inhabitants good and honest, the Obsidian Scale of Fire, meant ta control all fire within D'Hanin, the Amethyst Scale of Harmony ta prevent war breakin' out and causin' a divide amongst the people of D'Hanin, and las'ly the Emerald Scale of Plantation ta ensure all crops an' food would grow abundantly so we would never feel hungry."

I wasn't prepared to take in an overwhelming amount of information and did my best to keep up. Even though I could hardly stay awake in my U.S. History class, I was now getting a crash course in D'Hanin history. I took a swig of the Spider Ale without thinking. It was much better than expected; it perked me up, like drinking a potent energy drink. I think I felt a spider leg going down my throat though.

"So these scales, do they weigh how much good is in something? Or they weigh something?" I asked feeling stupid.

"No, No, No, they are not those kind of scales. They come from a dragon. You know like dragon scales." Lib paused for a moment, to make sure I was getting it.

"Right, dragon scales, got it. Makes sense." I said, now feeling really stupid.

Lib continued with his history lesson, "Ya see before Keahi was who he was, it was jus' everyone livin' in peace together. Until it stopped rainin' and caused the Great Drought which caused the Great Fire which destroyed half o' the world's crops, which in turn caused the Great War among the people, creatin' the territories, fightin' for what was left. It caused many people ta turn dark."

It was an exciting story, but I kept noticing the waitress look at me. I knew I must've been a sight to see, someone claiming to be from another world, but, besides my clothes and a lot paler skin, I looked exactly like them. I tried to act like I didn't notice her looking over, and concentrated on Lib's story.

"If ya can see the relation, Keahi collected tha scales from a dragon -- like I said before. No one knows what kind o' magic he used -- ta b--be able ta do it, but he harnessed the power o' the elements inside the dragon's scales to create the Elemental Scales for D'Hanin, to prevent anythin' bad like that ta happen again.

"So this Keahi guy, just waltz right into this dragon lair and plucks a couple scales off a dragon? Like, a real dragon?" I couldn't wrap my brain around someone talking about a dragon like it was a common animal. Lib looked at me strangely, *There's no way I'm alive right now,* I thought to myself.

"Yes," Lib said confused, "Dragons are terrifyin' but Keahi knew how ta handle 'em. Can I ge' back to the story?" Lib asked.

"Absolutely. Dragons and summoners, please continue." I said sarcastically.

Well, unfortunately, something even worse happened. There was a dark s--summoner who became powerful during tha' time and was unaffected by the Scales. Keahi kept 'im at bay and made D'Hanin the best place ta live. That is until 80 odd years ago 'e was confronted and killed on his quest to harness another element for tha fifth scale. Tha Four Scales were stolen by the dark summoner, Apaku and with tha Four Scales in the hands of a dark summoner their effects were reversed." Lib took a break and finished off his Spider Ale.

I looked down and realized I had drunk all of mine. Alina was immediately there to refill our glasses while Lib continued to talk. Patrons continued to bark orders at her, and since she was the only one that seemed to be working she didn't stay to hear the rest of Lib's story.

I started to put the pieces together and realized what he was talking about when he said it wasn't a mistake that I showed up here, "So these dragon scales have the elements in them, when the good guy had them they helped the elements thrive." Lib was nodding, looking to be concentrating as hard as I was so that we could get this story straight. "When the bad guy has them, the elements suffer? And you think - -"

"I think you are 'ere ta help get tha S--Scales back," Lib confirmed what I already knew.

"No, I can't just go get your scales for you! I don't know have a shred of knowledge about this world which should be enough to know that I'm not supposed to get them." I snapped back.

Lib sat back in his chair, "Maybe I have -- s-- said too much I just thought ya would have b-been excited to be a hero."

"What do I need to be a hero for? I'm not even a hero in my own world, and I'm perfectly happy with that."

"Why are you happy with that?" Lib said, "What is a life w--worth livin' if yer not a hero to at least one person?"

"Then let me go back to my own world and be a hero there!" I said, getting up and leaving the Unicorn's Nest. I wasn't a storming out type of person; I didn't like causing a scene, so I left Lib at the table quietly but as soon as I got outside, I had no idea where to go.

Lib followed me out shortly afterward, "Didn't mean ta get you upset. I just know if it w--were me I would be excited 'bout the chance."

"I just want to get back home, I'm not the one you guys were looking for, and I don't want to give you any false hopes that I'm meant to go on this quest to find these dragon scales."

"If tha's why you are even 'ere. Tha Fade will be tha one who will know." Lib said diffusing the situation, "Let me show you 'round the -- town there's nothin' we can do ta get you back home right now, so we might as well kill a bit o' time."

It didn't get my mind off anything, but I followed Lib anyway. The effects of losing the Four Scales were apparent now that I knew about them. Neighbors we're yelling at each other, kids were getting in fights, and the sun beat down on the already dried up plants, and with a strong wind, it looked as if 1 or 2 of these buildings might collapse.

Lib pointed out the essential shops, "That's tha Slayed Monster Smithy, you can get anythin' from an assassin blade to a bow and arrow made there, and there ya can learn how to use them weapons," he pointed out the fancier looking shop with big front windows. "If ya do start training I imagine the Fade will get your potions and drink from Okamai, over there. If ya need any clothes, books, or gifts, we have Lonua's."

I thought about why I would need to buy someone a gift right now, and I thought of my parents again, it was hard to wrap my brain around what was going on in this world, but what was even more difficult to grasp was the fact that I was dead in my world. Non-existent in the world I knew, existing in another world I knew nothing about. I had left my family heartbroken; I just wished I could let them know I was all right.

"Lib," he looked over at me, "I'm sorry, but I have a hard time understanding how I got here. I have family that believes I'm dead, because of this fire and now I ended up here?"

Lib thought for a moment, "I can't tell ya for s--sure, I've never heard anythin' like your story. I'm also not tha most well-rounded person here neither, I usually go to tha Fade with this kinda thing."

"Will he be able to help me understand?"

"I'm sure 'e will, he knows all the ins 'n outs o' this world. B--But my guess is you was needed here more than there, and somethin' greater than tha' brought ya here.

"But why me?" I understood what he was saying, but it didn't clear my mind at all.

"Cuz there is somethin' special about ya, I guess. Don't ask me what, I'm thinkin' too hard. Ya just gotta accept it sometimes."

Don't think, just do, is what he was telling me. My drum teacher in middle school gave me similar advice. He said I was overthinking about what my hands and feet were doing, and I just had to let them do their job.... I don't play drums anymore.

"You should not be so worried -- anyway there's no tellin' if that is what you are here for or not, I jus' know what I heard from tha Fade."

"But even so," I spat back, irritated, "By an unknown reason, I'm in a different universe. I feel completely lost."

"I understand. I have been on my own since I was 8 years old, I was lost more than I could even know I could be. Even b--back then I knew I wasn't real smart which made it all worse, then I found tha Fade here who was s--smart enough for both o' us. If it wasn't for him, I was gonna be like you -- almost was a freshly cooked meal fer the creatures."

I looked down at my feet as they kicked up little dust clouds, "What happened to your parents?"

"They lef' cuz they could not get me ta understand nothin.' They tried ta teach me how ta capture live creatures, but I kept ruinin' it. Ya see that was their business ta capture 'em and sell 'em ta breeders, farms, and tha what not. But I kept messin' the traps, I didn't understand how ta set 'em, and I set 'em off more times than anythin.' They couldn't take it no more, s--so they lef' me a little further away from where I found you."

"That's not really a reason to leave your child behind though is it?"

"I wouldn' think so. Tha Fade says they was killed by somethin.' Says 'e found 'em out there in the woods right before 'e found me," Lib looked away from me, his jaw clenched, "But I know."

I looked around the city, my situation didn't seem so bad anymore, "I'm glad you found me out there Lib. I don't know what I would've done if you weren't there."

He looked down at me and held back a gleaming smile. We stopped at the end of the road, and Lib held out a hand, presenting the large building I saw before we went into the Unicorn's Nest.

"This," Lib presented, "is the former home and arena of the legendary, Keahi Mehana.

I stared in awe of the building. It had been kept in such good shape, throughout the many years following Keahi's death. A stone statue of Keahi, wielding a blade stood at the foot of the entryway stairs.

"It was an arena as well?" I questioned, imagining the battles that took place and the entertainment that would bring joy to this sullen town.

"I s'pose I should've said a private arena. There wasn't a single person alive today that stood place in that arena. Only a handful of people left that heard the s--screams and s--sounds of clashing bronze -- and steel ringing through the city for hours all through the day and long through the night."

"A personal blood match? Sounds kind of dark doesn't it?"

"It was a differ'nt time," he said agreeing with me, "but let's get ya back ta the tavern, I'll have ta take ya ta meet tha Fade tomorra. His buildin' was closed up fer tha night."

I looked up and watched as the sun was setting in the distance and realized how long I had actually been here. We turned away from Keahi's home, and as the sun was setting, a giant moon was rising, almost in sync with the opposite wall surrounding D'Hanin.

It was chilling to see how close it was, it felt like I could walk to it if I just went outside of D'Hanin. It blew my mind just to think what was on the outside of these walls. This whole experience blew my mind, all of the new information I was struck with today; it was as if I was just a newborn infant seeing everything for the first time again. Even the thought of the possibility, and almost certainty, of other worlds other than just the world I knew and the world D'Hanin knew. The sheer greatness of it all made me appreciate life a little more.

\* \* \* \*

We walked back into the tavern at the Unicorn's Nest. My eyes ached and my head felt like a boulder on top of my neck, I was ready to drop to the ground and fall asleep, but my stomach was growling loud enough to keep me awake. I sat down at the table we were at before, expecting Lib to sit down with me, but he stayed standing up and waived at the waitress to come over. He looked down at me. "Aliner is gonna take care o' you, the rest o' the night. Get whatever ya wanna eat, and she will get ya a room made up in the meantime."

"Ok, but how am I suppose to pay for it?" I asked. There was no way they used American money, and even if they did, I didn't have enough to buy Dairy Queen for myself let alone get a room.

Lib smiled, and reassured me, "We've got ya covered, already discussed it wit' her," he patted me on the shoulder and headed for the door, "meet me down here in the mornin,' I'll be waitin' for ya." Lib stepped out the door and by that time Alina walked up to the table.

She sat down at the table as if it was her first chance to rest all night and smiled. I gave her a shaky smile; girls were not exactly my forte. Luckily, she broke the silence, "It's Finn, right?"

"Is what Finn?" I asked and choked on my words and corrected myself, "I mean yea, yea, my name. It's been a long day but from what I saw you, haven't had it too easy today either," hoping she understood I meant with the tavern. There really was no reason I should be nervous talking to her, but what's a fifteen-year-old guy to do?

She laughed and smiled. It was easy to make her laugh, "Yea, it hasn't gotten any easier the last few years, but I get by."

I smiled and nodded not too sure what to say. But once again she broke the silence, "What can I get you to eat?"

I gave her a blank look and looked around to see if anyone else had food on their table, unsure of what I could even order, I looked on the table for a menu, but there was nothing.

Alina stood up, "I'll get you what we have left of the nymph. I'll get outta your hair before you have a nervous breakdown." She smiled and winked then went back to the kitchen. She was much smoother than me.

I sat back in my chair. It was suddenly quiet without Alina to talk to. It was the first time I was alone since I got to D'Hanin. My eyelids got heavy fast without talking to anyone. A fat man, with raggedy, peasant-like clothes, coughed as he was walking past me and I opened my eyes and sat up. He was the last one to leave the dining area. I sat there and watched the flame on the candle at my table dance, I looked at the other candles and watched as they all danced and threw shadows across the tables and floors. Then the flames grew taller and danced wilder. I sat back in my chair and watched, was this normal for D'Hanin? But then I remembered the Obsidian Scale of Fire, were these flames losing control? But then they danced in unison. One would flick left, and they all would flick left, one would flick right, and they would all flick right.

Alina set a plate in front of me, and I snapped back into reality. The dish had a sparse helping of food on it. I looked back up at Alina and thanked her for the food. My focus shifted again at the candles, but they were back to their natural flame.

"Anytime. I'm sorry it couldn't be more," she explained herself, "with the Scales and what not."

"It's fine, it's plenty," I lied.

She smiled, embarrassed of sorts, "I'm gonna be closing down the kitchen, so when you're done." She handed me a rusty key that looked more like a lockpick than an actual key. "You're in room 5, it's the one with a view," she said sarcastically. I thanked her again. It seemed the only words I could say were thank you.

"Sleep tight," she said and walked away as I thanked her one more time.

I looked down at my plate and picked up the nymph. The only fact I knew about a nymph was it was a type of fairy, but this couldn't be the same nymph I knew. I looked down at my plate again, and sure enough, there were two wings on the edge of the

32

plate. I dropped the meat back onto my plate and buried my face in my hand.

"What kind of world was I in?" My stomach growled, and my mouth began watering. "Well, when in Rome," I said to myself, and I picked up the meat and took a bite. Juices ran down my chin and my mouth watered, and my eyes got huge. This was definitely the best meal I had ever eaten. The combination of spices I had never tasted with the crunch and tenderness of the meat was unreal. I quickly took another bite, savoring all the flavor.

The wings looked like they were more for decoration, even if they weren't I didn't feel I could eat the wings of a fairy, it felt too barbaric. But there were a couple bites of corn and beans and potatoes on the plate as well, something I was finally familiar with in this world but even somehow, the taste was similar but different than what I knew.

I cleaned my plate, scraping every last bit of beans and nymph I could, I wiped my mouth off with an oversized napkin and looked around. I didn't know what to do with my plate. It was rude to just leave it there. I stood up and wiped the table off with my napkin and set it on my plate. I walked it over to the kitchen doors and peaked my head in. There were grand stone fireplaces and cauldrons all throughout. All the flames were out, and Alina wasn't around. I saw the empty sink and set my plate in there.

"Thanks," I heard from behind me.
She was standing there with a towel wiping her hands and smiling. I nodded and said, "Thanks," as the word for the fourth time in a row came spilling out of my mouth, I had to say something else.

"It was delicious," at least it was something.

"Anytime," she smiled back, "have a nice night."

"Goodnight." I headed up to my room nervous to continue the night by myself.

I got up to the second floor of the tavern. It overlooked the entire dining area. I walked all the way along the railing and got to a door with the number 5 on it I got my key out and unlocked the door. With a click, the door swung open, and I walked in.

It was a small room, couldn't have been much more significant than a jail cell. An ugly, green plaid wallpaper curled off the walls and light spilled through my window. I walked over and looked out, I could see all of D'Hanin and the giant moon above. To someone living in D'Hanin, this might have not been anything but Alina was right, it was an excellent view.

I started to think of my parents again. It made me miss them. I was only gone a day, but the thought of possibly never seeing them again and not even existing in their world made my stomach churn.

Tears streamed down my face. I let it drip down onto the floor; there was no one around to see me, so I had nothing to be ashamed of. It wasn't just missing my parents either. I possibly had this whole world's future in my hands, at fifteen; I didn't think I'd ever be this important. I was going to let all off this get to me one last time, then I was going to focus on what I had to do from here, whether it be fighting or making my way home.

I walked over to my bed. It was just a twin size bed with one pillow and military-esque sheets. I sat down on it, took my shoes off and lied down. Another tear streamed down the side of my face, I closed my eyes and thought of my parents, and with the comfort of their pictures in my mind, I fell asleep.

# 3

## THE FADE AND KEAHI'S PROPHECY

I woke up to the sound of screams coming from outside. I sat up quickly, rubbed my eyes, and jumped off the bed to look out my window. There was a house on fire and a woman with her two children crying for help. Two men were arguing and prepared to fight. One was pointing to the house and yelling at the other man.

The house was far past saving. The door fell off its hinges and blew dust everywhere. It was heartbreaking to see the effects of what I would assume the Obsidian Scale and perhaps even the Sapphire Scale, making these men fall off their hinges.

I remembered I had to meet Lib at the tavern; I walked away from the window and could hear the screams and yelling all the way out of my room until I finally closed the door behind me. It wasn't exactly what I wanted to wake up to.

Lib and Alina were sitting at a table, as I came down the stairs. Lib saw me and waved me down like I would have tried to go start up a conversation with anyone else. "Mornin,' have a sit," Lib pulled out my chair; there was a plate with a bit of food that looked like it was scrounged together.

"What's this?" I asked.

"It's your breakfast, I made it special for you," Alina said, "I made up newt eggs and gnome strips straight from their burrows in our garden."

It all smelled exceptional, but I had to admit it was strange eating all these fairy tale creatures I once thought were just from the imagination. "It looks great, thanks," I said trying to be more relaxed with Alina. She noticed it as well and smiled at me.

"So what do we have planned for today," I asked Lib, anxious to know what I had in store for me.

Lib sat up in his chair, "I am gonna have ta take ya to tha Fade today, he'll decide what ta do with ya."

"And if he says I do have to stay, what then?"

"Then he'll train ya. Lots and lots o' trainin.' From 'ere until tha Fade thinks you are ready, you will be trainin' every day."

"What kind of training?"

"He will train ya in battle, how ta use a s--sword and what not."

I almost thought I didn't hear him right. A picture I saw in my history book immediately came to mind of a Civil War guy standing with a sword, his hand resting on the handle, but even they had guns at least.

"But Lib, I've never touched a sword in my life, I wouldn't know the most basic skills of fighting with a sword. It will take me years to even have a clue what I'm doing."

"It'll take a bit o' time, but tha Fade, 'e's tha bes' in our world."

"Why doesn't he fight Apaku and get the Scales back, if he's so great," I said with a little bit more attitude than I meant, but Lib didn't seem taken aback by it.

"Tha Fade's mind 'as always outmatched 'is ability. 'E was never an option ta fight for tha Scales but 'as always been tha one ta train."

"So, he's trained other's to fight for the Scales then?"

Lib broke eye contact with me, for a moment, "He has t--trained -- other's who have failed to get tha S--Scales."

"And what's happened to them? Why haven't they been able to get the Scales back, surely they know this world better than I do, probably have used a sword before."

"I don't know tha bes' answer for ya. They all died in battle. After about six of 'em, tha Fade refused to keep trainin' -- our people 'e said when the right person comes along 'e will train them and tha' person will get tha Scales back. It's been years since 'e's trained, 'e said it was 'is biggest regret lettin' tha other's go out."

"Why did he regret it, if he's got such a great mind, was it really his fault they failed?"

Lib leaned into the table; the tavern started to fill up with a miserable looking breakfast crowd. A good night's sleep didn't perk any of these people up.

"Tha Fade knew they were not tha ones ta get tha Scales, 'e was bullied and pushed inta trainin' these people. After six, they stopped fighting 'im, it's b--been years since then, and a lot o' us has lost faith. Tha Fade was no exception to tha effects o' them

37

Scales; I think that's why 'e broke and started trainin' in tha firs' place. I tell 'im that, but it is all on his shoulders now."

I looked back down at my plate and continued pushing my food around; I felt nauseated from talking about everything. "Make sure ya eat all your food," Lib said, just before a skeletal man with dark bags under his eyes came up and bumped into our table, spilling my Spider Ale.

"Well if 'e don't want his food, let us have it, there's no point in giving what we have away to a poor sap!" The man yelled at Lib.

Lib stood up, knocking into the man, "Jus' 'cause you've given up don't mean we all 'ave. Have a bit o' respec' fer yerself!" Lib's eyes looked as if they were going to pop out of his head.

I've never seen Lib get upset like that before, or even expected it; he was intimidating when he wanted to be.

Lib pushed the man away. The man fell into a table and gave Lib a disgusted look. The man walked away and sat at his booth.

Lib sat back down slowly, "Finish yer food, don' worry 'bout 'im, he'll be thankin' ya one day."

"If I'm even suppose to go," I said under my breath. I didn't feel like finishing my food now more than ever.

Alina saw the look on my face, she grabbed my glass and wiped up the Spider Ale, "You see, without the Emerald Scale all of our crops have shriveled up into nothing, leaving us with a great food shortage as well as not being able to feed our livestock." she paused, "It doesn't give anyone the right to act like that though."

"It is not his fault," Lib said, "the Emerald Scale ain't the only one that is getting to 'em."

"They know that, and if they let it get to them, we'll be no better off than any other abandoned city in

D'Hanin. We'll be in a war of our own before too long if these people don't perk up."

I pushed the food around on my plate, Alina took notice, "It's fine Finn," she said, "It will all get better for us one day, there's still a lot of beauty in this world. I can only imagine how great it was before the Scales were stolen." She took my glass from the table and forced a half smile, "I better go help that guy before he gets any more upset."

"She's righ', don't let it b--bother you if you can help it," Lib said.

I looked back down at my plate and began eating before anyone else could notice I still had food on my plate.

* * * *

Lib and I strolled through D'Hanin. Families were fighting other families and fires and dead crops everywhere. We walked passed two men who looked almost ready to rip each other apart. One man pulled out a dagger and held it up against the other man's throat, and blood trickled down. The man with the blade yelled and threw it into the side of a building and stormed off and took his family inside their house.

"You'll see more o' that tha longer you're here, migh' as well get used ta it."

We stopped in front of the building that was all windows. Now that we were up close I read the sign hanging above the door that read "The Fade Training, Established 523." I had no idea what year it was here, but I was sure they weren't on the same time we were.

"This'll be where ya start your trainin," Lib said, "Jus' go inside an' wait fer tha Fade, 'e knows ya'll be comin."

"Aren't you coming in with me?" I asked feeling hopeful.

"I've got things ta be takin' care of in Wood Grain; I'll be back tomarra ta see how it went. When you go in jus' wait for tha Fade ta speak ta ya. 'E does a lot o' meditatin, and ya can never be sure when 'e is," Lib explained. He looked down at me, "Don' be nervous; you will be fine."

Lib headed for the gates of D'Hanin, and I stood there with my stomach churning. I took a deep breath and slowly opened the door and walked in. I stood at the doorway and looked around, but there was no one there. Swords, daggers, bows, and axes all hung from the walls. There were punching bags and dummies hanging from the ceiling. The dummies swung slowly in circles in an unsettling way; it didn't help they all had faces stitched onto them.

The back door opened and a man, who I assumed must've been the Fade, stepped out and onto the mat. He was an older man with a white ducktail beard. He was unusually muscular for his age and had tribal tattoos running up both of his arms. He looked me in the eyes, and I noticed his bluish white eyes. I silently remembered not to speak until he spoke to me.

He stepped forward to me and finally spoke, as he got closer, "Finn Anderson," he spoke in a soft voice, as he looked me up and down. I could tell he was studying me. I hated when people stared at me, I gave him a forced smile as I stood like a statue before him. He then grabbed me by the back of the neck, I hated when people I didn't know would touch me, and guided me to the middle of the mat.

"If you didn't already know, I am the Fade. Lib told me of your story and your entrance into D'Hanin."

We sat down in the middle of the mat, facing each other. "It is an interesting arrival at the least, which is why I have accepted to train you. I will push you to your limits in body and mind to reveal you."

"To reveal —," I began, feeling as if he thought I was hiding something dark.

"To reveal, Keahi's Prophecy. I do not know if you are the one, my training will tell me. I must tell

40

you, I will not allow you to pursue the Scales if you are not the one and I cannot guarantee that if you are, that you will succeed. I only know that the one that has been undeniably chosen will be our only hope. That is why I will not take this training with you lightly."

"I don't feel like I am the one you're looking for. That's all anyone has thought since I got here and I don't know why."

"Lib told me about your entry into D'Hanin and where he found you, however his information on how it all came to be was lacking. What were the moments leading up to your "death" like?"

I thought about it for a moment, struggling to relive those moments, "I remember having a lot of anxiety and knowing my parents probably thought I was losing my mind, but, there was this bird that I swear was the cause of it all. I know that it burned my house down." I began to feel crazy again, the Fade was probably imagining a bird with a match, flicking it onto my house like a cartoon.

"That's interesting, and did this bird have any defining qualities?"

"It had unusually long wings and the fire didn't seem to bother it. In fact, right before I blacked out it sat on my chest staring at me before it burst into flame itself, and then, I'm pretty sure I died."

The Fade laughed, "I don't believe that you died, rather born again if you ask my opinion. You see it does make sense to me, your story. It is something I believe may be a key part of Keahi's Prophecy."

"What is Keahi's Prophecy," I questioned, feeling strange about possibly being a part of a prophecy.

"When I was a young boy, Keahi had taken a special interest in me near the end of his time here. He told me in my quest to return the Scales, death would fall upon me 8 times, in which the 7th time would immediately follow the 8th time death would fall upon me. The only death I can avoid is the 8th, which may fall upon the elements, so long as it happens when the wings reach the heart, a warrior will soar."

"And what does that mean?"

"As a young boy, I didn't much understand the power that Keahi held, I didn't understand his knowledge or greatness and as a child shrugged the prophecy off. My life needed to reach total darkness before I understood what he meant, and the prophecy came back to me in a cry for help sometime after Keahi's death when the amount of pressure put on me to succeed Keahi and train his warriors and overcome Apaku to return the Scales. He prophesied that I would choose 6 warriors that would die, plus my own in the quest to return the Scales. That would be the imminent 7 that would fall upon me. If I had chosen the 8th before the elements, I would have been held reponsible. My death would have immediately followed and the prophecy would have been completed, the Scales unreturned."

"But you stopped after the 6th warrior you sent to return the Scales and that's why I'm here, to be the 7th, chosen by the elements."

"Precisely."

"So that means I'm going to die for these Scales, and it'll be the elements' fault." I had already felt the hysteria of dying once and could already feel it again.

"The only death I can avoid is the 8th, which may fall upon the elements." He reiterated, "The prophecy does not tell if you will succeed or fail, it says you will soar, which means you will be our strongest hope in succeeding."

I began feeling the pressure of possibly being chosen; in the back of my mind it all seemed too coincidental to believe that I was not a part of the elements choice that Keahi prophesied.

"I will not take this decision lightly." I looked up at the Fade, and he could see the anguish in my eyes, "So far your entry into D'Hanin is very curious

42

and if you are a part of the prophecy, I will have to know from the elements that they have chosen you.

"And how will you know?"

"I can't say that I know for sure, but I have hopes that something will come to us in your training. It will be the deciding factor if you will go on the journey or not. D'Hanin will eventually cease to exist if we are wrong."

"That's a lot of pressure," I smirked, hiding my fear.

"You need not worry until we are sure you were chosen. We must first train you to be able to control your mind, and that starts with combat training. Are you ready?"

"No, I'm not ready," I said.

"It was a rhetorical question, Mr. Anderson, no one is ever really ready to start something like this."

"I just need to get home, if for nothing else to let my parents know that I'm all right. Can you please tell me if that is possible?"

"It is possible," the Fade said, "However, you will not learn that here. If the Elements can bring you to D'Hanin, I am led to believe that they can take you back to wherever you came from. It would be up to them."

I nodded my head without a single shred of confidence.

"We must start training; you may have been brought here for a purpose and as long as the Elements keep you here, we must prepare you. Please, stand up."

We both stood up. "Now take a sword," the Fade pointed at a sword on the wall, I took a step towards it as the sword jumped off the wall and hit me in the shoulder. I dropped to the ground and grabbed my shoulder.

"You've got to keep your eyes on everything at all times, or you'll be on the ground more times than not."

"How can I see everything at once?" I said a little upset.

"You're doing it now, you can see everything in this room, but you choose to focus on just one thing. Stretch your mind to focus on everything."

At that moment I was only focusing on the stinging pain in my shoulder. I took my hand off of it, and blood dripped from a deep gash. The Fade walked over and grabbed my shoulder. I screamed in pain until he let go. I stood up and backed away from him. I examined my shoulder and, besides the blood; you would have never known I had been cut.

"How did you do that?" I said astonished.

"I have willed my body, my mind, to perform and think at a much higher level to do this. It was a rare gift that I was blessed with and that I pursued with the help of Keahi."

"Will I be able to do that too?"

The Fade looked at me and smiled, "We are all blessed in one way or another, and it is those of us who have the heart to enhance them, that succeed and those who don't, that fail." He picked up the sword by the blade, "Please take the hilt."

I looked down at the sword, I assumed he meant the handle part and slowly reached out to grab it. I wrapped my hand around the hilt and felt the wear of the many that had used it before me. The Fade released his grip, and the sword fell to the ground almost bringing me with it. I looked back up at him, embarrassed, "How heavy is this? It has to weigh at least 60 pounds."

The Fade picked it back up like it was a feather and pushed it into my chest, "actually 30." I grabbed it with both hands and was able to hold it this time.

"It is a training sword," the Fade explained, "it's heavier, to improve your speed and strength, and duller than a real sword to prevent any serious injury."

"If it's duller, why did it still cut me?" I asked.

"Well," he said nonchalantly, "it's not much duller. I still want you to realize the consequences of getting hit by the blade."

I shifted the sword to another position. I tried to hide that my arms were starting to shake, but a drop of sweat rolled down the side of my face. The Fade looked at me with disappointment, "We've got a lot of work to do, more than what I would've hoped for."

I looked down, not daring to make eye contact with him. I had a great sense of shame wash over me, but I knew it only made me look weaker. I stood up straight and looked back into his eyes.

The Fade looked back at me, "We're going to work on your swordsmanship, the strength will come along with it." He stuck out his hand at a shield on the wall, and it flew towards him and landed right on his arm. He turned back towards me, "Now, try to hit me and I shall block the oncoming swings."

I faltered, deep down not wanting to try and hit him, "You want me to just swing it at you?" I asked.

"Yes, just like you're attacking me."

My mouth suddenly became dry, I didn't want to hit him, but he looked confident, much more than I. I took a tight grip on the sword and with all my might I gritted my teeth and swung the sword slowly. The Fade lifted the shield without any effort, and the sword bounced off sending a shock up my arms. I dropped the sword in pain.

The Fade wasted no time, "Pick it up and try again."

I looked up at him, wincing, I grabbed the sword again, out of anger and embarrassment, I yelled and swung it back. Once again it bounced off his shield, but I held my grip and lifted it up again with all my might and brought the sword down on him. He lifted the shield above himself much faster than I could get the sword there it ricocheted with a loud

CLANG that echoed throughout the room, then I lost my grip again, and the sword slid off, onto the ground.

My heart was pounding from the adrenaline coursing through my veins. It was strange to be sword fighting, but I liked it. The Fade didn't have to tell me again to pick it up. I picked it up quickly, and the Fade took a position. I swung the sword over and over, and every time the Fade would block it with ease. Sweat was dripping off my face and into my eyes. I could taste the saltiness from my lips. I swung the sword one more time, and it bounced off the shield making the Fade stumble backward slightly.

I didn't drop the sword this time, instead, I put the tip of the blade into the mat and leaned on it to keep myself from collapsing. The Fade lowered his shield, "That was good for your first time swinging a sword, very barbaric. I could see it in your eyes, swing hard, aim to kill, not to strike. That will only work in your favor once out of every 100 tries, but most likely you will not get to that 100th attempt in a real fight."

I looked at him finally catching my breath and lifted my sword up in what I would suspect to be a fighting position. The Fade smiled, "I see you are going to try for those 100 attempts."

I swung my sword at him high, he blocked it with force this time, and I had to use all my strength to control it. I brought it around to his other side and swung at his legs, he crouched down and blocked then spun around as he came up. I aimed for his chest and jabbed the sword forward. He moved to the side, and I stumbled forward, then something long and thin slammed against my back leaving a piercing pain, I dropped the sword and fell to the ground.

I grabbed my back and rolled on the ground screaming in pain. I looked at the Fade, and he was holding a fighting stick.

"Now you see if that had been a real sword, and I was an evil person, you would have been on the ground, split in half, dead. All your training would have gone to waste."

He grabbed my arm and pulled me to my feet, "Never go for the stomach or chest unless your enemy is weakened or only seconds away from death and you want to help him get there faster. It is a move easily shown by taking a new stance and pulling your arms back much farther than needed to acquire enough push to go through the enemy's body."

I wiped the sweat from my palms on my jeans and re-gripped the sword, "Let's go again then." The Fade lifted his shield and motioned for me to go.

I hopped forward bringing the sword down on him, with one formidable swing of his shield he bounced the sword out of my hand and across the room. He swung his fighting stick around in a blink of an eye and hit me in the shoulder, making me fall to the ground.

He stepped over me and simply said, "dead."

I stood up in anger, "It's impossible for me to swing that sword fast enough to hit you! No one could do it!"

He answered back irritated, "You are not using your mind, Finn. You depend solely on your strength to fight." He raised his fighting stick and lifted my sleeve up to reveal a large welt was growing, "it's obviously not working for you."

The Fade turned his back on me and reached out his hand towards the sword. It flew off the ground into his hand, and he spun around with his shield still in his hand. A dummy swung forward next to him.

"Don't let your mind control you, learn to control it and you can be limitless." He swung the sword upward across the dummy's body, and the dummy flew backward. The Fade held the sword out pointing straight up, and the dummy flew forward right in front of him again.

"See the exact spot you want to strike and be able to change it in an instant." He swung the sword again, aiming for the shoulder, and before I could process where he was going to hit, the legs of the dummy flew across the room and smacked against the wall. What he was saying finally made sense to me, it was like a juke in Madden, I had done it a hundred times in the game, and it always worked for me.

"Own the balance war, and you shall always be the one looking down on your opponent with the final jab." He swung his sword, and the dummy bounced back, the Fade stepped forward and hit again, the dummy bounced back. The Fade pushed the dummy back as far as he could without hesitation, and then chopped the rope holding the dummy, in half, and it fell to the ground. The Fade lifted his sword high and stuck it into the dummies chest.

I watched in amazement, the simplicity that he did this. I surely couldn't be the actual savior. If Apaku were half the swordsman that the Fade was, I would be torn apart in no time.

The Fade released his grip on the sword, and it stayed there, sticking out of the dummy's chest.

"This can't be right," I said, exhausted, "there has to be someone better than me for this job."

"It's not always about who is the best, but who has the most desire."

"But I can't even say that I have the most desire. I feel like so far I haven't even had an option."

"You must have an inkling of desire within you, because whether or not you think you have an option, you do. We're here training for this journey so it tells me you must want this."

I looked down at my feet, breaking eye contact with the Fade. It was a chance of a lifetime; I couldn't deny that sword fighting was awesome.

The Fade approached me, "I can not explain why the elements would have chosen you, I am not a part of that choice. But in their otherworldly knowledge, I do not question them. Keahi said they would choose, when they do, I will train that person to have the best chance of success."

"But I'll never be able to do what you can do. I'll be here for the rest of my life to even come close." I said in a panicky voice.

"Well we don't have that much time, but we'll do our best," he smiled taking this whole situation much more lightly than myself, "But this is going to require you to listen to me and trust me."

I nodded slowly; I knew he was going to be my best shot at helping me get out of here alive even if I had more desire to succeed than anyone else.

I walked over to the sword and pulled the sword as hard as I could, I had to shake it back and forth to loosen it, but I yanked one last time, and it finally gave and came out of the dummy trailed by stuffing. I held it up and looked back at the Fade, with a lot less confidence than I showed, "So you said it's about precision?"

He smiled, and we continued my training.

* * * *

We trained for hours, relentlessly. After it all, I finally dropped to the ground exhausted. Every muscle in my body ached, that whole endurance talk my P.E. Coach gave us over and over again did nothing to prepare me for this.

"Drink this," the Fade handed me a glass of murky brown liquid; I took a big gulp of it. It tasted terrible and almost made me sick to my stomach, but I needed anything to drink.

"We'll call lunch," the Fade said.

"Lunch?" I almost screamed at him.

"You've got an hour," he walked away from me, and before my eyes, he quickly faded away into oblivion. I almost didn't want to stand up; I was already tired and feeling defeated before the first day was over. My heart felt so heavy I could barely breathe, but I

49

forced myself to stand up.  Leaving the drink behind, I
headed for the Unicorn's Nest.

* * * *

I walked in and quietly closed the door behind
me.  There must not have been much to do in this
world because once again, the place was almost full.
The people closest to me took notice of my entrance.
They stared me up and down most likely noticing the
blood stains and the drained look I had on my face.

I continued in and sat down at the most secluded table, my legs aching as I plopped down into
the chair and leaned back.  I saw Alina across the tavern; she waved and finished taking someone's order so
she could see me.

"So," she said with a smile, "How was your first
day of training?"

"Well, I know now why I'm not considered in
shape," I said as I winced trying to sit up straight.

"I wouldn't get too relaxed; it'll only make it
worse."

"I know, can I just get more of that nymph so I
can get back to training, maybe that will get my spirits
up," I asked her, but she looked disappointed.

"I'm sorry but, I'm in charge of your food intake
as well, it's part of your training."

"Oh ok," I said, "that's fine."  Alina had cooked
for me before, so I wasn't too worried; everything she
had given me was delicious.

"I try to add in a little flavor to not make it so
bad on your stomach," she told me crushing my hopes
of having another delicious meal, "but it won't be forever, just to help in your training."  I just nodded and
accepted that I had to do, what I had to do.  She gave
me a warming smile, "I'll be right back."  She walked
away into the kitchen, and I sat there.

Most of the patrons at the tavern had forgotten
that I was there; I just sat quietly and kept to myself.  I

kept thinking about training, the moves going through my head that he performed. It gave me motivation to one day be able to do those, they were impressive and done so flawlessly.

I felt where he cut me on my shoulder; it was as if nothing was there. If I were able to do that, it would help me substantially to defeat Apaku. I looked around and grabbed my knife. I put it on the back of my hand and made a small cut. I dropped the knife and grabbed my hand. *"That was painful,"* I thought to myself stupidly.

I put my hand back on the table still covering it with my other hand and tried focusing my mind on healing the cut. I concentrated harder and harder and finally felt something. My entire body became warm, I could feel my blood heating up as it ran through my veins, I tried to focus that energy on my cut, and then the feeling disappeared. I removed my hand from the cut, but it was still there. A small amount of blood smeared over my hand.

I saw Alina walking over and wiped my hand off with my napkin and put my hand under the table. She set a bowl of bubbling green liquid down in front of me.

"Ogre finger soup," she said with a shameful smile, "Enjoy," and then walked away immediately.

I looked down at the bubbling green liquid in disgust and stirred it around. I took a scoop of it and found what appeared to be an ogre's finger. I felt my breakfast come back up into my throat and in disgust, dropped the spoon onto the table. The "ogre finger" rolled around and with a closer look I saw that it was just a baby carrot.

I took a deep breath, *"maybe that's just a funny name for it."* I took another scoop and bravely took a bite. *"Nope, not just a funny name."* It tasted terrible; I did my best to get it down. There was no way I would've been able to eat this, but I knew I had to. I took a deep breath and held it, then started shoveling the soup, doing my best to contain my taste buds from tasting it.

I emptied the bowl and stood up to go outside worried that I was going to puke. I hurried passed Alina, "It was that good, huh," she said sarcastically. I put my hand over my mouth and got outside. The fresh air helped. I leaned against the wall and tried my best to take my mind off the ogre finger soup. I walked around the village to try and digest it before going back to the Fade.

\* \* \* \*

As I walked in, he was waiting for me, "What took you so long?"

"The food didn't go down so well," I replied knowing he had probably heard this excuse a million times before.

"You'll get used to it," he replied and handed me the sword as I stepped back onto the mat, "We're going to continue sparring."

The sword hadn't gotten any lighter, and my arms were still shaking under the weight. I put the sword up, and the Fade lifted his shield and nodded.

We sparred, or should I say I swung the sword around and he blocked it every time effortlessly. My arms were burning, but I continued to fight. A glazed look came over the Fade's face as if he was getting bored. I could feel anger rising in me and a need to prove myself. I gritted my teeth and swung hard at his head. He blocked it, but the shield went up. I turned the sword back around as fast as I could at his waist, he got the shield down and blocked the sword but fell off balance as I swung again, and he stopped it, but finally, I made him hit the ground.

I looked down at him in utter amazement. "Impressive," he said with excitement, "now help me up." I dropped the sword and grabbed his hand to help him stand up. "Very impressive," he said again,

"I could finally see your precision and speed. You knew where you were going to strike, three steps ahead of where you were." He paused, "That's what I was teaching you before, you had your mind under control, you weren't thinking about this one single move, you were thinking about the next three or possibly four or five if you needed them."

I finally understood what he meant by controlling my mind. It was as if those few moments were in slow motion. I wanted to keep going; I finally felt like I had taken a step forward and didn't want to stop.

* * * *

We sparred until I could see the giant moon casting a blue light into the training center. I didn't make him fall to the ground the rest of the night, no matter how hard I tried to control my mind; I couldn't quite get that moment back. The Fade was much more concentrated the rest of the night as well which may have been why I couldn't do it again.

With a final clang of my sword against his shield, I stepped back and pointed the sword down into the mat so I could rest and lean on it.

"Ok," the Fade said, "That's enough for today. We'll continue training tomorrow."

"Ok," I said with the last of my breath. I hung the sword back up on the wall, and the Fade came back up to me with another glass of the murky liquid.

"Drink it," the Fade told me sternly, "Meet back here tomorrow, same time."

I took the drink from him and chugged it. He left the room, and I hurried out the door. I limped down the empty street, my body aching more and more with every step. I heard a loud creaking sound and stopped. The gates of D'Hanin were slowly opening, and Lib was walking towards me.

He spotted me and squinted his eyes to see if it was me. He quickly limped over to me with a big bag slung over his shoulder, "What are ya still doin' out here, you need ta get -- rest fer yer trainin' tomorrow!"

"I just got out; I was heading back to the Unicorn's Nest," I snapped back defensively.

Lib eyes got wide, "Ya jus' got out? 'E's gonna kill ya!"

The Fade apparently didn't train this long with any of the others, "I guess I just needed more training than the others."

"Don' worry, I'll talk to 'im for ya, hurry off and get a bit o' shut eye." Lib patted me on the shoulder and walked off. I hurried off before there were any more interruptions so I could finally get to my bed.

# 4

## PLAYING WITH FIRE

I woke up feeling better than I have in my entire life. An
entire month
had passed
since I started
my training,
and it's finally
starting to pay
off.

Swinging
my feet off my
bed, I went to
my mirror. I
flexed and could
tell I had gained
a lot of bulk
since initially
arriving here; it
made me look
much older. I
tried to pat my
hair down, but it was getting so long I couldn't do any-
thing with it.

The new clothes that Lib had gotten me looked
more like peasant clothes, just plain, with different
shades of brown and tan, but they moved with me as if

they had a mind of their own, which led me to believe they weren't your everyday peasant clothes.

I made my way to the training center after a quick breakfast. Strangely enough, the town had even begun to feel like home, like I had lived there my entire life, my new clothes helped me blend in, I had learned where everything was in the town, and there weren't so many strange looks from the villagers anymore however it was exchanged for dirty looks to the ones that let the Scales get the better of them.

The Fade was not present as usual when I entered the training center. It had become a regular thing, so I stood in the middle of the mat and warmed up, doing stretches, lunges, jumping jacks, push-ups, the usual that I was accustomed to in my world. I started to break a small sweat, so I pulled a dummy up and went to get my training sword off the wall. There were dents and chips in the blade from using it so much; the handle was starting to wear as well. I swung it around in one hand and switched to the other and swung it in a circle a few times to warm up my wrists. The sword felt a considerable amount lighter than when I first started my training.

"You take a painfully long time to prepare," I heard from behind me. I turned around still twirling the sword. The Fade was standing in the middle of the mat, where I did my warm-ups.

"I was just waiting for you," I replied back.

"I arrive when you are ready to train, I don't have time to stand around and watch you "warm up," he said.

"Well I don't want to hurt myself, we both know the effects of the Four Scales aren't gonna be put on hold while I nurse a torn hamstring," I tried to reason with him."

"Apaku isn't going to wait around either while you do your "warm-ups," he reasoned with me, "You can't come down off your training, you must be ready to fight at any moment. Do you understand?"

"Of course, you're always right," I said going through the motions.

"If you give your muscles time to relax at the wrong moment, they could be relaxed for eternity."

I swung the sword around, practicing moves he had shown me. It wasn't that I didn't care what he said, I just knew he was right, and so I just listened and didn't waste thoughts on trying to come up with excuses, I just accepted everything he told me.

"Alright," he said, "let's get back to work." The Fade motioned for the dummy to come closer, and it slid right in front of me. It was the same drill we had been practicing for the past few days. As I improved, he used the dummies more and more so he wouldn't take such a beating every day.

"Go on," he told me. I took my stance and started with a diagonally downward slash as the Fade moved the dummy out of the way. I stepped closer to it and swung again this time from the other side; the Fade moved the dummy once again.

"Should we do 25 strikes?" He called to me.

"30," I yelled back. The goal of this training was not to stop sparring with the dummy until I hit that 30 mark. The training helped my endurance and speed since the Fade continued to move the dummy faster as I had more strikes. By the end, I would be leaping from one side of the mat to the other.

I got the first 5 strikes in reasonably quickly. The sword felt heavier and heavier as I reached 15 hits, then 20. Sweat was dripping off my face, and I started seeing double. I focused in on the dummy and hit 21, 22, 23. I stood in the center of the mat catching my breath, trying to zone in on the dummy. I heard a CRACK! Then a stinging pain across my back.

"Watch your surroundings! Do not lose sight of the whole, for the sake of being tired! Keep fighting!" The Fade yelled encouragingly at me. I went after the dummy again.

15 minutes had passed before I reached 25 but with a double move, I quickly got to 27. My arms were shaking, and my heart was pounding against my chest. The dummy seemed to be apparating all over the mat. I watched for a pattern and found one, I guessed the dummy's next move and met him on the left side of the mat, landing a perfect strike. The dummy's lower half was flown across the room.

"Excellent!" The Fade cried out, "Control your mind! You finally did it!"

I stood up tenaciously; a rush of adrenaline controlled my breathing and gave me the strength to stand there proud. The Fade walked up to me smiling, "Your mind is getting strong Finn, don't stop training it."

"Of course," I replied.

"You have shown me great strides in your training but don't let that get the best of you, you still have a long way to go."

I nodded, still smiling.

The Fade made me another drink, "We must keep going through lunch to beat sundown."

I took the drink and gulped it down; I had become accustomed to the terrible taste of the food and drink. I could feel how much it was helping me in training and decided to not complain about it anymore.

We continued our training. The sun quickly dropped from the sky, leaving increasingly elongated shadows across the grounds and through the training center. Even in this world, it meant winter was approaching.

The Fade lit burners around the room so we could have more time to train. The lamps didn't cast much light, but I guess nobody ever said I could control the light in a real fight.

The Fade had stepped in to spar with me, this time we both had a sword and a shield. He fought with me mercilessly. He had a lighter sword and was much faster than me, but I did my best to block his every move.

We danced around the mat, taking an equal number of swings at each other. He got a solid hit against my shield and made me fall off balance; he pushed me back with every swing. I tucked and rolled out of the way of a finishing strike, but it didn't help me. He quickly recovered and kept pushing me back. I needed something before he got me on my back.

"*I need a way out, I've lost the balance war*," I thought to myself, and without consciously thinking about it I waved my shield around the room with a spin and every flame went out leaving the room pitch black. I spun back around not knowing exactly where the Fade was.

I aimed low and felt my sword connect with something and then a loud thud and a grunt. I stood up, and the flames quickly rose back up alongside me, filling the room with light. I looked down at my feet; the Fade was laying there in awe.

I helped him up and he took my sword from me. I must have done something terrible. He hung my sword on the wall and stood back. He turned around and looked at me seriously, "We're done training in combat for now."

The Fade left me with that. Pushing me out of the training center and leaving me outside in the darkness, confused trying to wrap my brain around this day. There was no way that I was going to be able to sleep tonight.

I decided to explore the city a little more, to wind down from training. Everyone had turned in for the night, and the town was peaceful, at least on the outside. I was able to stroll through the village, finally being able to take in the buildings and the atmosphere. Normally, I wouldn't be able to get passed the scowls of the villagers, but with their anger consumed by their homes, I was at ease to keep my head up and admire.

I thought about what happened at training; I could still feel a burning sensation that I just couldn't shake. Anxiety filled me to the core to continue training; I was still so far away from having the talent of the average warrior in D'Hanin and finally when I get a good hit on the Fade, he kicks me out of the training center. However, it helped to get my mind off of things when I heard a rustling of horses.

I followed the noise to the back of the Unicorn's Nest, revealing a large farm, few animals were out of their burrows and huts, presumably already turned in for the night. But on the other side of the stables, something caught my eye. It wasn't a stable of flawless white horses, but the tangled, dark brown hair and the tattered clothing and muddy boots of the girl that was brushing them. I hesitated to approach her for only a moment before making my way to the fence of the stable, "Hey, Alina."

She turned around quickly, her face dripping with sweat, as I gave her a nervous smile. She wiped her face off and quickly ran a hand through her hair, "Hey, Hi."

I had never seen her act like... Well, like me. She always seemed so collected in the tavern. It had become easier to talk to her in the tavern in the past couple weeks. We had a lot of time to spend together which was great. I think she liked it too.

"Sorry, I thought I heard a noise back here after I got out of training and was curious."

"Just me," She smiled, "I didn't see you come in at the normal time, and I thought you might've had a bad day or something and just gone to bed."

"No, I was just admiring the town."

"Did you want me to get you something to eat then? I can fire up something real quick; you must be hungry."

"No, it's fine," I smiled; it was nice to be on the cool side for once.

She smiled as she looked away and wiped the sweat from her forehead and ran her fingers through her bangs again, "I'm sorry I'm a mess right now, I was just finishing up out here before I turned in for the night."

"You do a good job out here, I mean I could've sworn those horses were shining when I walked up," I laughed trying to make a joke, but I instantly lost my cool when she gave me a confused smile. "Sorry, I was just saying ---"

"Horses?" She questioned and smiled, her confidence coming back.

"Yea, I ----" I took a second look, this time I recognized these creatures from the long protruding horns that graced their foreheads. My mouth was left agape.

"They were found when I was 12 years old, and the Fade came to me to capture them.

"You caught them?" I asked.

"Yea, I remember it was late at night, and my mother was singing me to sleep when my father came in and told us what was happening. I was terrified; I imagined these beasts with long horns and legs that could kill me with one kick and I didn't understand why the Fade was taking me. But, my parents trusted him, so I went, and when we arrived it was beautiful; the five of them were just roaming, gracefully, shining. The Fade instructed me to walk out to the field with them and as I did the unicorns came to me, as if they knew me for thousands of years. I brought them back here and had been taking care of them, protecting them ever since."

"That's amazing, and they've always been that obedient?"

She nodded and slowly took my hand; my heart skipped a beat, my palms started sweating as she led me through the gate. She guided me towards the unicorn she was brushing before, but I still kept my eyes on her. She lifted my hand and guided it onto the unicorns back, it snorted air through its nose, looking back at us as she placed her other hand on its neck. Together, we ran our hands over the silky fur.

"Their horns possess magical attributes that the Fade can tap into to strengthen his healing. That's why he wanted them here; it doesn't bother them, they are pure creatures and can sense purity in others."

"Why did the Fade want you to capture them?"

She laughed nervously, "While they can sense purity, only a virgin can capture and tame them." She walked me back to the fence, not letting go of my hand. "It's been such a blessing having them, it's given me a purpose in this life, but it has come with heart ache in learning to take care of them."

Her hand tightened on mine as she reminisced, "What do you mean?" I asked, sympathetically.

"When I first had the unicorns I was terrified of them. I lost both of my parents a year after I found the unicorns, in a battle that they could have survived if I had been able to ride with the Fade, into battle."

"How do you know that you were the deciding factor in their death?" I asked.

"Because nobody has ever told me I wasn't. I've heard all the comforting words I can stand except the ones I wanted to hear. It wasn't your fault." She looked down at her feet with a look I could only imagine resembled the way she looked down at her parent's lifeless bodies.

I knew she wanted to hear that it wasn't her fault; however, I didn't think that it would've meant the same coming from me, so I took her hand and pulled her into my arms to comfort her.

Without resistance she came in, lying her head on my shoulder, "I'm sorry," she laughed, "I don't mean to bring this up, it's just been such a big part of my purpose with the unicorns and taking care of the Nest." She looked me in the eyes one last time, tears welling up, she let go of my hand. "I can't believe myself," She forced a laugh again, "I must be tired. I think I should probably head in."

"Yea, no problem," I told her, "I'll see you in the morning, right?"

"Of course," she replied with a small smile before she hung her head low, on her walk back to the stables.

This whole world felt as real as back home when I saw the pain in Alina's eyes that this war had caused. I looked around in the stables at the unicorns. It all was real. Undeniably real. D'Hanin deserved peace just as much as anyone else.

\* \* \* \*

I lied in my bed, thoughts of unicorns, training, and Alina ran through my head keeping me awake. I closed my eyes trying to fall asleep, but with my thoughts so jumbled, it did no good. I couldn't shake this feeling and sat up on the edge of the bed, looking out my window.

My bedroom door swung open, and I jumped off my bed, putting my hands up, ready to fight. It was the Fade. He was holding a candle, lighting only his face.

"Good, you're awake. Come with me."

I threw my clothes on and followed him out of the tavern.

The Fade quickly explained to me, "What you did in the Training Center was miraculous. You truly do not know what this means for D'Hanin."

We headed for the gates, and they swung open for the Fade and me. We walked out, the candle being our only light to guide us. This was the first time I would be exploring outside these walls; the trees swayed and creaked with the breeze and the sound of animals scratching their claws along the branches as they scurried across them. The deeper we went the darker it became.

However, it didn't keep the Fade from rushing into the forest until we reached a clearing in a heavily wooded area. The Fade set the candle down in the middle, only giving us enough light to tell where each other were. He got close to me.

"You are a Fire Element Bearer, my friend."

My face went white, "So that means the elements did choose me?" I asked concerned.

The Fade laughed, "Yes! There is no doubt in my mind that you are the chosen one!

"Then there's really no arguing now, is there?"

"This is a clear sign from the elements that they have chosen you to retrieve the Scales. You can control any fire around you; you can throw it, put it out, raise it, guide it. If you can think it, you can do it." He said excitedly.

"I can?" I said almost unable to believe it, "I don't remember ever being able to do any of those things with fire."

"Of course not, while you were in your world, but when you dropped into our world, a fire element must have clung onto you and lived deep within your heart until you could use it."

"A fire element?"

"Yes, the elements all across our world have just been waiting to cling to someone who holds greatness in their heart."

"And I have that greatness?" I asked still confused about all of this element talk and clinging to my heart.

"Very few people have had an element cling to them since Keahi's time. There is a small group of us still around, for the most part, good people, which have an element. The effects of the Four Scales limited the elements reactions to humans. Which means they must have gone to other worlds to find someone that was capable and unaffected by the Scales. I'm not sure what will come of it, knowing you are not from

D'Hanin.  But let's find out."  He said, turning and walked towards the candle.

He pulled out a small yellow rock from his pocket and put on a glove.  With the gloved hand, he held the rock over the candle, and it caught fire.  He held it up, "I'm going to throw this at you."

I braced myself and prepared to dive out of the way.

"Do not move, use your mind to avoid the fire hitting you, concentrate and you will feel the element coursing through your veins as you control the fire."

The Fade pulled back and threw the rock right at me.  My heart started pounding, but I tried to stand firm.  The little ball of fire was flying right at my face like a shooting star.  I finally closed my eyes and ducked feeling the flaming rock connecting with the back of my head, knocking me to the ground.  I grabbed the back of my head feeling a bump, but thankfully, none of my hair had burned off.

I rolled over.  The Fade picked the rock up and stomped out a small fire in the grass.  He looked at the flaming rock and threw it at me again, hitting my chest I tried to grab it, but I couldn't control my skin from searing and dropped it once more.

The Fade ran over and picked it up again as I got out of the way.  "Without the Scales, this fire will rapidly get out of hand."

"Well stop throwing it at me, it burns!"

Before I could even finish the ball of fire was flying through the air, I dove out of the way, "What are you doing, what do you want me to do!"

"Channel the fire Finn; you have the ability to do it."

He had the fire in his hand once again, so I squared him up and he threw the fire at me; I finally understood what it was like to be a Goomba as Mario launches fireballs at them.

I watched the flame closing in on me, I stayed active in my panic, but it didn't keep me from flinching, my eyes snapping shut, prepared to get hit but luckily it must have missed me because I didn't feel the impact. I slowly opened my eyes seeing the ground illuminated. I stood up straight and the ball of fire was hovering right in front of my face. The heat of the flame made my face warm; I could feel the same burning sensation as I had had before, slowly encapsulating the warmth on my face and releasing it throughout my entire body.

The Fade walked up and grabbed the fire out of the air and tossed it to me. I held out my hand; the flame hovered right above it.

"You must practice, keep opening your mind up to the element, train yourself to understand it, but do not lose control to it, that is the most important thing. In my many years, I have met few people blessed with an element, and many of them, nearly inevitably, had lost control of it," the Fade was more stern than I have ever seen him. I nodded my head.

"It is something I cannot teach you; you must know your limits and not break them. We will continue your element training."

The fireball became extremely hot against my palm so I switched it to my other hand, the Fade noticing the move.

"You'll get used to the heat; you'll be able to control more at a single time as well. As for now keep practicing with this," he pointed to the ball of fire, "and controlling the light on a candle."

I looked at the ball and switched it back to my other hand watching it hover. I was beyond asking, *"why me?"* I've learned that whatever we are given, good or bad, is because we have the ability to handle it.

We continued to throw the ball of fire around, like a father teaching his son to play baseball, for about an hour. Every time the ball would start to go out he would challenge me to raise the fire. I wasn't able to every time, but I could feel the burn in my arms much like the night I tried to heal myself.

* * * *

We finished up training for the night; the sun was just starting to leak light through the trees as we walked back to the village.

"Are you able to cure wounds because of an element?" I asked curious to know more about what had clung to my heart.

He smiled, "Yes, I have the Angel Element. It is the oldest known elements, and not to boast, but the most challenging to master.

"What are the others?"

"Well, there's Water and Plantation, similar to the Fire Element. There's also the Karma Element, giving the master abilities to bring wrath or happiness to anyone they desire. It's the one most easily lost control of."

I interrupted him, "What happens if you lose control of your element?"

"It controls you... eventually you will believe you can lay waste on anyone in your path, that you are an almighty being and you are killed, either by someone or yourself when you or they have had enough." He paused for a moment, regaining his thoughts, "the last one, which I would never have believed existed if it weren't for the Amethyst Scale, is the Harmony element, which gives the bearer an ability to bring inner peace to anyone. I have never known or heard of anyone to acquire the Harmony element for him or herself. I believe it's because no world is meant to be in complete peace, and if it were, we'd be dead," he smiled.

I'm not sure I saw the humor in that, or completely understood what he meant, "So the Scales, are the elements, well, four of them?"

"That is correct. Keahi was the only one to be able to harness the power of an element and put it in the Scales. However, he did not have any of them. It was a feat that frightened many people."

"So why didn't he do all of them?"

"I believe he was, but as you know his time was cut short. He planned to make D'Hanin a Utopia, a perfect place, but as much as he denied it, the Scales were not perfect. They are great, but even with the Scales, crops will die and wars will break out; however, it does prevent them from reaching terrible heights. In the short time that we had the Scales, it was indeed perfect." The Fade stared off into the night sky, deep in thought.

"Keahi sounds like an incredible person," I said, breaking his thought.

"That he was. There was nothing more beautiful than this world to Keahi, and all he wanted was for everyone, no matter his or her class or health, to have a chance to experience it at the highest of its glory."

"It's still an amazing world to be in," I said.

"Keahi would've appreciated that, however, it would not have kept him from being heartbroken, seeing his world in the state that it is in."

We finally reached the gates and went in. I was exhausted, the Fade told me I could have the morning off to get rest, and I wasn't going to deny that. I hurried back to the Unicorn's Nest by myself and walked in. The place was empty; I almost thought I was in the wrong place.

"There you are!" I heard from upstairs. I looked up and saw Lib hanging off the balcony. He ran downstairs and grabbed me by the shoulders.

"Are you ok, is t--there anythin' w--wrong with -- you!" He looked all over my body.

"I'm fine, what's wrong?"

"Where 'ave you b--been? I have s--searched tha entire village for you!"

"I was in training with the Fade," I said trying to calm him down.

By that time Alina came out of the back room in a hurry, "Oh good, you found him. Finn, we've got to warn the Fade."

With no surprise, there was something else I didn't know about, "Lib! What's going on?"

He pushed me out the door, Alina followed out running behind the Unicorn's Nest while Lib limped towards the Training Center dragging me along.

"The g--garmec, Apaku's army. Tha guards 'ave seen 'em only minutes -- away the blasted things they have infested this w--world, destroyin' anythin tha's in their path."

The Fade and I must have been so close to them without even knowing it. I had to go into hiding, or get out of here somehow; if the garmec got me there would be no hope.

"Where am I gonna go, there's no way I'm ready to go after the Scales!"

"Go?" Lib said, my heart dropping, "You are gonna figh.'" My heart dropped again.

# 5

## THE FIRST OF MANY

Lib barreled through the doors of the Training Center, dragging me along with him. The Fade must have just gotten in because he was just walking onto the mat as he turned around quickly.

"We have gotta ge' Finn prepared!" Lib yelled, "The garmec are approachin'!"

"How much time do we have?" The Fade said back.

"Minutes, we have already got troops on tha front, and tha guards are p--prepared ta kill."

The Fade walked quickly to his wall of weapons, "Leave him with me, you must go to the front and get prepared, we shall be close behind."

Lib patted me on the shoulder giving me a nod then running out the door. I turned back around, and a sword was flying towards my face. I quickly grabbed it out of the air and swung it around much more comfortably than expected.

"How does that feel?" The Fade asked.

"Light," I said back as I swung it back and forth like a feather.

"Good, take this," he handed me a rather small, round shield. I put it on my left arm immediately, and he dragged me out the door with his shield and sword in hand.

"Just stay close to me, we can't afford to lose you, but we need all the help we can get. Do not try and use your element no matter what happens; you are not ready to use it," he instructed me, as we got closer to the gates. My heart pounded against my chest, and I started to feel dizzy.

"Am I even ready to use this," I asked holding up my sword.

"You are more than ready; the garmec are barbarians, you are a precision striker with more training than they have ever had with a sword."

The encouraging words didn't help much; I still felt like I was about to drop to the ground. The gates started to swing open as we ran through I could already see about twenty of our men standing, suited up, ready to fight. I spotted Lib, and we ran towards him in the back as the gates closed behind us.

He was holding a giant hammer with spikes coming out of each end and looked down at me confidently, "Do not be afraid, I will die before I let one o' them monsters get at ya, and trust me," he paused for a moment, looking ahead, "this is not where I'm gonna die."

Then I heard the sound of a horse trotting up behind me, I looked back and saw hooves land right behind me. I looked up at the beautiful white coat and all the way up to its dark eyes. It leaned its head down to look at me and revealed its horn.

I looked around it and saw Alina with her knife sitting bareback on the unicorn; my mouth was left agape, talk about a warrior!

"Compose yourself!" I heard the Fade yelling at me.

"Did you not think I could actually ride?" Alina smiled. She was much much more brave than I was. I snapped back around and saw something much less beautiful than the unicorn; at least two hundred of them rushing forward at us which I assumed were the garmec.

They weren't much taller than I was, standing on two legs much like horses back legs, galloping towards us screaming, spit flying from their mouths, barring their twisted and crooked yellow teeth. Their faces looked much like an English bulldog with the greening skin of the old lady from "*The Shining*."

They gained on us quickly; I gripped my sword tightly as the troops fanned out into a giant C and charged at the garmec. Alina charged with them on her magnificent steed at full force, Lib, the Fade, and I walked forward trailing, not far behind.

Our troops collided with the garmec; blood sprayed almost instantly. I watch tentatively as heads and limbs of garmec rolled upon the ground. Even our men were bleeding out on the ground, watching the battle as the light slowly faded from their eyes.

It stopped me dead in my tracks; the smell of blood and dirt filled the air. I had difficulty breathing, watching lives end right before my eyes. I managed to gasp out a few words, "Can't you help these people!" I yelled at the Fade as he fought off two garmec.

"I'm a little busy right now!" He yelled back.

Shocked by the bloodshed, I didn't even notice the Fade and Lib were fighting along with everybody else. A surge of adrenaline ran through my body; I had to focus on my training and help the people I cared for. I jumped alongside the Fade and chopped

the arm off a garmec much simpler than I had expected.

The garmec and I screamed together, one in
pain and one terror-stricken.

"Be calm Finn! We need you!" I looked back at
Lib as I could see the pain in his eyes for me. He killed
two garmec that he was fighting and ran over to me;
killing two more that I had no idea were closing in on
me.

"Nobody in their righ' mind wants ta do this;
they do this for a love o' their p--people and tha world
they know. Find tha' s--strength, Finn, or there is
'bout 10,000 garmec in D'Hanin that already have that
strength ta kill -- you. Now go protec' tha Fade, 'e
needs ta be healin,'" Lib yelled as he pushed me farther into the bloodshed.

I walked around looking for the Fade, dodging
oncoming attacks, and letting the others massacre the
garmec. I saw Alina, still atop the unicorn, fighting
much more valiantly than I. She was looping around
in circles, creating a perimeter and realized she must
be close to the Fade; he needs the magic of the unicorn
horn. I ran towards her, seeing a horde of garmec barring their teeth, and trying to get to the unicorn more
than the Fade or her.

I braced myself before I dove into battle, and
then all at once, I went for it. I stabbed a garmec
through the chest, killing it; I spun around and
chopped the head off the other garmec the Fade was
fighting.

"I've got you covered; you need to heal our people!" I yelled at the Fade.

He nodded and ran up to a man, whose arm
was barely hanging onto his body. I followed the
Fade, as Alina ran off the other garmec and circled
back around.

A garmec came at me from the side, and I
blocked his swing with my shield. The force of the
swing was much stronger than I expected and my arm

fell, almost crippled, but with my speed, I stuck my sword straight out, and the garmec impaled itself. I ripped my sword out, and a wave of blood followed spilling onto the ground.

The Fade stood up and fought off another garmec, the man's arm was completely healed, but he still rolled on the ground in pain.

"I didn't save you for nothing, now get up and continue fighting!" The Fade ordered and pulled the man to his feet.

We ran over to another man with a significant cut on his arm, but who was still fighting. I took on the garmec while the Fade healed him in a matter of seconds. I could move this sword much more effortlessly than the training sword; I could barely believe the precision and speed I had.

The man thanked him, and pushed me to the side, "This is my kill!" He yelled and chopped the garmec's head off with a forceful swing.

I looked around and found Lib who was taking on three garmec by himself. The biggest one swung violently cutting him across the chest; blood began flowing immediately. I grabbed the Fade, and we ran over to Lib.

We each took on a garmec, slaying them within a matter of minutes.

Sweat dripped down my face as I looked around the blood-soaked battlefield. The Fade was taking time to heal Lib. I saw arrows flying from our guards by the gate, impaling the garmec with impressive accuracy. Alina galloped past a group of garmec overpowering a soldier, trampling a majority of them, but unfortunately, it wasn't in time to save him.

I fought more garmec, one after the other. The Fade continued to try and heal people but just couldn't keep up with the bloodshed.

"I can't keep healing; it's taking all my energy out of me!" He yelled after healing a young kid who couldn't have been much older than me.

"Then we've got to finish this!" I yelled back feeling more like a warrior than I could've ever imagined.

"I agree!" Lib yelled as he charged after another group of garmec. As he left me behind, the Fade ran off with Alina; I felt, what seemed like, a linebacker tackling me from behind. I wrestled, with what I now knew was a garmec, until something happened I couldn't explain.

Fire flowed out of my hands, like a volcano, catapulting the garmec off of me it collided with a tree, engulfed in a flame, which grew up the tree.

"Finn!" I looked up to see the Fade running towards me. "What did you do! I told you not to use your element!"

"I didn't mean to; I don't know how it happened!" I said panicked, seeing the flame grow wildly out of control.

"Control the fire, bring it back down immediately!"

I stood up unsure of what to do; I was in shock as I watched the fire spread to another tree, a large branch that was consumed, broke away from the tree and fell on a group of unsuspecting garmec and soldiers.

"Finn! Do something!" The Fade yelled at me, "Channel the fire to return to you!"

I closed my eyes tight as the battle raged on around me. I screamed inside of my head, ordering the fire to put itself out. I inched closer; feeling the fire radiating more intense heat, but it was of no use.

I was shoved to the side as three of our soldiers, started chopping the tree with axes, allowing it to fall to the ground. The rest of the soldiers scrambled out of the way.

The Fade grabbed me to get out of their way, "Move towards Kautun, there is less garmec back there. Fight as needed, the soldiers will control the fire as best as they can, do not try to help!"

Shame washed over me as I backed away from the battle. The soldiers cut down two more trees, tipping them down onto one another, creating a giant bonfire. It burned bright, the soldiers did their best to contain it and fight off the garmec that saw an opportunity. The smallest of ashes floating off, alarmed the soldiers as they chased them down, and stomping them out before they caused any more fires.

I could feel warmness in my fingertips that rose up my arms and eventually into my body. I concentrated on the feeling finally seeing the fire dim slightly. I knew the Fade told me not to help, but I didn't feel like I was, it was the same feeling that I had when the fire was released. I didn't fight it. It was allowing the soldiers to protect themselves, and that's all I wanted.

I didn't want to be responsible for any more of our own soldiers' deaths.

I continued to fight for what seemed like hours more, my life flashing before my eyes on more than one account. The fire died down enough to a point it was no longer a threat to any more of the forest.

We could see the end of the battle as garmec started retreating. The garmec I was fighting began to back off; I lowered my sword keeping eye contact with him, I let him withdraw with his army, I couldn't kill anymore, and felt a sense of relief when he ran.

I looked around, the last of the garmec were running away or slain by our men.

I saw about 15 or so of our men lying dead on the battlefield, almost too bloody and mangled to be sure they were ours. The Fade, covered in blood, continued healing the rest of the exhausted soldiers.

Alina's white unicorn no longer looked as if it was a peaceful, beautiful creature, now with bloodstains covering its coat. She trotted away leaving the battlegrounds as quickly as possible, not wanting to look back.

Lib was carrying bodies of soldiers back through the gates for a proper burial.

The healed or unwounded soldiers started piling the bodies of the dead garmec into the fire I had caused, throwing the limbs and heads into the pile as well.

I stood by myself, wandering around, confused and lost. My mind couldn't grip onto reality. It ached my heart, even if these were brutal beasts trying to kill us, seeing the lifeless bodies, of the garmec and our own, sent a chill up my spine.

I saw a soldier, about a foot and a half taller than the rest with arms the size of my head, approaching the fire in what looked like a ceremonious way, with three soldiers following behind them as they walked to the flaming pile of bodies surrounded by soldiers watching.

The lead soldier stood in front, looking at the rest of the army, "To Apaku! We send the ashes of your warriors into the sky to show you; we will not fall to a dark summoner! And though you have taken some of our own with yours, we pray that they know they have not gone in vain and will forever be remembered throughout D'Hanin for the rest of history!" The soldier yelled into the sky. They all watched the burning corpses silently still.

The Fade walked up to me and grabbed me by the arm with his bloody hand, "the garmec are patrolling our lands, watch out for them on your journey, you don't want to run into a group like that when you're alone. If you do, pray they hadn't already seen you and hide." He pulled me slowly back through the gates without saying another word.

# 6

# THE WARRIORS OF KEAHI

We cleaned ourselves up, washing away the blood of battle, and met back at the training center. I almost didn't make it again, I hadn't slept in the past 30 hours, and it didn't look like I was going to be able to rest anytime soon.

"This is it, Finn, do you know this?" The Fade asked me. I stood in front of him with a blank look. "The time has come for you to begin your journey, we will prepare you, and then you will be off."

It was not the news I wanted to hear after the battle I just had to endure, "I still have so much to learn though, I can't go yet," I said frantically.

"The rest will come with the journey; I have nothing else worth teaching you that you would have to wait here any longer for."

I continued to argue knowing it wouldn't get me anywhere with the

Fade, "Where do I even start, I don't know anything about this world!"

"Apaku has control of the entire Western Nation, for him to send a group of garmec that size to Kautun has only one meaning. He's planning on overtaking the Central Curve. If Kautun falls, it will be his."

"Then why isn't this the worst time for me to be leaving? I need to stay here and protect Kautun."

"No, you need to go out there and protect D'Hanin and it starts with getting the Scales back. Apaku has distributed the Scales to his most faithful followers. He kept the Amethyst Scale for himself, gave the Obsidian Scale to his right-hand man, Raigor, the Sapphire Scale to his next in line, Kuyper, and the Emerald Scale to Abanyu. You must go after Abanyu."

I thought I was only going to have to fight Apaku! Now you're telling me there's 3 more people!" I yelled frantically.

"You need to trust me, Finn. You don't want to go after Apaku yet. He and his nation are too strong, however, Abanyu will be his weakest asset. Destroying him and returning the Emerald Scale will send a message and empower our own people."

I couldn't find the words to argue, however, I was angry. This quest that I was suppose to go on just became infinitely more difficult and I couldn't understand why this information was held from me.

The Fade noticed my irritation, "You will not win this war by yourself, Finn. The elements have chosen you to lead the war, not to fight it yourself."

I nodded, it taking every ounce of my being not to release my outrage onto the Fade, it would just be that much longer and difficult before I could get home.

The Fade understood my frustration, I didn't need to take it out on him for him to know I was about to break, "Follow me," he said calmly.

We exited the training center, the sun was already going down, and the moon was rising. A chilling breeze blew my hair to the side, and a shiver went through my body. I expected to see snowfall at any moment.

The streets were empty. Every surviving soldier retreated to their homes, comforting their families or finding privacy to mourn. The only sound being the wind, as the village was completely silent. The Fade walked lightly through the town.

"Your greatest asset you will have on your journey will be your weapon. We are short on time; I will supply you with a dagger, a shield, and proper attire." He looked at my clothes, which were torn and tattered from the battle.

"However," he continued, "No warrior can go on without his best friend, that is why we must put off your journey one more day while it's shaped."

We stopped in front of the Slayed Monster Smithy. You could feel the heat billowing out of the open building. A man could be seen in the shadows, examining a sword.

The Fade cleared his throat to reach his attention. The bladesmith stopped what he was doing, and looked up at us, "Good to see you made it out alive, Fade." He stood up and walked out of the shadow.

I recognized him immediately as the soldier carrying the torch in the burning ceremony. He had a sword still in his hand with bloodstains covering it.

"You as well, Tor'oos," the Fade spoke first and then turned to me, "This is Tor'oos Tanzec, he will craft your sword."

I nodded at Tor'oos Tanzec, however, I noticed an irritated look before he spoke, "You don't have to introduce me by that name. Tor'oos is enough."

"Of course, my apologies. This is Finn Anderson; he is with me to be fitted for a sword."

Tor'oos raised the tip of his sword slightly and nodded, "It's been a long day, Fade."

"It has for all of us, including Finn."

I couldn't look him in the face but could feel the angry scowl on his face burning a hole in the top of my head.

"You know this is part of your duty---"

"Bring him in here."

The Fade guided me under the roof and stepped back. There were jars of eyeballs, razor-sharp teeth, and algae or a type of moss among other materials lining the walls. Pelts hung from the ceiling and piles of bones lay in the corner. It wasn't what I expected to see in a blacksmith shop.

"Hold out your arms," he instructed me, and I stuck them out to my sides.

"In front of you."

I quickly swung them in front of me. He grabbed my wrists, his fingers easily overlapping in the grip. With his right hand, he grabbed my bicep and squeezed, then stepped back, "Put your arms down, look me in the eyes."

I looked him in the eyes trying not to blink, *"What could he possibly be trying to figure out,"* I thought to myself.

"Ok, bring him back tomorrow, I will work tirelessly through the night once again, but I'm done after this Fade," he receded into the shadows, "I will not continue to have my best work destroyed by unfit warriors."

"I believe this will be our last," the Fade responded and pulled me back into the frosty night air.

He walked me back to the training center, and we stopped in front of the doors, "There is nothing else left for you to finish tonight that would keep you from getting rest. You had come a long way from where you were when you first arrived in D'Hanin. However, after the glimpse of real war we just experienced, I do not believe you are mentally prepared to begin your journey and will need help. With Kautun now on the garmec's radar, I do believe they will be back, so there is no option of you staying any longer and risking your life for Kautun when you have all of D'Hanin to worry about. I will have choices prepared for you when you return tomorrow."

"Choices?"

The Fade looked up at the moon before patting me on the shoulder, "There's nothing else left for you to finish tonight that should keep you from getting any rest," he reiterated and gave me a half smile before retreating into the training center.

That could have kept me up for most of the night, but at times you just need to trust that if it doesn't keep them up at night, it shouldn't keep you up at night. So, I didn't waste any more time getting back to my room, and as soon as I hit my pillow, I fell into dark oblivion.

\* \* \* \*

I woke up the next morning feeling more sluggish than I ever have. I pulled my covers up not wanting to get out into the brisk morning air, and to top it off knowing this could've very well have been my last night in a real bed; I found few reasons to throw the covers off and start my day. But I did it anyway and walked down to the tavern, Alina was the only one there.

"Morning," I said to her. She looked up, not noticing that I was coming down the stairs, and smiled.

"Good morning," she said back subdued, "I hear today's the day."

I nodded with a forced smile.

Alina looked at me with sad eyes, "Let me make you one last breakfast before you head out."

"There's nothing that would cheer me up more," I gratefully replied, although aware, another meal from her would make it that much harder for me to leave.

She walked back into the kitchen, out of sight.

I waited for about ten minutes before she came back out with a small plate covered with gnome bacon, a large egg, toast, potatoes, sprinkled with a red seasoning, I had seen before but wasn't sure what it was only that it was delicious, and a steaming mug of hot chocolate.

I ate quickly, knowing I had to meet the Fade but savoring each bite as much as I could. Alina sat with me, quietly letting me enjoy my last meal. She was always great company to have whether or not we were talking.

I finished off the last few bites of my breakfast and set my fork down and wiped my mouth, "Thanks, Alina, that was really what I needed.

"It was my pleasure; I just hate to see you go."

I nodded, "Me too," I looked down at my plate, I had a lot on my mind that I hadn't felt ok talking to anybody about until I sat there with Alina. "I'm not sure how to talk to anybody about this, but I know you're the only one I want to talk to about it."

She leaned back not sure whether to be flattered or worried, "What is it?"

"I don't know how I felt about killing yesterday. I was terrified from the first moment to the last, but it gave me a rush of adrenaline," I paused for a moment remembering it, "But I don't know if I'm ready to do it again, and that makes me question if I'm ready to leave."

I looked up at her, and she grabbed my hands, "I know you're ready, and everyone else will tell you as well. You're ready. The Fade can't teach you how to feel when you're out there. It's something you will have to deal with and strengthen."

"But if I did what I did yesterday, without you guys there, I'll be picked off in minutes. I feel like I won't have a chance to cope with that feeling of guilt and adrenaline."

"Well, I hate to tell you this, but I've never done it myself before. I'm involved solely on healing and taking care of our injured. What I have learned though, from being in battle, when it comes down to life or death, no one will blame you for choosing life. Especially you."

My heart wasn't so heavy after talking to Alina; She was one of those people that you know actually care to make you feel better.

Patrons began coming in, we both stood up, knowing it was time for me to leave.

She wrapped her arms around me tightly, "I have great faith in you Finn," she stood back and looked me in the eyes with her hands still on my shoulders, "but promise you'll take care of yourself out there."

I nodded and closed my eyes wanting to freeze time at that moment. She gently squeezed tighter for a brief second but the moment couldn't last forever, as I leaned back, "I'll see you again soon Alina," I slowly turned, heading for the training center.

I met the Fade outside the training center. He was standing motionless; his eyes closed softly.

*"Was this the time to be meditating? I just hope he snaps out of this soon."* I watched his eyes under his eyelids and could tell they were rapidly shifting back and forth, up and down. I decided to sit down at his feet and wait.

I waited and waited. The cold wind blew, and I squeezed my legs in closer to me trying to get warm.

"Oh good, you've arrived."

I looked up, and the Fade was looking down at me.

I stood up, "Yea, a little while ago."

"Sorry if you waited too long, today is a big day, and I needed time to mentally prepare myself for your decision today."

"My decision?" I asked, "You mean I get to decide if I can go home or go on with the journey?"

The Fade smiled at me, catching on to the sarcasm, "Follow me, we started walking forward, "today, we will pick a companion."

We walked slowly towards Keahi's home; the place Lib said was an arena for the personal enjoyment of Keahi.

As we neared the building, the Fade explained what we were indeed there for, "This is it," he said to me, "we're going to go in, I have narrowed down the warriors for you, and you will choose from them."

"Excuse me? Did you say warriors?"

"Yes, Keahi's Warriors," the Fade smiled, "Each one has been trained by Keahi himself."

"How? They would have to be ancient by now," I asked.

"I can explain inside, too many wandering ears for my comfort out here," after a brief pause he looked down on me, "are you ready?"

I prepared myself to stand in front of a room with warriors fighting a bloodbath to win my choice. I just hoped there weren't going to be any real fights yet," I looked up at the Fade, "as ready as I can be, I guess."

We entered the building, the Fade swinging the heavy metal doors open for me. I walked in. It was completely dark, so I stood patiently for the Fade. I could only see him from the light leaking in through the doors, but as they slammed closed the room was covered in complete darkness, which ended shortly with a loud clang.

Two high windows on either side of the room opened up; the sunlight illuminating about 20 feet in front of us then another noise from the next pair of windows and the room brightened another 20 feet. Windows continued to clang down a long narrow hallway for about 100 feet, revealing two tall chambers evenly spaced out.

The Fade began walking forward, and I followed him. With a closer look, each chamber held a different warrior encased in ice.

"What is this? Why is everyone in ice?"

The Fade looked down at me and smiled, "I'm sure you've heard the rumors of this place. An arena, a show held only for Keahi's thirst for blood?"

"I heard something of the sort."

"This must be kept between us; this was not an arena. It was Keahi's Training Center. He knew the complications the Scales could bring, and the hatred that could fall upon him by so many people. He prepared an army of highly trained warriors, within these walls. There's warriors that know how to use a bow, some know how to use a blade, and some a hammer for when the worst presented itself to Keahi."

"Do any of them have the ability to use any of the elements?" I interjected.

"As I said before, an element is a rare occurrence in our world, rare enough for only one warrior to be blessed with an element."

Naturally, I desired to choose that warrior first.

"However," the Fade crushed that desire with one word, "that young boy was I. I trained alongside Keahi, while the other's trained for him and when Keahi died I was left to decide for the warriors."

"Why didn't you just send all of these people off to fight then? A war was obviously set in motion after Keahi's death."

"Because I knew of Keahi's Prophecy. My choice to hold them was indeed amongst the most difficult of my life, however, I would not consider this to be an undesirable choice in my life. One will follow you into battle, but they all will fight in the war. We will hold this secret until that time has come."

"But how do people not know already, don't they wonder what happened to all the warriors in the arena?

"As the years went on, the people of Kautun heard the noise of battles within these walls less and less, eventually the last clang of a sword on shield would ring through the city and no one would hear another noise from Keahi's Arena again. Naturally, interrogated by everyone; I simply told them the warriors moved on to other cities. The Fade smirked, "I'm not well liked throughout D'Hanin. My many choices following Keahi's death have been unlikeable to say the least.

"Well Lib spoke highly of you." I said, trying to lift his spirits.

The Fade let out a genuine laugh, "He is in the company of my favorites in D'Hanin as well," he said, and guided me forward, "Take a look around; there's a short description for each warrior underneath them. Choose your warrior wisely and they will help you on your journey through D'Hanin."

I slowly walked forward to the first warrior on the right side. It was a man; he looked to be in his fifties with completely gray hair and a slim build. His eyes were closed gently almost making him look dead. I looked down at the description, it read:

Warrior: Aloisio Luen
Weapon: Bow
Secondary: Short Sword
Height: 6'00"
Weight: 160
Description: Aloisio is a peaceful warrior, in touch with nature. Known for his speed and precision, he will improve your speed and precision by pushing you to match his.

I knew now that each description was tailored precisely for me. Aloisio almost felt like the perfect match for me. I stepped back and looked at him. *I can't be sold on the first warrior; I have to keep an open mind,"* I thought to myself.

I moved on to the ice chamber directly across the hall. This time it was a girl. Her eyes were opened and looked straight ahead. Her hair stretched down her back, touching the sword on her hip. She looked about my age:

Warrior: Aneira Kanelé
Weapon: Long Sword
Secondary: Dagger
Height: 5'02"
Weight: 120
Description: Aneira is ready for battle at any moment. Her small stature will benefit you knowing that she can go wherever you go. She does exceptionally well, maybe even better in cold climates, which your journey will begin in.

This decision was already getting difficult; both warriors seemed like great matches. I looked back at the Fade, who just smiled and nodded. I had to think for myself before seeing the last eight, who did I want, who would I picture my partner being.

I closed my eyes and pictured a big guy, someone who could compliment my abilities, not someone who could match them. I also needed someone who could strike from a distance.

I opened my eyes and began walking down the hallway and taking a good look at each warrior, without reading the descriptions. I came upon a massive man, about the fifth chamber down, and walked over to him. He had a big belly and round face.

Warrior: Berea Bon
Weapon: Hammer
Secondary: None
Height: 5'09"
Weight: 350
Description: Berea likes to eat, you can be sure you'll never go without a meal with him on your side.

He does not have a secondary weapon but makes up for it by being able to launch his hammer up to 40 yards. He insists that his fists are his secondary.

He looked like a jolly man, able to lighten the mood if situations got harsh, but it still wasn't what I was looking for. I continued down the rows. There were an excellent variety of women, men, big warriors and small warriors.

There was another warrior; I believe the seventh choice. I almost couldn't see any distinct features in him until I was just inches away from the glass. He had long jet-black hair pulled back into a ponytail; he wore all black, including black gloves. I looked down to read his description:

Warrior: Shadow
Weapon: Rope
Secondary: Dagger
Height: 5'09"
Weight: 165
Description: His name defines him, Shadow, stays hidden in the night and the shadows of anything casting. He is quiet and kills his enemies as quick as the grim reaper.

He was disparate from me in almost every way, but not in a way to compliment my abilities. It would be challenging for me to move quietly enough to let him work. I couldn't see the reasoning, the Fade had for Shadow being my partner, but then again, I don't doubt he had a good reason.

Before turning to look at the other warrior, I noticed the one next to Shadow. It was a burly man, with a big beard and long scraggly hair; he looked like the picture perfect outdoorsmen. He wore basic clothes but heavily layered. He had a stern look to him, frozen in the ice:

Warrior: Scahl Kemrec
Weapon: Axe
Secondary: Throwing Axe
Height: 6'06"
Weight: 260
Description: Scahl will be able to provide you with shelter wherever you are. His large stature will make it difficult to hide from enemies but makes up for it with his strength and ability to throw an axe.

I stepped back to look at him, he looked like a serious warrior, ready to get the job done. He intimidated me, which could be a positive attribute; it would prepare me for anything worse. This was my warrior; I could feel it.

I looked back at the last two warriors I didn't even bother checking out. One was a hideous looking ogre type monster and the other was a diminutive, stocky, angry looking person. I looked back at Scahl, and then down the hallway, the Fade was already making his way down.

"This is it," I told him relieved, "Scahl. I think he will be a good match."

"He will be a good match," the Fade confirmed as he stood next to me looking up at Scahl, "You did good, I will prepare Scahl, for the journey."

The Fade made his way to the center of the room and pulled a lever that was connected to a rope that disappeared into the ceiling. The line started to move up as the rest of the ice chambers began dropping to the ground slowly, leaving Scahl the only one still in the hallway.

"Go back to Tor'oos; he should be ready for you now. I will meet back with you shortly."

I backed up away from Scahl, and the Fade then turned to leave the building.

I walked a short distance to the blacksmith. I was nervous to meet with him again after our intimidating first meeting. I could hear a pounding hammer and grunts, as I got nearer to the Slayed Monster. I walked up and peaked my head in. He was facing me, but was zoned into, what I presume, was a shield. I almost didn't want to interrupt him, but I knew I must.

I knocked on a pillar, but he didn't look up. I beat harder, but still nothing.

"Tor'oos!"

I looked behind me, and Lib was standing there. I looked back around, and Tor'oos was looking up at me.

"So you've returned," Tor'oos said.

I looked up at Lib, and he pushed me forward, "Do not be 'fraid o' 'im."

"Um. Um. Yes, the Fade told me you'd be ready for me."

Tor'oos set his hammer down and walked away from his project. He went behind a wall. I looked back at Lib, "You are gonna 'ave ta be more assertive, Finn. It was a good thin' I came, or you would be standin 'ere waitin' for a long time."

"Thanks," I replied, "I wasn't sure I'd see you before I left."

"I would not 'ave let ya go if I was not the one sendin' ya off," he said with a smile.

Tor'oos came back around the wall with a pristine sword that glimmered in the light. I was in awe of its beauty. He flipped it around and held the blade, pointing the hilt towards me to take. I wrapped my hand around it; it immediately felt like an extension of my arm.

"Swing it around a little," Tor'oos said.

I stepped back and swung it around flawlessly executing moves the Fade had taught me that I hadn't been able to do with precision previously. I stopped and looked the sword over. I could see myself in the reflection of the sword. Shifting my eyes down, I noticed a symbol on the shoulder of the blade.

"I mark all of my work, no matter what it is," he said when he saw that I had noticed the mark. He retook the sword from me; I didn't want to let go.

"I gave you a slightly curved blade, point it out to injure your opponent, point it in to kill," he explained, and I nodded.

"The crossguard is designed to mold around your hand, and only your hand, when you are wielding it. The grip is wrapped in troll skin leather, only I have been able to attain. It will never wear or need to be replaced." He swung the sword, pointing it down, "The pommel has the petrified eye of a berserker, and with every strike of the sword it will instill fear into your opponent because we know it's not going to come from your size."

I looked at Lib who was smiling; he gave me a nod as to ensure that it was just a joke; however, I was confident he was earnest. I looked back at the petrified eye. It didn't seem like an eye besides the shape; it was just a transparent foggy white ball. I studied the elegant design of the sword; his description didn't do the sword justice.

Tor'oos put the blade into a sheath and handed the sword back to me, "You did all of this in one night?" I asked.

"I forged it in one night; I've been preparing it for much longer." He said back seriously, "You must go now, I have other works to be attending to."

I attached the sheath to my hip. Lib and I exited the building walking towards the gate.

"That is a mighty fine sword ya got there," Lib told me in just as much awe as I was.

I kept my hand on the hilt, "I couldn't have imagined a better one."

"That is Tor'oos for ya, 'e makes every sword with a grudge, which makes 'em grea.' Ya s--see, 'e was always overshadowed by 'is brothers. They was much more famous then 'im. 'E's always goin out to find whatever -- 'e can to make a sword unique and claims they give 'em special powers, but I dunno. Never got to experience a Tor'oos sword for myself. 'E's the most unconventional o' the three, most unconventional o' anybody."

I desperately wanted to try my new sword out, in a strange way it empowered me, I stood tall, my chest puffed out, with this sword attached to my hip.

Lib and I reached the gate, as we waited snow began to fall lightly. It had been getting cold for the past week now. I stuck out my hand, Lib noticed.

"I can not say this is tha bes' conditions for ya ta be startin' in, but hopefully the weather will break before ya get too far." He pulled out what looked like a dead coyote from his back pocket, "I was gonna wai' till ya were leavin,' but, it's startin' to get chilly now."

He held it out to me, and I took it. I held it up and could now see it was a coat, which looked homemade out of an animal. I swung it around my shoulders, and pulled my arms through; it radiated a heat that would keep me warm throughout the snowfall.

"Thanks," I said, "It'll be a great help."

He nodded, his eyes starting to water.

It felt like Christmas, with the snow and getting the sword and coat. I was going to miss this place; especially since I knew it was going to be rough traveling from here on out.

My mind was quickly averted from that thought when what I was most nervous about came walking toward us as we waited at the gate. They moved quickly, Scahl, towering over the Fade, with a giant axe in his hand and a belt with small axes going around his waist. The Fade was carrying a bag over his shoulder.

They stopped in front of us, the Fade gave me a short introduction, "This is Scahl Kemrec."

Scahl nodded at me, "I'm grateful to have been chosen. I'm prepared to start our journey."

His beard completely covered his mouth; I could only tell he was talking because his beard moved with every word.

"Don't be so eager yet." The Fade interjected, "We have the small matter of supplies to attend to." He pulled a bag off his back and flipped it around revealing a shield hanging off it. He tapped his fingers on it, "Your shield, I apologize it couldn't have been made personal but we just didn't have the time, it is attached to the bag, but you can easily detach it and strap it onto your arm if the need arises."

It was a simple shield, small and round like the one I used in battle, definitely used but not quite as tattered.

The Fade opened the bag, moving onto the next item. He reached his hand in and dug around, then pulled out a small second-hand dagger.

"Your dagger," he said and held the hilt out for me to take, "This will go on your waist; you can see the sheath for it right there." I looked down on the right side of my hip, opposite the sword was a small sheath for the dagger, I put it in and waited for my next Christmas pres--- I mean supplies.

The Fade handed me the entire bag, "You've got extra clothes, a couple of tents, and a few pieces of food in there to help you with your travels, we couldn't pack too much. We don't want you to be slowed down."

I looked back up from the bag, my heart pounding against my chest, praying that he had a million more supplies to give me to delay walking out of that gate.

But with the bag now slung over my shoulder and his hand placed onto the opposite, he paused, "You're a great warrior, Finn. I believe with all my heart that you can complete this quest, but with every great accomplishment it does not come easy. This is not a quest that will be over quickly."

He took his hand off my shoulder, and the gates started opening. Scahl stood next to me facing the gate boldly.

The Fade gave me a fatherly hug then stood back, "Do not back down, do not falter, do not doubt, and always be prepared for the fight of your life because this will be just that. I will see you on the other side, Finn."

I nodded at him, Lib pulling me in for a quick hug, "I will see you when you ge' back, we can share a spider ale over your victree."

"Can't wait," I said back. Scahl followed alongside me as we walked out the giant gates. I couldn't force myself to look back as the gates closed behind us, possibly for good.

# 7

## A SHADED START

Scahl and I stood at the gates for a moment, snow lightly falling on us. I looked up at him, feeling a bit shy, "I'm Finley, Finn, Finn for short," I stammered out my name and reached out a hand, "An, Anderson."

Scahl nodded and grabbed my hand, "It's a pleasure, it feels good to be out. A bit warm though."

I faked a laugh, until realizing he meant because he had been frozen, "So, is it a long trip?" I asked.

Scahl looked down at me, "How skilled are you with your sword?"

"I do pretty well, I'm still learning though."

"It's gonna be a long trip," Scahl smirked through his beard.

"Well, we better keep moving. I'll let you lead the way." I picked my bag off the ground, and we started forward, our footprints trailing behind us in the snow.

A few hours quickly passed, trekking through the forest, most of the snow being stopped by the bare tree branches before hitting the ground. I trailed behind Scahl for the most part, his strides were much longer than mine, and I had to jog to catch up to him on numerous occasions.

"So, where is Abanyu?" I asked him.

"He is where the South Eastern Curve meets the South Western Curve down the Potens River."

"And where exactly are we?"

He looked down at me, "You don't know much about D'Hanin do you?"

"I've only been here a month, how much do you expect me to know?"

"No need to get feisty," he said with a smirk, "We are in the Central Curve, within the Shaded Forest. We have approximately a month to the nearest town. From there, towns are closer together, and we'll only have to camp for a few nights or so between towns."

"A month!" I almost shouted, "In this!" I gestured to the falling snow.

"Calm down, no need to get all upset, we're men, the snow is no match for us," he exclaimed swatting me on the back, "and besides, the Fade told me you had the fire element."

"Well I haven't mastered it yet, we only practiced once before they shipped me off."

Then you must practice before nightfall." He walked up to a tree then pulled his axe off his back and with one big swing chopped a branch about the width of my body cleanly off the tree. It fell, smaller branches breaking off as it hit the ground, the noise echoing through the forest.

I stood by the branch, "What do you want me to do with this?"

"Set it on fire," he said plainly.

I just looked at him.

"Well?" He asked.

I can't just set it on fire; I'm not that good with it yet."

"How do you know? You've only used the element once. Come on, go for it," he instructed.

I looked at the branch, "Ok, I'll try."

"I need you to do it, I would prefer not to spend a night out here in the snow, and I know you won't either."

I looked back at him, then back at the branch. I closed my eyes and tried imagining the branch on fire. I focused, but my toes were getting colder and colder as I stood on the frozen ground. Then the noise of twigs and dead leaves crunching under Scahl's feet didn't help my concentration either.

I had to keep focusing on the fire pushing it out, of my body onto the branch. I could feel my insides warming. I could feel the fire coursing through my veins. *"What was Scahl thinking of this? Would he think less of me if I didn't start the branch on fire?"* He was watching me like a judge; I was confident he was preparing to hold up a number card.

I opened my eyes and looked over; Scahl was standing impatiently, waiting for something to happen.

"I need you to go away; I can't concentrate."

Scahl looked at me like he didn't know what he did.

"I'm sorry, I just really need to concentrate."

"The pressure should help you, can you imagine Keahi's eye's burning a hole in you every time you were training?"

"No, I can't. I never knew him." I snapped back.

Scahl didn't flinch, he just looked down on me more, "All right, I'll get us food, please try to have the fire ready when I get back," Scahl said calmly. He pulled out a small axe from his hip and walked off through the trees.

I stood alone; I didn't appreciate the commands I was getting from him. I'd been bullied enough times in my life and this felt the same. I shrugged it off taking in my surroundings, the barren trees, the frozen ground and the daylight slowly fading. I was vulnerable to any animal that may have been lurking in the branches. I hesitated to close my eyes again, but pulled my dagger out of its sheath and held it in my hand to feel secure enough to light the branch on fire.

But then, I couldn't concentrate on burning a branch with my toes feeling like they were about to fall off, so I focused on warming my toes, I concentrated harder then heard a hoot from a bird lurking nearby.

I looked around and gritted my teeth. I closed my eyes again. *"I have to block the noise out."* I imagined the fire, in my body, the warming feeling it gave me every time it channeled. The world had gone completely quiet, the cold was gone, and everything was black. I felt my chest grow increasingly warmer, then my arms, then my hands. I focused on that warmth.

Excitement rose, and the heat stopped. I didn't want to lose the warmth, but I could feel it dwindling away.

I concentrated harder than ever, and the warmth came back. My eyes shot back open; sweat dripped from the back of my neck and down my temples. The warmth stayed in my chest for a few moments after opening my eyes, then it disappeared.

Exhaustion crept up on me from the simple task, which grew doubts that I wouldn't be able to create fire, or only control prelit fire. I remembered what the Fade said about not doubting myself, but he wasn't out here with me, he didn't see me struggling with this simple task.

A cold gust of wind blew and gave me a chill. I had to keep trying to make fire; I couldn't doubt my abilities all ready, I shook it off and walked up to the branch and broke a smaller branch off of it. I held it out in front of me and closed my eyes once again. The complete concentration came once again, much quicker this time. I felt the warmness in my hands, as it slowly got warmer. *"Maybe if I could get it warm enough."* I pushed the warmness until it started to get hot. I winced, the heat was almost too much to handle. I continued to drive it until it felt like my hand was on fire. I dropped the branch and opened my eyes; the heat took longer to leave my palm. I looked up, and Scahl was back with a couple of dead animals.

"No luck?" He asked.

I shook my head, "I could feel it. I just can't create the fire out of nothing."

"Yes you can, if you have the fire element, you can create fire."

"Then what do you suggest?"

"We're going to have to keep moving." he latched the dead animals to a hook on his chest and walked past me, "We'll freeze if we stop here."

"I'm going to freeze either way!" I already can't feel my feet!" I yelled at him.

Scahl stopped and turned around, "Then figure out a way to create fire! You have the element!"

Scahl picked up the small branch I broke off earlier, it burned where my hand wrapped around it, "You have to keep pushing it, figure it out."

I turned away from Scahl; I broke another small branch off and gripped it tightly. I closed my eyes and channeled the element to my hand; it burned

100

as if I was grabbing a hot panhandle. I could smell smoke rising from my hand.

"Release it!" I heard Scahl yell.

I dropped the stick and grabbed my hand. My palm was entirely red.

"You had it," Scahl said as he approached me, "you need to release the fire, you're letting it build inside you, release the fire."

"How am I supposed to do that?" I placed my hand on the cold ground to soothe the burn.

"I don't know; you must have an idea how your element works if you can control it enough to direct it to your hand. Use that knowledge to create fire."

I broke another stick off the branch; I took a deep breath and closed my eyes. The warming sensation quickly arose in my hand again. I concentrated on creating the fire; I could feel it burning under my skin. My palm began to sweat; I could feel the sweat pouring out of my pores onto the stick. My eyes opened, still concentrating; the stick started to catch fire! The fire was rolling out of my pores; what I had mistaken for sweat, it lit the stick on fire. I let go of the stick, and it floated above my hand, engulfed in flames.

The flame grew larger and larger. I looked over at Scahl with concern; his eyes were wide, "now, bring that over here," he motioned to the fallen branch. I walked over slowly guiding the engulfed stick, but the fire kept growing. Scahl pulled out his axe and began chopping up the large branch and arranging it into a pile. "You're releasing too much fire. Bring the element back in."

I placed the stick on top, and with intense concentration, I guided the flame to spread. It slowly spread with my command; the blaze grew more massive and hotter.

"Finn! Bring the element back in!" Scahl shouted at me.

I tried to bring it in, but the fire expanded off the branches, "I can't stop it!"

Scahl began kicking and throwing dirt onto the excess fire, "Concentrate on the element, not the fire!"

My heart was racing as the fire acted like it stuck onto me. I yelled inside of my head, *That's enough! No more fire! No more fire!"*

Eventually, my hand began to cool and dry, I opened my eyes.

"Help me control this!" Scahl pleaded.

I jumped in, kicking dirt on it, forcing a perimeter to guide it into a small campfire. I didn't feel comfortable releasing my element back out to control it.

Scahl stepped back, catching his breath, "We will continue practicing with your element another time, begin making your shelter."

My heart kept racing. This was worse than during the battle. If the fire kept continuing to grow, Scahl and I wouldn't have been able to put it out as the soldiers had. It could've taken out the entire Shaded Forest.

I opened the bag given to me from the Fade and shuffled through it, Scahl sat by the fire and began skinning the squirrels to prepare for dinner. There was a lot more in there than I had expected. I found the tents and pulled them out, I threw one to Scahl, and he caught it in one hand. "What is this?"

"It's a tent," I replied.

He tossed it back to me, and I dropped my tent. "Are you going to sleep in the open tonight?" I said irritated.

"I will take the first watch while you get your rest."

"First watch of what!" I stood up just barely towering over Scahl even when he was sitting down, "We're only a few hours outside of Kautun."

Scahl stood up, showing off his height, "The moment your guard is down, especially in the Shaded

Forest, you will be killed. Didn't the Fade prepare you for anything out here?"

I tried not to let fear show on my face; I knew this was going to be dangerous but couldn't imagine anything being that bad yet. Scahl could tell how naive I was and didn't shy away from putting it in my face, "Do you even know why it's called the Shaded Forest?"

I didn't have to say a word for him to know I didn't have a clue.

"It's called the Shaded Forest because there's always something bigger than you, above you, casting their shadows down. If you try to hide, it's too late; it's already been watching you, if you try to climb, it will climb higher than you, if you reach the top of the tallest tree, it will fly above."

I looked up and could see the stars through the dead tree branches, "What is "it"?"

"It is everything in this forest," he said gravely.

"So you left me alone to go hunt when you knew this forest could kill me?"

"You think all I could catch is a couple measly furlet? I'm a big man, I need more than that, I just needed you to think you were alone so you could concentrate," he motioned to the fire.

"Ok." I held my head low, "Wake me when you feel tired." I was done arguing with him; it wasn't doing me any good.

Scahl sat back down, and I went to the opposite side of the fire. I unraveled the tent and tried to make sense of the sticks and fabric. I looked back at Scahl as he just watched me. I stood the rods up and struggled to push them into the frozen ground.

"Eventually you will have to do something on your own."

"It's fine; I can do this." I pressed my hand against the ground directing the warmth of the fire to my palm, careful not to release any more fire. As soon as it felt warm, I reached the stake high above my head and slammed it into the ground, finally breaking dirt.

I looked back at Scahl who was focusing on cooking and didn't take any interest if I made the tent or not.

Scahl was eating by the time I had finished the tent. I crawled in and laid down, not feeling like eating. The first day had not been encouraging; we didn't get nearly as far as we had hoped and Scahl wasn't much for encouragement.

\* \* \* \*

I awoke from a deep sleep to Scahl pulling me out of my tent.

"What! I'm awake, I'm awake," I said with my eyes half closed.

"We've got to move."

I noticed it was still dark out when I completely opened my eyes.

"We stayed still too long; something is watching us."

With that, I was completely awake. I grabbed the hilt of my sword ready for action.

"Put out the fire; I'll get everything together, quickly."

I ran over to the fire and used my total concentration to put it out. It had dimmed since I had fallen asleep which made it easier. Smoke rose into the starry night sky as Scahl grabbed me by the shoulder and pushed me along.

I was at a full jog trying to keep up with him. "Why are we hurrying? I don't see anything," I said as I heard a long scratch against a tree. Scahl turned and looked around at the top of the trees.

"Come on!" He yelled at me. I started running next to him, but he was taking bounds much farther than mine. Then I heard the sound of a branch breaking under the weight of something massive. I turned around and looked up into the trees and looking down at me were two bright white eyes. The beast leaped from the tree, silhouetted, it spread its full body out revealing a long spiked tail and long arms with wings. It looked like a sugar glider as it fell through the air onto another branch as it cracked under the beast's weight.

The beast opened its mouth revealing sharp teeth and letting out a horrendous scream. I covered my ears and closed my eyes. Scahl grabbed me by the back of my shirt and threw me over his shoulder and started running at full pace. I watched the beast leaping from tree to tree gaining on us, its muscles flexed with every bound, and its black skin was covered in a disgusting looking slime that dripped all throughout the forest. The beast was getting closer. We entered a small clearing in the woods, and Scahl threw me off his shoulder into the snow.

Scahl turned around quickly, as the beast landed on him taking him to the ground, it was slightly bigger than him, but with a strong kick the creature was launched into the air but fell gracefully onto a tree branch. I struggled to move in the freezing snow but managed to stand up, my numb hands prevented me from getting my sword out of its sheath. I heard the loud screeching again and looked up to see the beast's wide-open mouth coming straight at me.

A small axe came spinning through the air colliding with the beast, knocking it off course and narrowly missing me.

"Get over here!" Scahl yelled at me. I didn't hesitate and ran as fast as I could by his side as he threw axes whizzing past me, I could hear the beast charging behind me.

"Dive!" Scahl yelled, and I dove as he pulled out his axe and swung it at the beast ripping a hole in its wing. It screeched again, this time in pain. I stood up and finally unsheathed my sword, then stood next to Scahl.

"Just stay back! I'll tell you when to jump in!" Scahl yelled once again at me then ran towards the beast screaming at the top of his lungs.

I stood back, feeling helpless. I knew this wasn't right; I needed to jump in and help.

Scahl brought the axe down on it, but it dove out of the way, the beast fully extended its jaws going for Scahl's head, but he brought his axe up and blocked the bite. The creature shook its head and went back in for the kill, I watched, finally finding my opportunity. I jumped forward before it was in full flight, and brought my sword down upon it, causing it to be thrown to the side past Scahl.

Scahl threw his last two axes at the beast as it regained its footing, one bounced off the rubber-like skin, and the other lodged itself into the shoulder of the beast. Scahl charged it, and they collided. He grabbed it by its bottom jaw; they swung around, the creature trying to get free. It finally shook its head furiously, and Scahl released his grip.

The beast turned, ready to leap away into the trees, but Scahl grabbed it by the tail, "Finn!" He yelled as he swung the creature around and launched it at me. The beast flew through the air skidding to a halt right next to me. I lifted my sword and stabbed it in the heart, it screeched and looked at me with its mean, glowing white eyes.

"Its head!" I heard Scahl yell at me, "Chop it off!" I pulled my sword out of its chest, pointing the blade in, I sliced through the beast's neck.

I watched the head roll to the side, my heart pounding. Scahl collected his axes, as I stood paralysed over it, "Did we have to kill it?" I asked, "I think it was going to fly away."

"It wasn't done, it was going to get help. When you jumped in like that, it knew it was outmatched."

I looked back down at it, "Well what was it?"

Scahl walked up to me and pulled his last axe out of its shoulder and placed it on his belt, "It was a vulansiran, very common, deadly creature, but not our worst nightmare in the Shaded Forest."

I kept my focus on the vulansiran, "Well it wasn't so bad to fight."

"With your help it wasn't," Scahl added, "we will outmatch any creature the Shaded Forest is equipped with. I need you to fight alongside me in every battle as you did just then. I know you're new to this world, but it's time to hold your own."

I nodded, "The Fade didn't prepare me for what lies beyond the walls of D'Hanin, but I know I can fight, so that's what I'll do."

"That's what I need." Scahl replied, slapping me on the back as he walked around the dead beast, "We better get out of here, before anything else shows up, the vulansiran should avert the attention away from us for at least a little while."

My stomach grumbled as I walked around it, "Shouldn't we salvage the meat?"

"No, if something looks that evil, you should know it won't do any good for you."

"Makes sense," I shrugged.

"We need to be able to move quicker; there's nothing we can do while in the Shaded Forest, but we'll be an easy target if we're moving this slow all the way to Abanyu."

"What do you suggest?" I asked.

He looked over at me, "We've got to get you a ride. After this whole mess, we have no time to move at your pace."

"What kind of ride?"

"I'll think about it," he replied in thought as we kept moving forward.

# 8

## CAPTURING A TORADRAC

The rest of the night quickly went by; I was able to sleep for another two hours before we had to keep moving again. Scahl had the fire out by the time I crawled out of the tent. He was still shaken from the vulansiran encounter. I felt we handled the fight pretty well, at least for the size and ferocity of the beast.

Scahl stayed close to me, moving at a much slower pace than usual, "All right," he said breaking the silence, "we're going to get you a toradrac. I spent the remainder of the night thinking about it, and it clicked when I heard an echo of their call that couldn't be far away from here. It will be the easiest to train and the fastest to grow, however not the easiest to catch."

Everything he said utterly went over my head after, toradrac, "What's a toradrac?"

"It's a type of flightless dragon. It's very hot-tempered and is a solid creature. Most say the females were too heavy to fly, so, over the years, it lost its wings. The males kept to the ground to protect and feed their mates and eventually lost their wings as well. There should be a second litter of eggs that should be hatching before the end of winter."

"An egg?" I asked.

"There's no way you would be able to capture an adult, and even if you did you wouldn't be able to train it, as I said, they're hot-tempered."

"So I can't imagine stealing an egg could be that much easier," I said.

"That's right, but having the toradrac's first sight of this world be you, will make you mama and will make it that much easier to train."

"All right, so where do we start?"

"Just keep following me," he smiled.

I continued to follow him for a few more hours; the forest was becoming hillier. We stayed on a path, a small creek rushing along passed us. I knelt down and scooped up a handful of icy cold water to take a drink. Scahl continued at my pace but he still had much better stamina than I had, he could probably walk for days without a break if I weren't with him.

We reached the edge of a hill; Scahl stopped abruptly and pulled me behind a tree. The slope went almost straight down for at least 25 feet. I looked out over an area with about 10 caves lining the hill.

What I assumed were toradracs, ran up and down the slope, fighting or playing, and just scaling the hill minding their own business. They were beautiful creatures. At least the height of a horse, but stockier, looking more like bulls than dragons but were covered in glimmering scales. I saw blue ones, gray ones, green ones, and yellow ones. They all had two horns coming from their heads and tails like a dragon's.

"This is it?" I asked in wonder.

Scahl nodded, almost in as much wonder as I was, "This is it."

Then a thought came to my head; I wasn't stealing an egg from one toradrac. There had to be at least 20 of them I would have to sneak passed.

"How am I suppose to steal an egg with all these toradracs around?" I said a bit more panicky now, "You didn't tell me there would be so many of them!"

"Keep it down," Scahl hushed at me, "We don't want them to know we're here just yet."

"Yet?" I said having trouble keeping my voice down.

"Yes, toradracs are pack animals, they always live in herds like these. I have to go through the herd and walk a distance away. They will not bother me if I keep my head down, they will not be threatened by one human traveling alone."

"So I'm supposed to get one by myself? I'm guessing you're going to tell me that part?"

"You will wait here until nightfall, watch the tops of the trees and I will give you the signal to go for it. I'll need you to start me a torch, then I'll wave it back and forth, and you'll know to go. Head quietly to the cave at the bottom of the hill, I saw a male walk into it with a dead animal and come out seconds later without it. That means he was hunting for his mate, who is too busy guarding the eggs."

Scahl took a breath and looked down at me, "Once you have retrieved the egg, run for your life towards me. Every male is malnourished, they'll be too weak to chase you very long, and the females are most likely to heavy to keep up with you."

I nodded, "So what do I do when I'm in the cave?"

He pulled out his axe and cut off a small tree branch, "Steal the egg."

"Yea," I said, "but how?"

Scahl shrugged, "I don't know, I've never had to do this before, if you're successful though you'll have to let me know how you did it, just in case I'm ever in this situation again."

He held out the branch with a smile, "Light me up."

I set the branch on fire, and he set off down the slope. Toradracs watched him, many snorting with smoke coming from their nostrils. Scahl walked confidently through the herd with his torch held up. Many of the toradracs went on minding their own business.

I watched Scahl reach the bottom of the hill and peek into the cave I would be exploring. He looked back at me and nodded, then continued walking.

I sat against a tree watching the sun go down. The toradracs were finding their way into their caves and bringing back the last of their catches from hunting.

I had a wrenching feeling in my stomach, not because what I was about to do was dangerous, but because I was stealing these creature's baby. My morals were challenged in this adventure, but I reasoned with myself that the help this creature would bring me to successfully completing my quest would be for a more significant cause that could even help the animals in this world immensely. I was going to take great care of this toradrac. If I made it out alive, that is.

\* \* \* \*

I waited an hour and a half after sunset and finally saw the signal. At the peak of a tree in the distance, I could see a flame slowly going back and forth.

I quickly shot up and collected myself, then as swiftly and quietly as I could, I started down the hill, sliding most of the way.

I took glances into each of the caves, trying to see what I could but they were all pitch black inside. I got to the bottom of the hill and looked around for any late roaming, toradracs; there were none, so I headed towards the cave and stood at the edge, and peaked my head in. It was as pitch black as the others; I couldn't see more than 3 feet in front of me.

I was going to need to use my element. I knew it was going to make the situation even more danger-ous, but I needed just enough light to see. I didn't need a big flame, I found a small twig nearby and held it out in front of me. Using all my concentration and successfully to my surprise, I lit it on fire like a match.

I raised it into midair, eye level and directed it into the cave. It lit the cave enough to where I could see the cave sloped downwards into the mountain. I kept the twig floating a few feet in front of me being cautious not to make myself visible or lose control of the flame.

I walked down further in and at 20 feet into the cave the twig cast a light on the female toradrac. I stopped, frozen like a statue, my heart beating as the flame circled the cave eventually casting on a toradrac watched the floating twig, teeth bared.

I needed to know where everything was in the cave, so I directed it around, eventually revealing the second, sleeping toradrac. I continued going around the cave with the twig finally casting light on 3 giant eggs lying right behind the awoken toradrac.

I tried to control my breathing, being as silent as possible I sent the twig to the back of the tunnel. I brightened the light just enough to see the toradrac watching it closely and tightening its tail around the eggs. I crept up slowly towards the eggs being careful to stay in the shadows. Even the smallest of the eggs was the size of a bike tire, but the only one I could grab was one that was not touching the toradracs tail, but it was still too risky. I was close enough to be able to reach down and grab an egg.

My palms were becoming sweaty and it became increasingly more difficult to hold the flame at an even burn. I took a deep slow breath as I directed the twig over by the other toradrac who was still asleep, leaving me in total darkness with the awoken toradrac. But just as I hoped, I saw the toradrac enter into the light, and I knew she had just left her eggs unattended.

I reached down slowly, keeping an eye on her as she sniffed the flame; I felt the warm shell and picked it up. I slowly backed up towards the entrance of the cave, but before I got more than 10 feet away, I watched her bite down onto the twig in aggression, the flame went out, leaving me in total darkness, I heard her huffing and puffing in pain. I knew the other one had to be awake from the stomping of the other.

I turned and ran for it, the egg cradled in my arms. The noises stopped than a sound of hooves stampeding towards me broke the silence. I ran for my life in pitch-blackness for only a second until I reached the entrance of the tunnel. Other toradracs were making their way out of the caves as well to see the commotion.

I sprinted towards Scahl, hearing even more hooves stomping behind me at a terrifyingly fast pace. I looked back only once to see the toradrac from the cave skidding out of it and making eye contact with me. I looked forward again and could see the torch a hundred yards away.

The toradracs were faster than me; however, I weaved through trees, the forest getting more densely wooded. The toradracs were too big to get through them quickly, but they continued following me as fast as they could, breaking through smaller branches and weaving through the rest of them.

I was able to distance myself from the toradracs by the time I reached the tree Scahl was in, "Put out the flame," he quietly ordered me.

The flame was out in an instant I tossed the egg up to Scahl and climbed up the tree about 10 feet and sat next to Scahl on a branch breathing heavily. He held a finger up to his mouth to tell me to be quiet. I did my best to catch my breath. The stomping hooves quickly got louder and louder the closer they got.

We waited under the moonlight in the branches of the trees for about an hour before we no longer heard the hooves. They must have finally given up and went back to their caves, to now more securely watch over the eggs.

Scahl began climbing down the tree, and I followed. We got to the bottom, and he still didn't say a word, just motioned for me to follow him. We walked for about another hour in complete silence until he thought we were finally far enough away from the caves.

"I think we're in the clear," he said, breaking out into laughter, "I forgot how big those eggs were!"

I handed him the egg, "It looks a lot smaller when you're holding it."

"Wow," he said, his eyes glowing, "This is amazing, I can't believe we pulled that off."

"I pulled it off... Barely," I said.

He handed the egg back to me, "You deserve it, and with the right training it will be a great companion for you."

I went to put it in my bag, but Scahl stopped me, "It would be best if you held it until it hatches, it might sound crazy, but the smell and the touch of your skin against the shell will help the baby toradrac grow accustomed to you before it hatches."

I held it against my body, both arms around it and we kept walking.

\* \* \* \*

I sluggishly walked behind Scahl for days through the Shaded Forest, carrying the toradrac egg. I thought it would never end, but Scahl assured me we were getting closer to the edge of the forest. Being able to practice my element every night helped me to use it much more naturally at will, but I was afraid my swordsmanship was dwindling.

Other than finishing the vulansiran off, I had not used my sword. I needed to continue my training somehow, and we had not seen any real threats since the vulansiran. I heard them frequently off into the distance, but something must have gotten around that we were not an easy meal. I suppose that was fortunate, but it made the travels extremely dull.

The sun began to cast long shadows on the trees, telling me that night would be approaching soon, "We wouldn't happen to be nearing a town or anything," I asked, "I could use a night in a real bed."

Scahl laughed, "From what I remember, Keahi told us of a town a few days outside of the Shaded Forest, so not really."

As much as I didn't like that answer, I had a feeling that's what it would be. Besides seeing strange animals burrowing into the ground, colorful birds of all kinds and the furrets we hunted, there was not much life in the Shaded Forest. It was an eerie feeling knowing we were the only humans out here; it made me think we were the only ones dumb enough to go this deep into it.

"Don't you have a map?" Scahl asked.

"No, it was amongst the first items I looked for in the bag."

"60 years frozen and this place is still lacking a map."

"Why is that?" I asked.

"There aren't a lot of people traveling farther than a couple of days outside their home village."

I would think someone in this world would be teeming with curiosity what the rest of their world held. I mean how far behind would Americans be if it weren't for Chris Columbus? Or how ahead would the Indians be? "So what's the next town?" My curiosity was starting to teem.

Scahl looked down at me for a moment, "I'm not exactly sure, my memory has faded over the years. For all I know there could be more towns built since then."

"You're not exactly sure?" I said a little more hotly than intended, "How are you supposed to know where to be going?"

"We're supposed to be following the rising sun, so wherever it rises we go in that direction, and we'll get to Abanyu."

Scahl looked slightly embarrassed, and there was an awkward pause, "Listen, Keahi has traveled more of this land than anyone. He trained all of us in more ways than sparring, and that includes the land. But times have changed since I last walked, there may be new towns, forests, there could be new mountains, but the one thing we do know is Apaku, and his garmec have not moved, and I remember those locations better than anything else that could be on a map."

"How do you know they haven't moved if you can't be certain on anything else on the map?"

"Apaku is on the strongest mountain range in D'Hanin, and hundreds of garmec guard the rest of them in near equal locations. They've never had a reason to move. Until they find out about us, that is."

I hid my worry as best as I could, he hadn't led me astray yet..... As far as I knew.

We walked for a few more hours; I practiced a variety of cuts with my sword, as Scahl carried the egg to give me a small break. I was pleased to see my abilities hadn't dwindled much. My custom sword contributed a great deal to that, making each move much more effortless than the training sword.

Scahl slowed his pace, and I stopped swinging my sword, he looked around, "I think we should rest here, it's been quiet for the past hour."

"I'm not sure that's something to be pleased about," I said searching the trees for any sign of movement.

Scahl smiled, "You're catching on, we need to be on guard now."

"I'll take first watch," I was still full of energy, and with any luck, I was hoping we were attacked, not by anything too dangerous but something just challenging enough so I could try out my sword.

# 9

## AN INNOCENT BYSTANDER

"When do you think the egg will hatch?" I asked Scahl as I felt a long scratch against the inside of the egg as the toradrac inside shuffled into a more comfortable spot.

Scahl was finding it challenging to slow his pace to match mine. He looked back at me, "Maybe another

week," he looked up at the sky, "it looks like winter has broken."

I shifted the egg to my other arm and could feel shuffling on the inside of the egg, *"this is how women must feel,"* I thought, making myself laugh.

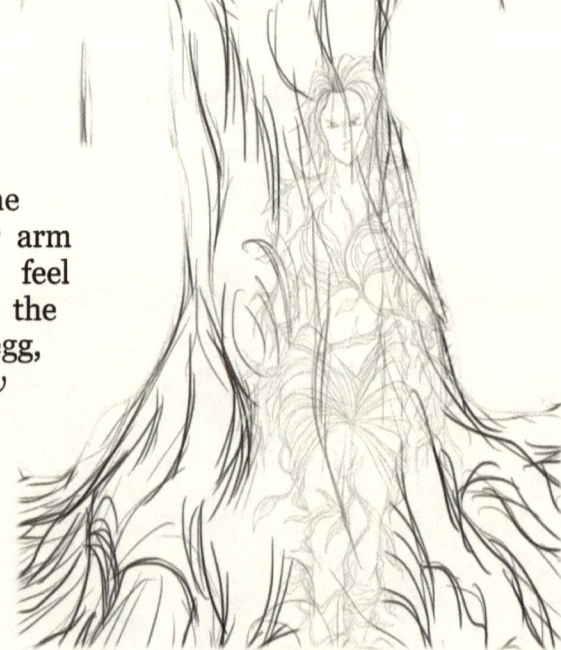

I positioned the egg comfortably under my arm and kept it still. 4 days later, in the dead of night, as I was curled up around the egg I heard the egg hatching.

CRRRRAACK!

I woke up with a jolt, Scahl whipped open the tent from the outside, prepared to fight. We shuffled around looking from where the noise came from until we heard it again.

CRRRRAACK!

I covered my ears, looking around, "What is that?" I yelled to Scahl.

"It's the egg, step back from it!"

CRRACK!

The sound came slightly quieter this time. I looked down, and the toradrac egg was wobbling with several long cracks in it, "It's hatching!" I said as a piece of the egg broke off, hitting the ground like a piece of metal. I could see movement inside the egg, but it was too dark to see.

Scahl closed the tent door just enough to be able to peek through, "I need to stay away, we need to make sure it sees you first."

I moved the egg closer to me, putting both hands on the egg in complete bliss. Under my hands, I felt the rigidness of each crack, and as I angled the egg so I could see inside, I saw another golden eye looking back out at me.

CRRAACK!

My heart was pounding with excitement, seeing me it must have felt the same merriment I was feeling, and it finally came charging out of the egg, pieces flying around and knocking me back as the enormous body fell onto me. Its scales shined yellowish gold with a dark brown mane around its neck and face. The young toradrac looked up at me, struggling to stand up.

It was about the size of a newborn horse but fatter. It panted heavily as I helped it off of me. After a couple of tries to stand, it failed and laid down still. I stroked its mane trying to calm it down, I worried for it, that it might be sick.

"Don't worry, it's just tired," Scahl said through the tent.

I picked it up with all my might and nestled it on my lap, instantly the toradrac felt calmer.

"This is amazing," I said, "I can't believe it."

The toradrac fell asleep on my lap almost instantly. Scahl finally came into the tent and stroked its head, "We'll let it get rest tonight, but we must start training tomorrow; remember that it is not a pet," he said seriously, but I had already grown attached to it.

We cleaned up the eggshells and Scahl went back to sleep. I couldn't fall asleep; I took the last watch and sat with the toradrac in amazement for the rest of the night.

* * * *

We walked for miles, upon miles, upon miles without a break. Scahl claimed it was to strengthen the toradrac quickly. My feet felt like 50-pound blocks as I dragged them through the snow. The snow began to fall harder, and the wind blew stronger. The wind would freeze my eyeballs; I could barely keep them open, or even keep my head up as the falling snowflakes pelted my face like needles.

I called out to Scahl, who I could barely see in the snow. He was getting farther ahead of me. I called again, and he turned around, "I thought you said winter had broken!"

"I thought it did; it looks like it came back for one last fight!"

I looked down at the toradrac who was keeping pace with me but trudged through the snow, miserable, "I think we need to make camp!" I yelled out to him.

I listened intently for a response but only heard a muffled yell coming back. I closed my eyes and wiped the snow from my face. I looked back up, and Scahl wasn't there. "Scahl!" I yelled and ran towards where he last stood.

Scahl came back into view with his axe out, he charged at me. I braced myself for impact, but as he dove towards me, there was a black flash and a slimy tail that collided with me, knocking me to the side.

I regained my composure and looked through the falling snow. I stood up and ran back to Scahl's aid, who was pinned to the ground by another vulansiran. I unsheathed my sword, and the vulansiran turned its ugly head to look at me.

It jumped off Scahl, as he screamed at the top of his lungs, and charged me. I swung my sword at it, and it dodged the move. Scahl's scream was bloodcurdling. I knew there wasn't something right about it.

I continued swinging, and the vulansiran relentlessly dodged each move. It snapped at me but kept having to abandon his attacks to avoid mine; I still couldn't see Scahl, waiting for him to jump in, and help me take care of this monster.

The vulansiran circled me, but his gaze was locked onto the toradrac, which cowered behind me. Drool dripped from the vulansiran's mouth as it charged again, I realized it wasn't trying to fight me; it was trying to get to the toradrac.

We were evenly matched. My attacks were my defenses, and my defenses were my attacks. The vulansiran jumped and glided onto a nearby tree branch. It stared daggers at me, trying to get a better angle at the toradrac, then jumped from tree to tree. If it weren't for its jet-black skin, I would have lost it in the falling snow. But I carefully watched each jump until it jumped down towards the toradrac; I jumped in the way off it, bringing my sword around and connecting with its leg.

It limped around and squared back up with me about 10 feet away. I grabbed my dagger from my belt and threw it as hard as I could. With the luck of the Gods it impaled the vulansiran in the eye, and it screeched, bowing its head and scratching at the dagger trying to get it out. I wasted no time and charged it, my sword held high, and my steps as quiet as possible. I pointed the tip in and brought the sword down across the vulansiran's head, and it dropped to the ground, a pool of blood spilling out.

I fell to the ground, using more force than I should have but the adrenaline that threw me into that move took over. I stood up, dusting the snow off me and stared down at the lifeless vulansiran as I walked around it to look for Scahl. I saw him walking over to me through the harsh falling snow.

I tried to catch my breath, the cold consuming my lungs, "I think the vulansiran was after the toradrac, we're all right though."

"Not quite," he said back lifting his hand from his rib cage, blood covering his hand and coat, "it's claw sunk into me when it jumped off me."

"I'm sorry, I was just coming to help," I said back knowing I couldn't make it through this without him.

"No, the outcome would've been worse if you didn't steal its attention away from me," he assured me with a wince. He wobbled a bit then fell to his knees with a grunt.

"We're going to have to set up camp here," I said and turned and melted a large enough area of snow so we could set up camp. I helped him into the clearing and helped him take his coat off. He had a long gash going from under his chest all the way around to the side of his rib cage.

He took his shirt off and tightly gripped it around his wound to stop the bleeding as much as possible. He handed the knotted end for me to hold onto since I had much more strength than him at the moment.

I tried to hide my fear, I didn't know anything about first aid, but Scahl watched my reaction.

"Don't panic," he said, "Do not panic."

"W-- What am I suppose to do?"

He opened the cut up and looked at it, "It's not as bad as it looks," his head rolled back, and I helped him support his head, "We just need to close the cut to stop the bleeding."

"And you expect me to do that," I said to him. The worst cut I ever had was covered with a band-aid, and I didn't think that would help us at all.

Scahl's eyes rolled back, and his body went limp. I knew I had to act quickly; I needed a string and needle. Or at least a needle, I could use the fibers from my clothes to make the thread. But I didn't have a needle, that wasn't going to work. My heart started racing.

Could I maybe call on the Angel Element, somehow harness that power. I tried concentrating on it, calling out for its help. I opened my eyes hoping to see it standing before me but I was alone, the snow continued to fall, covering us both. I sent the element through my body and melted the snow off of myself; the cold snow on Scahl's body was most likely the only prevention from him bleeding out.

I then realized I had my own element; I knew I wasn't going to be able to harness the power of the rarest and most challenging element in a matter of minutes. I had to start thinking about what I had and not what I needed. I thought for a moment and pulled out my dagger, I released the shirt covering the wound and set a steady flame onto the blade of the dagger. It glowed, red hot, I grabbed hold of Scahl as tight as I could, and quickly placed the sweltering knife on the cut.

It made a horrible sizzling sound and Scahl suddenly awoke, screaming at the top of his lungs. He wrestled around a little bit until he realized what I was doing. His body tensed up trying to endure the pain, before going limp again. I pulled the dagger away, and the cut was welded together, I engulfed the blade once again and held it against his body. He didn't move this time, completely blacked out.

I continued until the entire wound was closed up and there was a terrible smell of burning flesh in the air. I fell back, exhausted. I took a clean cloth out of the pack and wrapped it around Scahl's torso, covering the wound. He continued to lay unconscious.

I set the tent up and struggled to pull him in, out of the cold. I took a small axe from his belt and went out to collect wood for a fire bringing the toradrac with me in fear it would wander off.

I didn't walk a significant distance away from the tent, knowing anything that saw him lying there would be there in seconds to finish him off for their next meal. I would set fire to a branch to weaken it, being cautious not to place the entire forest on fire. Once it was dwindled, I would smother the flame, and with a few easy chops I cut the branch off.

I gathered a couple of armfuls of wood and placed them close enough to the tent and started a roaring fire. I went into the tent to check on Scahl; his chest was slowly moving up and down.

I went back outside and sat against a tree knowing this was going to be a long watch. The toradrac nestled up to me, shivering, I placed my arm around it.

\* \* \* \*

I waited for hours; the night came quickly, the snow slowly stopped. I heard Scahl shuffle and groaned only a few times, but it was enough to know he was still alive.

\* \* \* \*

124

I kept checking on Scahl throughout the night; I decided it would be best to pile snow onto his wound to prevent infection. I could see the sun shining through the tree branches, slowly rising. I had made it through the night and decided if I were going to get any sleep the best time would be now.

Chances were all the creatures that were going to eat had done their hunting in the night. I checked on Scahl one last time then closed my eyes and drifted off into sleep.

* * * *

Scahl was unconscious for an entire day. I began to worry what my options were at this point but decided to wait it out a little longer. I sat against a tree in the quiet. The wind blew, and the fire flickered. I concentrated on keeping it alive. I looked up into the sky through the dead branches and saw a flock of birds flying overhead.

I sat in the cold, directing the element through my body to stay warm. The toradrac nestled up against me, enjoying the warmth that I radiated. The wind silenced the entire forest, except for the creaking of trees; all the noises of animals and bugs had disappeared. The wind calmed for a moment, and the woods were completely silent.

Then in my subconscious, I heard, *"The legend in the flesh."* I sat up and tried to focus on the soft voice. I stood up and looked around placing a hand on the hilt of my sword.

*"Well, maybe legend is a bit much,"* I heard once again. I didn't know if I should talk back or if tiredness was getting the best of me.

I heard a feminine laugh, *"There's no need to be frightened."* A transparent figure stepped out from behind a tree in a billowy motion. I stepped back as she stepped forward towards me. Her feet left no tracks in the snow, but her hair blew in the wind as if it was a part of it. She smiled at me. Her face was young and flawless.

"Who are you?" I relaxed my grip from the hilt of my sword; I knew something like her was nothing I could affect with my sword.

"*Is it really of any importance, who I am?*" Her words were ringing in my mind. I stood frozen; it was imperative to me that I knew who she was.

"*If it's that important to you, then I am the trees,*" she absorbed herself into a nearby tree and it swayed back and forth, "*I am the breeze,*" a gust of wind blew my hair back. She once again appeared out of a shadow, "*I am the grass in the summer, and the flowers in spring, I am a plantation element.*"

She stood close to me; I looked at her in awe. I reached my hand out to touch her face, but my hand felt only air, "*You can not feel me, nor I, you, in my pure form.*" I brought my hand down to my side.

"What are you here for?" I asked knowing that these encounters could not have happened often.

"*For you to understand I must explain my first encounter with your kind.*" She paused and walked away from me next to a tree, gently touching it, "*it was in this spot, when I came across Keahi, the creator of what you know as the Four Scales. He called out to us; I foolishly came into this form and revealed myself to him. He told me of his plan to harbor each element in order to protect us, and leave us at our most dominant power. I quickly agreed and helped him in making the Emerald Scale.*"

She turned back towards me, fear in her eye. "*After the elements began to see how the plantations were flourishing, they slowly began to want their own Scales. Keahi was a hero even among our kind; we never blamed him for what has come of the Scales. It was not his choice to be murdered, the Scales seized from him by the dark summoner, but it was our choice to let the Scales into existence. We were blinded by glory and severely overlooked the most*

126

terrible of outcomes. There is an unseen barrier causing us not to be able to control our individual elements; we cannot control what makes us, us. They have desperately attempted to attach themselves to your kind, but it has been nearly impossible without the Scales. It would give us the best chance of releasing our elements, but that has only gotten us so far."

"Gotten us so far?" This time an unfamiliar man's voice was taking over my conscious.

The plantation element starred daggers at me; my first reaction was to grab my sword, as quickly as something so beautiful could go to looking so vengeful.

"It's quite all right Finn, we've met before," I heard the new voice calmly. "I have been successful in bringing you here, something no other element was capable of doing."

"Capability was not the issue," I was in the middle of an argument that was now going on in my head. "We can all see it, what you have done is not perfect, it was a cheap way into the soul of another."

"His power will grow, as will I; regaining my strength through him to become powerful once again."

"We are ALL trying to be powerful once again, but not at the risk of becoming evil."

"There is no evil in the elements! Only in the person!" The voices continued to get louder as the Plantation element circled me. I could feel the fire element coursing through my veins, unwilled.

"But you can be a strong influence. Do not risk this opportunity!"

"I would do nothing to risk what I have created!"

"Begone! It would benefit us all if you left it all up to this boy you have selfishly taken."

"We were running out of time! Your kind has dwindled to near extinction; we have a chance now!"

"A CHANCE? You have done nothing for our chances; you knew what Keahi prophesied for the elements!"

I intervened, "Please stop, I can't listen to it anymore," I spoke softly, not sure if I was speaking out loud or in my mind at that point, "what was the prophecy?"

"Prophecies are for the foolish and weak-minded mortals. Our future has not been written in stone and prophecies are no exception. You know not what was laid out for us in other worlds."

"Not even a man or woman you could find, but a mere boy."

"He has the heart to embody me, and that's all I saw."

"Only his journeys will ease our minds, our fates have been set into motion now."

I couldn't take the battle in my head anymore; the anger was flaring up in me when I did not want to feel anger, but terror. I grabbed my ears, failing to silence the noise.

The Plantation Element came within inches of me, "Recede to the soul! You have exceeded your part in his journey and must recede!"

I started to wobble in place, trying to regrip reality. I grabbed onto a tree and slid down, my eyes clenched shut.

"You will not hear from me on this journey again, but in my choices, I still have a part to play." My element spat back.

The anger and the heat left my body, the cold night air immediately chilling me to the bone and my conscious becoming silent again. My eyes peaked open feeling exhausted from the fight.

The Plantation Element made its final approach to me as I sat there. "We need full control of our elements returned, and we will be beside you on your journey because it is as much ours, as it is yours."

I felt even more pressure befall unto me; now another race was relying on me to save them.

She smiled at me, "*To fight for something with no benefit unto yourself is a noble act indeed, but in the end, you should know, the benefit will arise right before your eyes.*"

I smiled back at her, and we held eye contact for a moment, she walked away into the shadows and was gone.

I looked back over at the tent were Scahl lay unconscious. The fire was dimmed and barely flickered. I hesitated to use my element, in fear that the voices would come back, but with no effort from myself, the fire began to rise again, enough to feel the heat where I was seated.

\* \* \* \*

I rested for another hour; the argument had taken a toll on me but spent the rest of the afternoon keeping the fire going and putting snow onto Scahl's wound. My stomach growled, and I knew I had to get something to eat. I couldn't get too far away from the camp was the problem, and if I didn't know my way back, I could easily get lost among the hundreds of trees.

There was no other option than to go hunt though, and I knew Scahl would need food when he awoke so I headed out into the trees, with the toradrac, burning the bark of trees that I passed so I could find my way back.

I didn't see much life besides a few birds flying too high to catch. I wasted too much time wandering and knew I didn't have much time before I had to get back to Scahl. I thought about what I could do for a moment, and then remembered what Scahl had said about the Shaded Forest, "*there's always something above you.*"

I began climbing the nearest tree, I then also remembered what else he said, *"if you climb, it will climb higher."* Every animal in this forest couldn't possibly climb higher than me though. I continued climbing for about 15 feet. I positioned myself and looked down at the forest.

I could now see a few small animals scurrying across tree branches in every direction now, getting a new perspective on the forest, revealed a whole new world. I aimed at a few different squirrel-looking animals, I believe Scahl called them furlet, and threw fireballs at them, connecting with each of them. They all fell to the ground. The animals began scurrying into hiding, and I had to act quickly. I threw fireball after fireball, only connecting with one more before they were all hidden.

I climbed down the tree and collected them all, counting out 5 of them. It wasn't much but it would sustain us. I headed back for the camp only getting turned around a couple of times. I set my haul down next to the fire and was pleased to see nothing was out of place. I peaked my head into the tent at Scahl, and he was still lying there, sweat beading on his forehead. I crawled in and knelt down next to him to look at the wound. It seemed better considering what it looked like previously.

I never knew anyone that had been in a coma, but what I did know from the movies was to test for reactions. I pulled my dagger out from my waist and put the tip into his finger. Nothing happened. I tried again, this time with a little more pressure, and now feeling a twitch.

It wasn't much but it gave me the hope I desperately needed, that he would wake up, and I wouldn't have to find my way out of this forest alone.

I sat next to the fire and began stripping the meat as best as I could. I then pierced the flesh onto a sharpened stick and held it over the fire. Moments later I heard, "Morning, sunshine." I heard from behind me in a raspy voice. I turned around and saw Scahl exiting the tent his eyes squinted and hunched over in pain. I jumped up, "I didn't think you were gonna make it!"

"How long have I been out?" He said as he grabbed my shoulder, slowly sitting down by the fire, holding his side in pain.

"Almost two days," I replied and sat next to him, "here, eat this, you've got to be starving," I handed him a piece of the meat, and he took a small bite.

"Only two days, huh?" He said, and I nodded, "It felt like weeks, terrible nightmares."

"Nightmares?"

"Yea, if you're infected by the slime on its skin and survive, you have to live through terrible night-mares until it's out of your system and you can finally wake up," Scahl closed his eyes, remembering the nightmares. There was a pain in his face that I had never seen before.

"Are you going to be able to continue?" I asked him.

He opened his eyes back up, "Give me one more night to heal and we'll head out in the morning."

I sat there for a moment too long, contemplating if I should tell Scahl about the argument. I didn't want to relive it trying to explain it to Scahl at that moment. It would only make it feel more real repeating, "*It would benefit us all if you left it all up to this boy you have selfishly taken.*"

"*We were running out of time! Your kind has dwindled to near extinction; we have a chance now!*"

I wasn't ready to face it, but Scahl had gotten a sense of distress, his eyes opened up, staring me down.

"Everything all right?" He asked reluctantly.

I stood up feeling reluctant myself to talk about it, but if I wanted to sleep maybe it would help, "It's just been a strange night, I don't even know what happened it happened so fast."

131

"What happened?" Scahl was finally showing concern.

"I guess a Plantation Element visited me, I don't know why, but all it did was fight with my element. I could hear the entire fight in my head."

"A Plantation Element visited you? That's something of Keahi's level with the elements!" Scahl said.

"I was so immersed into the fight; I could barely think for myself what was happening."

"What were they fighting about?"

"I don't know. There were talks about prophecies and Keahi and stuff."

"Well, what was the prophecy?" Scahl said, starting to get impatient.

I stood up and paced back and forth, "I don't know for sure, they didn't say. I just didn't understand what they were talking about; it was all too intense for me."

Scahl stared at me for a moment before moving up against a tree, "Why don't you go rest. I can wait a little while."

I nodded appreciating a moment to fall asleep and get my mind off the argument. I was embarrassed. I couldn't tell Scahl that the argument led me to believe that I wasn't suppose to be here. All hope would be lost, and the Fade would end my journey. I wasn't ready for it to be over, I was better than I have ever been and I had a purpose here. I had the elements on my side, and mine chose me. That had to mean something; I wanted to be on this journey, I wanted to save this world. I would figure out what it all meant later.

# 10

## THE SOLITARY MAN

The next morning, as Scahl and I went hunting for something to eat, we were silent. There were two different understandings of the situation with the elements, and I was all right with that as long as I didn't press the issue he wouldn't worry about it. I knew what

I had to do and the risks involved, and I wasn't going to jeopardize that by trying to analyze what the elements were talking about. They understood I was the choice, whether or not it was the right one, it was final. I was going to have become the right choice.

Scahl broke the silence with a grunt, his axe flying through the air at a sizable bird, much bigger than the furlet, roosting on a tall tree, it just missed, the axe falling to the ground, the bird took flight. Scahl quickly reacted and threw another one, this time connecting with it. I watched as it fell to the ground and Scahl rushing over to pick it up, stomping through the forest.

"You know if I heard stomps that loud in the forest, I'd run for the hills."

Scahl smirked back as he slung the dead bird over his shoulder, "I'm not the reason the animal population is sparse."

"Well I can't imagine stomping through the forest is helping anything."

"What can I say, I got excited to have a real meal."

Scahl walked slower through the forest, and I kept up. We saw another bird, roosting on a nearby tree.

"Your turn," Scahl nodded towards me. I quietly walked closer to it hiding behind trees. I created a ball of fire in my hand, this time feeling more in tune with my element directly. It was as if I knew who to talk to now, and it made it much easier to create the ball of fire warming my hand. I stepped out from behind the tree before the bird realized I was there and threw it with all my might. It connected with it, and the bird fell to the ground. The toradrac ran through the snow towards a small trail of smoke rising where it landed. He picked it up the bird by its tail, and brought it back to me, "Look at that, mine's already cooked," I said to Scahl with a laugh.

"Yea, enjoy the feathers, I'll take mine plucked." He said back.

We settled in a small clearing, and I started a fire to cook our breakfast. It wasn't as good as the meals Alina prepared for me, but it was good enough for where we were. After a month out here, I had become accustomed to living without all of life's essentials, but that was one thing I didn't think I would ever again become accustomed to living without. I sat on the frozen ground and began to miss the many meals I shared with her in the warm and cozy tavern.

The rest of the morning consisted of Scahl teaching me how a "real" wilderness man prepares his meals, burning his portion of the meat to a crisp.

"Ten bucks you won't be able to chew through that," we laughed, and I began eating when I couldn't see any more red in the meat. "Whatever that is, I'll take it," he bit down on it like it was a belt and gnawed on it for a minute, finally ripping a portion off. "See, cooked to perfection," he said, his jaw clearly getting tired.

After we finished breakfast we packed up, I put the fire out with a single thought and began walking again.

I began to get tired of looking at dead trees covered in snow; I started looking at minor details in the branches, in the trunks, in the stacks of snow on a single branch. I could see were birds and an unknown species of animals roosted on the branches. It wasn't very exciting, but it was very much the most exciting activity I could do at that moment.

The toradrac and I trailed behind Scahl, he kept a closer eye on us this time, to not create too much distance between ourselves. I had to focus on keeping the toradrac going in a straight line with us, but he would wander off the second I took my mind off of him. He was an inquisitive creature, I could imagine by instinct, this was all very strange for him growing up.

\* \* \* \*

The forest trees had begun to thin out, and the snow had an icy gleam to it. It hadn't snowed for the past couple days, and I was able to shed a layer of my heavier clothes and finally, another couple of days would pass, and we saw nothing but hills, scattered trees, and sky. The change of view was encouraging. It made me feel we were getting somewhere. Snow was only in patches throughout the hills, and the trees were still as dead as ever.

In the distance I could see a pillar of smoke, rising slowly into the sky.

"We must be getting close to town," Scahl said.

"Don't you think there would be more smoke-stacks if that were from a town?"

"Yea, I guess, but even so, nobody goes outside their town more than a few days. It might just be somebody on a hunting trip. He's probably setting up camp for the night," Scahl looked around, "Maybe we should do the same, I don't want to be crossing paths with a stranger in the middle of the night."

The sun was still about an hour from setting but Scahl was right, it would be pitch black by the time we reached that camp.

We went to the bottom of a hill and set up the fire and tent.

"This reminds me of a time my Dad and I went camping when I was six," I said as I laid on the cool ground looking up at the stars that slowly appeared as the light was vanishing, "We got lost on the way to the campsite and ended up having to sleep in the car on the side of the road."

Scahl looked over at me, sitting right next to the fire to keep warm, "Hopefully it wasn't as cold as it is now."

"I don't remember how cold it was; it didn't matter, I just remember sitting on top of the car and my Dad showing me all the star constellations. I can't find any of them here."

Scahl looked up at the stars, "Do you think they could even be the same stars?"

"If I looked at these stars in a different perspective, I believe I would be looking at the same stars. It is one part of this world that looks all too familiar."

I smiled and sat up, "I think that was my first memory," I paused thinking back through the years, "Probably my last great one with my Dad." I couldn't talk about it anymore; it just made me wonder what his fate was with the fire at home and if I would get another chance to make a memory with him even if it wasn't a great one.

Scahl looked away from the stars, back to me, "Memories are an interesting thing, are minds recall them but our hearts decide which ones to keep." He looked back up at the stars, pausing for a moment, "It doesn't always take two to create a great memory and I'm sure your father has more great memories of you than you could ever imagine."

"Thanks for making me feel worse for not having any memories." I said light heartedly.

When we're fighting the dark summoners and after we defeat them, standing in eternal glory, with the Scales in our possession. We will have all the great memories we can possibly remember."

I laughed at the thought of eternal glory, "A lumberjack and a kid from another world, that's exactly who you think of when you think eternal glory."

"Well it's that or death," he laughed.

I forced a smile snapping back to reality, "I guess it's gonna be eternal glory. "

We sat around the fire, making light conversation for a couple more hours, and then I receded into the tent, the toradrac attempting to crawl in with me, to sleep.

I woke up before Scahl did; both of us finally getting a decent night sleep without having to keep a constant eye out under the Shaded Forest. The sun was still rising as I sat by the fire, noticing the pillar of smoke in the distance, was gone; whoever was there must have pushed on in the middle of the night.

Scahl shuffled then rolled over and rubbed his eyes. He sat up, "Are you tired of sleeping on the ground yet?" he said as he massaged his neck.

"I've gotten used to it," I said with a shrug.

"Hopefully we can get to town today, I think we could if we walked through the night and just got an entires day rest in a nice warm bed."

"I'm up for it if you are."

"I'm up for it," he stood up groaning and his bones cracking. He stretched his back out, "All right let's get a move on."

We packed up camp, I brought the fire down, and we began walking.

"I noticed the smoke was gone this morning, "I said to Scahl.

"Oh yeah, I forgot about that, it's good, I didn't want to run into any trouble."

"Are the people of D'Hanin troublemakers, or something?"

"Not necessarily," he replied, "But like anywhere you've got your bad people, especially with the Amethyst Scale gone and we've got to watch out for garmec patrolling."

"Garmec patrolling?" I asked intrigued, "When are we going to run into them?"

Scahl shrugged, "Hopefully we don't, this is going to be hard enough without running into them," he looked down at me and noticed the intrigue, "Don't worry, there will be plenty guarding Abanyu."

"Yea, I just don't want to get rusty."

"I'm not judging," he said back, "it's thrilling to fight, I know."

I looked down at my feet as we continued walking for about five more hours, across hills and open skies. We got to the top of one hill and finally found where the smoke was coming from. A small house that looked as if it had many renovations done by an

138

amateur, and a tall chimney standing about a story above the actual house, constructed in the only flat area of the hilly terrain. We both stopped and looked at it.

"Is it safe to go past there?" I said to Scahl.

"I'm not sure; we better go check it out." I heard an unfamiliar, raspy voice say.

Scahl and I looked over our shoulders, and an ancient man, hunched over with a cane supporting him, stood smiling, looking at the house.

Scahl and I stood back, more in shock than fear. The old man looked as if he didn't know where he was.

"Nice place isn't it?" He said, "Built it myself."

He looked over at us still smiling, "The name's Èrund Orlow, he switched his cane to his left hand and held out his other. We shook his hand and introduced ourselves. The toradrac grunted, steam coming from its nose.

Érund smiled at it, "Gold toradracs have always been my favorite, makes me want one for myself again," he said with a laugh.

I looked down at the toradrac, which nestled under my hand, and looked back up, "Yea, I captured the egg a few weeks back into the Shaded Forest."

"Impressive, hard to believe you got away with one. I remember when I was just a boy; my father had a whole herd of 'em. Magnificent creatures," Èrund said, reminiscing.

"Yes they are, Scahl said, "But we didn't mean to bother you we were just passing through."

"The Fade said you two would be passing through here; he'll be happy to know you made it through the Shaded Forest."

"What business do you have with the Fade?" Scahl said.

"Not a lot of business anymore," Érund smiled, "Just a bit of communication every now and again."

I saw Scahl taking notice of a chain hidden underneath Érund's shirt, "Give the Fade our best, we'll be out of your hair," Scahl grabbed me by the shirt, but not before Érund grabbed my opposite sleeve. I began to feel like the rope in a game of tug 'o war.

"Don't rush off in such a hurry. The Fade would never forgive me if I let his warriors go on without a meal, "Érund smiled and nodded, "Follow me." Èrund began walking ahead towards his home; we'll get you something to eat."

Scahl looked over at me, feeling like he just got trapped into forcing awkward conversation," he looks harmless, I don't think we have anything to worry about."

"It's not fear that bothers me," Scahl said turning to follow Érund struggling to walk as slow as he was. I could tell he was itching to just run to the house and wait for us there.

Before too long we reached the house, I noticed the dead plants surrounding the house and a little step up to the front door. I tied the toradrac up to the house, giving him enough rope to roam around a bit.

"Follow me inside, make yourselves at home."

Èrund swung the door open, and we followed him inside, Scahl having to duck under the door. Three old couches were lining the walls and a couple of big fluffy chairs surrounding a banged up coffee table. The room was overly crowded.

"Do you have a lot of company out here?" I asked.

"No, hardly ever, but you have to be prepared to give your guests plenty of options to get comfortable." He said walking into another room, "Feel free to make yourselves comfortable."

Scahl and I sat in the big fluffy chairs. My feet barely reached the ground. The fireplace sat directly opposite of us, unlit.

"We won't be able to stay here long, "Scahl said in a hushed voice, "We don't have any options but to keep moving forward."

"I'm sure he won't expect us to stay, he's just doing a favor for the Fade." I could smell something brewing in the next room, which I presumed to be the kitchen.

"I'm not sure about that; he has to get lonely out here all by himself."

I shrugged, "Let's just enjoy getting our minds off the travel."

"This all just makes me uncomfortable, I knew the Fade before I was frozen in ice, and he wouldn't have any communication with this man anymore. I just want to know how he knew we were coming."

By that time Èrund walked back into the room carrying three cups, with steam rising from them.

"My favorite winter drink," he said, "I've got to get as many cups in before it gets too warm."

He set the cups in front of us, and we took them. I sipped a small swig, and it tasted like hot chocolate. It was full-flavored and creamy with a generous helping of whipped topping on it. "It's terrific," I said, "thanks."

Èrund held his glass up to me, "The trick is to use furlet milk, not water." He took a sip and leaned back in the couch, "Were you able to harvest any while you were in the forest?"

"No, I prefer them for their meat," Scahl said back.

"It's a shame, with all of them scurrying through the trees, they're an easy source of energy for long travels." He paused for a moment awkwardly, "either way, I have a small roast in the oven, the Fade said you gentlemen might like a good meal."

With every mention of the Fade, Scahl looked more skeptical, "Thank you, but we probably shouldn't stay that long, as I'm sure you know we have a long way to go," Scahl said as politely as he could.

"All the more reason to stay!" He replied, "You can't just keep traveling endlessly, take time to break up the trip!"

"Well we wouldn't want to intrude, we could just stay in the next town," Scahl said.

"Well, I would think you would be staying anyway! The Vita Festus is in three days; you can't miss that."

Scahl looked over at me, silently asking if I had any ideas to get us out. I didn't. Especially after getting a whiff of the roast, I didn't think to stay would be all that bad.

"Then it's settled," Èrund said, breaking the silence, "You'll stay here overnight and tomorrow we will head to the Vita Festus." He jumped off the couch, "OH! I better check the roast."

Èrund quickly limped out of the room into the kitchen.

"I don't think it will hurt to stay," I said when Èrund was completely out of the room, "It sounds like it's on the way anyway."

"Yes, but walking at his pace will put us a week behind!"

"Well once I can ride the toradrac we'll be walking double time, and we'll make it up."

Scahl sat back in his chair, "Fine; I'm done talking about it, he wouldn't dare do anything against us, he owes us to be the finest host."

We both sat in silence until Èrund came back out with a tray with three plates, each with a small serving of meat on them. He handed them to us and sat down, "Sorry for the absence of any vegetables, my garden didn't do so well at all last year, and it left me with no reserves for the winter."

"Not a problem at all, you've been more than a great host," I said taking a bite from a hunk of meat.

He smiled, "I can hardly enjoy a meal anymore without my garden. I used to make feasts with a great mix of meats and vegetables and fruits," he sighed, "Now it's just meats and more meats. And I must say it gets harder and harder to catch these blasted animals out here all by myself."

"Why don't you move closer to town?" I asked.

"It wouldn't do me much good, they're as bad off as me, and the only time they do have plenty of food is during the Vita Festus. They won't eat for days so that they can have a decent feast. Before the Scales were stolen, they had enough food to serve all of D'Hanin. It was truly a magnificent feast."

Èrund, reminisced, clearly missing his younger days, for the rest of the night.

"If there's any reason I still fight for every breath, it's to see those Scales returned, one last good feast with my recipes is what I want."

"If we have anything to say about it, you'll get that last feast," I said with a mouthful of roast.

"I'm sure you will, the Fade was confident. It's a shame you were put into this position though, still so young and so much put on your shoulders. I knew one day these Scales would cause someone problems. I never believed you could harness that kind of power without any complications."

Scahl chimed in after slowly nibbling on his roast, "Well if I recall it was pity error that lost the Scales. Something that, possibly put into better hands, would not have put us in this position."

Érund sighed, hurt in his eyes, he set down his plate, "I think it's about time I start a fire," he said as he walked over to the fireplace. He knelt down by it and tossed in a couple of logs and began trying to light it with not much success. "I'm sorry, but it takes me awhile to get it started, without the, well you know." He continued to try and light it, "Once I get it lit I can usually keep it under control, except for one time, the fire went mad like it had a mind of its own and almost took the house."

He continued trying to light it getting more upset, "Damn Scales," he said under his breath, "I wish I could be of more assistance to you. I squandered a great opportunity in my younger days that I cannot take back.  Most days it hurts me even more that I am stuck on the sidelines as I near death."

I figured he had had enough with trying to start a fire, and I was beginning to see my breath as the sunset.  I caught a spark from Èrund and turned it into a fire.

"There we go," he said, feeling accomplished.

He stood up and dusted his hands off, "That should keep us warm through the night.  I'm going to head to sleep.  Just make yourselves comfortable on the couches.  If you see me come in here in the middle of the night just ignore it, I like to keep an eye on the fire."

We both nodded as Èrund shuffled out of the room with our plates, looking a bit more disheartened than when we first met him.  I looked at Scahl, to let him know he needs to let off a little bit.

Scahl finished off his drink, "I'm ready for a real drink."  He laid out on the couch and quickly fell asleep.  I followed soon after into a deep sleep, sinking into the cushions of the sofa.

# 11

## VITA FESTUS

The next morning brought an early start, Érund paced around the room, bursting with excitement; until Scahl and I were finally ready to leave.

Scahl and Èrund strolled ahead, Scahl looking more and more anxious to walk faster. "We've got to pick up the pace a little bit if we want to make it," Scahl said to us.

"Well you've got an ancient old man and a young toradrac, what do you expect?" Èrund spat back, "Learn to enjoy these times; you could just be hurrying towards your death."

"If I live or die on this quest, the people of D'Hanin have a right to know as soon as possible; they've been going through this Hell long enough."

"You remind me a lot of myself as a young lad," his smile then fading, "if I were still in my prime, I'd kick your ass." Érund got heated quickly standing taller than I've ever seen him.

I interjected before Èrund had a chance to try, "Everybody calm down, if we lose ourselves now, we will shame ourselves more than if we died fighting Abanyu. So let's keep it together."

"The legends I've heard have taught me other-wise," Scahl said sharply, unfazed by Érund's threats. Until a THUNK! On his head by Érund's walking stick and Érund belting out in a laugh, made him keep a closer eye on him.

"Érund, that's enough," I exclaimed.

"My apologies, I look back on my old self and always thought I could've used a clunk on the head by a wiser."

"All right," Scahl said out loud, obviously irri-tated, "I think your toradrac is falling behind."

I looked down at my feet, and he wasn't there. I looked back, and he was 10 yards behind us, with the most pathetic looking face, he would put one foot for-ward but then would scratch at his head, I walked back towards him trying to comfort him.

"Don't let him become too dependent on you, he's gonna have to walk on his own sooner or later," Scahl said looking over his shoulder as he kept walk-ing on without me.

"There's something wrong with his head!" I yelled back, Scahl not even saying a word.

"It's just his horns," Érund replied, "He's about that age that they should be peaking."

I spoke to the toradrac, and he finally kept moving forward with us as we all just kept walking in silence. Every so often I would look over at him and notice him fidgeting with his head, where I could see his horns slowly coming in under the skin.

\* \* \* \*

146

Two uneventful days and nights had come and gone. Scahl was still on edge, Èrund was just Èrund, and the toradrac, who I had begun calling Farley, had started filling out. It just didn't seem right, Farley had become a part of the group and deserved to be called something other than the toradrac.

Èrund stopped us and held his ear to the sky. With a smirk, he said, "hear that?" There was a faint noise of music playing.

"The Vita Festus has started!" He said like a child on Christmas morning, and he continued walking, still slow, but at a much quicker pace than before.

We walked, the music getting louder and louder. Èrund hummed along, and even Scahl looked as if he was finally happy to be there.

Farley jumped around ramming his head into trees, trying to imitate playing with his littermates I guessed. He started to get away from us, so I called out to him, "Farley!" He looked back and walked back over to us looking disappointed he had to stop playing.

Scahl looked back at me, "Farley?" He asked.

"Yea, like the actor," I said, "I always thought he was funny."

"Never heard of him," he said with a smirk, "But it will be a unique name around these parts."

I heard Èrund let out a loud laugh and looked back. He was looking ahead, his eyes wide, "We're here!" He held up his walking stick and pointed.

I looked forward, and there it was, the Vita Festus. Small shops and booths lined the streets, hundreds of people walking along, singing, dancing, and buying goods. A band played on a high stage and even further down another band performed on another stage.

A portly man with white hair and a cheerful face walked up to us, "Welcome, Èrund! Glad you're back to help us celebrate! And welcome friends of

147

Èrund!" He shook our hands, "Oh! And what do we have here?"

I looked down at Farley, who had smoke coming out of his nostrils; I patted him on the back of the head to calm him down.

"Not to worry little guy!" We welcome our guest's pets as well!" He said to Farley then straightened back up to look at me, "We have a pets holding area for you that my assistant," he motioned for a small, scrawny kid to come over, "will be glad to take your toradrac to."

I looked over at Èrund, and he nodded to me. I looked at Farley, "Go with this man; he'll take care of you. Farley followed the scrawny kid out of sight; my stomach lurched, being away from Farley for the first time since he was born.

"Now please go enjoy yourself!" The portly man exclaimed, "your toradrac will be waiting for you at the end of the festival, sure to of had as much fun as you!"

We kept walking as the portly man walked to another group of people welcoming them to the Vita Festus.

Èrund walked with a great smile, singing along to the music, "I can hardly stand to be in this town when the Vita Festus is not present. It's just a hoard of wistful people, trying to make it another day closer to today. This is the only time I care to be around these people; I'd be the same as them if I did."

Scahl pointed to a wooden awning with tables underneath, "That's what I've been craving," he said, pulling us over to the crowded area. Drinks were being handed out left and right. A waitress slid three drinks all the way from the other side of the table to us. Èrund grabbed one and took a small drink. Scahl intercepted mine, and downed his, "We gotta keep your senses sharp."

Scahl drank and laughed with everyone at the table, while Èrund and I slowly made our way out from under the awning after he finished his drink.

"I think he'll be fine there for now," Èrund said, "there's still a lot for us to see."

We walked the street, certain areas quieter than others but no matter where we went there was a sense of happiness, which I had not yet seen in D'Hanin.

"I was overjoyed to bring you here today," Érund said grinning as we pushed our way through crowds of people.

"Why is that?"

"The Fade had good words to say about you with little concern."

"I'm glad he thinks so," I said back not sure if I was following.

"You won't understand everything in this world at first glance, but it will always present itself eventually." Èrund grabbed my shirt and pulled me over to a ring with people surrounding it, "Tell me what's going on?" He asked since he was too hunched over to see over everyone's shoulders. I stood on my tiptoes and could see a guy get hit with what I assumed was a training sword, after he stood up fine, only his ego slightly damaged. A small portion of the crowd roared.

"I think they just finished fighting," I told him. He pulled me to the front of the crowd and with an unexpected force, pushed me into the center of the ring.

"We gots us an eager un 'ere!" I heard over the crowd. Everyone continued to cheer, and Èrund smiled and nodded. Another man, slightly taller and much older than I was, stepped into the ring and picked up a sword.

"Pick up the other sword!" I heard Èrund yell with a smile.

Before I was prepared, the man rushed me. I blocked all of his moves with ease. The Fade had trained me well.

The cheers grew louder as everyone expected much less from me.

"We gots us a double up bet!" I heard the announcer yell.

Another man from the crowd jumped into the ring, and they both started fighting me.

I used all my concentration to parry all the blows.

"I tink we know why 'e 'as such a fantastic sword now!" The announcer yelled, and I looked down wanting to unsheathe my sword, which I could be even better with.

The crowd grew louder in amazement. I counter attacked a strike from the first guy and took out his legs. There were thuds and roars from the crowd, then I spun around and countered another blow from the second man and hit him square in the shoulder making him fall to the ground at least 6 feet away from me.

The crowd roared again. I smiled at all the cheering fans and waved my free hand at them. Èrund made his way to the front of the group and grabbed me, I set my sword down and continued gesturing to the crowd as two more people entered the ring and picked up the swords. I got lost in the sea of people before I could see them fight.

As we got away from the crowd Èrund laughed, "My favorite part of the Vita Festus when I was your age," he handed me a handful of silver coins.

"You were betting on me?" I asked finally making the connection.

"Well, I can't bet on myself anymore! You did great kid!" He pulled out a bigger bag and shook it. I heard a rattle of coins.

A rush of adrenaline went through me, "Let's go back; we could make more!"

"Oh no, they'll never let you back in after a show like that. You're a sure bet; they'd never make any money if you kept fighting, everyone would bet on you!"

150

I smiled feeling a sense of pride. We continued walking down the busy street; we stopped at a stage, a band playing mainly percussion instruments.

We sat and watched them for a little while, just enjoying the relaxation. This is what was great about the Vita Festus, it blocked the outside world for an entire day so you could just relax and enjoy yourself without any worries of the Scales and there were plenty of options for you to choose how you enjoyed your relaxation. Whether it was listening to music, fighting, betting, eating, shopping, or drinking, they had it here.

I looked over at Èrund who was sitting on a tree stump, "So where's this feast you were talking about?"

He looked up at me, "You read my mind, let's eat like kings tonight!"

He stood up, and we walked almost to the end of the street, the smell of food getting stronger, making my mouth water.

We reached the end of the street and walked into a big building, it was dimly lit, with six long tables packed with people but spaced out enough, so you were comfortable. Èrund sat down at the central table closest to the kitchen. People streamed in and out of the kitchen doors carrying trays full of food out and carrying empty ones back in.

Èrund pulled his bag of coins out of his pocket and dumped a handful of them into his hand; there were varied sizes, shapes, and colors of coins, he picked out a large silver one and kissed it, "Here's to a good feast."

I reached into my pocket to pull my silver out, but he stopped me, "Don't worry I'll take care of this, buy yourself something nice."

And within seconds a large woman, who resembled a warthog, rushed to our side and laid down two small piles of food right onto the table. Èrund thanked her and placed the coins into her hand then rushed to the next people with surprising quickness.

Érund stared at the food with disappointment. I shuffled through mine, not sure if everything in front of me was real food, but it still smelled and looked pretty good.

I heard him mumble under his breath, "Damn Scales." He looked back up at me, "I feel embarrassed, I spoke so highly of this feast; however it has failed to excite this year."

"It's fine," I reassured him.

"It's fine, you're right, but the Vita Festus isn't supposed to be about just being fine and when you can count how many Vita Festus' you have left on the one hand." He trailed off in thought.

"This reminds me of a scene in this movie I used to watch. It was about a bunch of kids in a faraway land, they had absolutely no food in front of them, but somehow they made me envious of the enormous feast they were all digging into, even though I knew it was nothing."

"I guess this is still far from nothing." He said picking through his food. You're right, you're right, I'm letting the Scales get the best of me, I don't have time anymore for that, let's dig in," Èrund said already shoveling food into his mouth.

I didn't know where to start, so I grabbed something that looked like a chicken leg and dug in. It was all delicious; I didn't care what it was that I was eating, I only knew that any other feast I would have in my life would not live up to this one.

We both finished all the food, and before I had time to sit back, the warthog faced woman was back, dumping another small pile of food in front of us, this time Èrund didn't even have to pay.

"I thought we were finished?"

"No, I bought us a feast, and while they can't call this a feast, we must keep going!"

"Well I don't want to let it go to waste," I said, amazed and we both continued eating.

"They'll cook anything and everything and make it taste great; it's the only way they can get enough food for everyone."

I tried to talk with my mouth full but the only thing that came out were bits of food, but Èrund understood; it tasted great!

We finished our second helping, and a busboy ran over and scooped all the bones and whatever remained into a large trash bag, and he wiped the table off in front of us.

We sat there for a moment, Érund glanced around the room, "Well, normally they would be rushing out again with more food."

I sat back and put a hand on my bulging stomach, "Really, it's fine, I couldn't eat another bite," but as I was saying that, the warthog faced lady rushed over and scooped two mountains of what looked like ice cream, and made two desserts for Èrund and me.

As I thought there was no way I could eat all of that, Èrund looked at me and said, "That's the sign for dessert," he pointed at my hand on my stomach and laughed then started digging in.

We finished off our sundaes, comfortably full from a delicious mystery meat feast. Èrund stood up slowly, "Let's get out of here before the Festus is over." He thanked the warthog lady personally as we made our way out.

We stepped outside, the warm air warming my body almost put me to sleep on the spot. But we continued to walk around the Vita Festus trying to digest the food. We played a few games, similar to backyard games that I was accustomed to. The crowd died out a little bit each hour.

We walked towards a little shop displaying a large variety of saddles, "You said you would be riding Farley, correct?" Érund asked.

"Yea that's the plan."

"Well, then we must get you a saddle with the money you earned. It only takes about a month for a toradrac to be strong enough to carry a small person like yourself."

He wasn't wrong about me being small, I knew that from the many lockers I had experienced from the inside of, but I couldn't help trying to stand up a little straighter. By that time the shopkeeper greeted us, "How you gentlemen doing? Enjoying the Vita Festus?

"Like always," Èrund said.

"Good, so are you looking for a saddle?"

"Yea, my friend here has a young toradrac."

The shopkeeper's eyes got wide, "A toradrac? How'd you get that?" He said to me.

"I stole an egg," I replied.

"You're able to capture an egg from one of them ornery beasts, and you need me to provide you a saddle?"

I looked at Èrund feeling a little embarrassed.

"We haven't had much time to spend making a saddle during our travels," Èrund said.

"Didn't mean any offense by it. What color is it?" He asked me.

"Gold."

He turned around and sorted through his collection, he pulled an armful of them out and laid them on the counter for me to see.

"He'll be able to grow into these, and they won't be torn up by his scales."

I looked them over, not seeing a big difference in any of them. I picked out an attractive dark brown leather one, which felt the softest.

"Good choice," the shopkeeper said, "It'll cost you fifty denicks."

Èrund motioned for me to hand him the silver he gave me earlier. I placed it in my hand, and he counted it out. The shopkeeper looked at us curiously but accepted the money. I grabbed the saddle off the counter and said, "Thanks."

"Enjoy the rest of the Vita Festus!" He yelled at us, Èrund waved back.

There wasn't much left of the Vita Festus, the sun was down, and the streets were clearing. The music turned into a soft relaxing tune.

We found Scahl exactly where we left him; this time passed out with empty mugs surrounding him. Èrund shook him awake, or at least partially conscious.

"We better get him to an inn," he said to me, "I don't think he could handle anymore fun today."

We lifted him up onto our shoulders supporting him all the way to an inn that was nearly full. We checked into our room and threw Scahl onto the bed, who immediately passed out. Èrund sat on the edge of his bed and took off his shoes, "So how was your first Vita Festus?"

I set the saddle next to my bed and sat down, "Let's just say I hope I can make it again next year."

Èrund smiled, "It was nice to have such wonderful company this year, I'm glad you came along. Even with Scahl, I'm glad to have been able to enjoy a Vita Festus amongst friends."

"He has been acting strange lately; I don't think he means any harm by it, it might just be the travels."

"I understand, I would've acted the same way in my younger years. I hold no grudges against him, and would gladly travel to another Vita Festus with him as well."

I nodded, "I can't guarantee how much longer I'll be around, but if I am, you know you can count on going with me."

Èrund smiled and laid back on his bed, "Well this old man has to get his sleep."

I yawned, "Me too, I've been looking forward to this for a long time."

I lied down on the bed, looking out the window at the stars, just enjoying the comfort of a bed and being able to pull blankets up to my chin.

# 12

## A FOND FAREWELL

We stood on the outskirts of the deserted Vita Festus. Farley back at my side with his brand new saddle strapped to his back.

Stray trash blew in the warm newly spring wind. I think we all felt refreshed, and sometimes just one day is all you need to restore yourself.

"Well, I've gotta say Èrund, it was undoubtedly worth the setback to come here," Scahl said, "But we must keep going now," he stepped away to give me a moment to say goodbye.

Èrund held out his arms and gave me a grandfatherly hug. "Thank you again for sticking around to give me company," he said with a smile.

"You don't have to thank me; I wanted to be here as much as you wanted me to."

"Either way it was nice to have your company," he put his hand on my shoulder, "have a safe trip and please return soon."

"I'll do my best," I nodded.

"The words of an unconfident person," he smiled, "Your best will get you far, Finn, but you can go far more than you believe you can do."

"Then I'll go above and beyond my best," I smiled back.

The eerie silence of the finished Vita Festus was suddenly broken, with sounds of stomping in unison. I turned to look at Scahl, who was listening intently and frozen in concentration.

The stomping began to grow louder. Stragglers from the Vita Festus began to emerge, curious about the sound.

"Don't worry yet," Scahl told us, "It doesn't sound like a sizable group, probably just patrollers."

A sudden panic from the stragglers sent them all running in the opposite direction, and a loud crashing sent a jolt through all of our stomachs. Farley began stomping the ground with his hooves.

"All right, still not the time to panic, but get ready to fight Finn. Èrund, you better head back home as fast as you can, we'll hold them off long enough for you to get a head start," Scahl directed us and pulled out his axe, ready to fight.

"I've got one last fight in me; I will send you lads off in honor," Érund stepped forward seriously, Scahl laughing back.

"Érund, we have this taken care of, please go this is not your battle," I stepped in front of him.

Érund looked at me with sorrow in his eyes, which threw me off guard, "I have one last fight in me, I won't bother you passed this and will recede once again waiting in silence until I can once again see the world like it was in Keahi's time."

Scahl pushed me out of the way, "We have fully capable men coming from the Festus to help us, you had your time to protect the Scales, and it is not now. Go now before you make a fool of all of us."

Érund's eyes fell to the ground, "My last hope is to see the Scale's back in our hands. I will find a way to help fight once again. I hope to see you again, Finn." Érund's eyes never left the ground. He turned away and walked back to the village for safety.

I slowly turned away; knowing what I was going to be looking at on the other side of me wasn't going to be much better. I took a step up next to Scahl with my sword drawn, Farley stomping up next to me.

"What are we going to do with Farley?" I asked Scahl.

Scahl looked down, "I don't know, he'll have to protect himself."

I knelt down next to him, and looked him in his yellow eyes hoping he would understand, "Protect yourself, whatever you have to do, don't let them hurt you."

He stared back at me blankly; I could only hope he would understand. I looked back to Èrund, and he was already out of sight. I just prayed that we could fight them off long enough for him to get back home.

Scahl and I waited, watching the top of the hills for any sign of the garmec. The stomping began to get louder, and then in a flash, they came over the top of the peak, between 30 and 40 of them, pulling something by rope. They spotted us and gave a hideous yell and tugged on the leash and before our very eyes a 12-foot giant, bruised and battered, came over the hill. They let go of the rope, and the giant charged us, making the ground shake at every step.

The giant closed in on us, the garmec following close behind. The stragglers from the Vita Festus that had stuck around to help us fight stood steadfastly. I only counted 10 of them but for the first time I had confidence in my abilities, my heart wasn't pounding against my chest, I had a mission and understood the possible outcomes and were at peace with them.

Then out of the corner of my eye, I saw Èrund falling from a tree. But with a closer look, he wasn't falling; he was leaping from a tree what seemed to be in slow motion, he was headed for the unaware giant. Èrund held his walking stick up high and brought it down on the side of the giant's head, making it collapse. Èrund landed on the ground and rolled not so gracefully. Scahl and I charged at the oncoming garmec. Èrund jumped up and started fighting on his own.

The giant recomposed itself, looking for what had hit it. It spotted Èrund and brought a giant fist down. Èrund dove out of the way and the fist smashed into a garmec.

I watched Èrund in amazement; he looked over to me, "Nobody wants to bother a weak old man, a strong old man is a different story, I would've never gotten any peace!" He laughed and continued fighting.

Scahl and I stood by Èrund's side to help him fight off the garmec, Farley ran around looking lost.

"Farley!" I called out to him so he would stand next to my side and I could protect him. But it was too late. A garmec brought its hammer down, and it collided with Farley, throwing him to the ground with a sad whimper. I tried to make my way over to him, but the giant blocked my path. I dodged attacks and watched as Farley stood up smoke billowing out of his nostrils with every grunt. He charged at the garmec that hit him, and rammed him into the ground, then swung his tail colliding with another garmec, throwing him off its feet.

Another garmec with a sword slashed Farley's side, but his diamond-hard scales ricocheted the sword away, and Farley charged him into the ground.

Now that I knew Farley would be all right I had matters to attend on my own, as a giant fist swung at my face, missing by inches.

I tried to find a way out, I couldn't get close enough to the giant to strike him, and I was running out of energy much faster than him.

Scahl and Èrund were getting overwhelmed; I could only spot four of the stragglers left, struggling on their own. I desperately wanted to get over there and help them, but we had no chance if I lured the giant over there.

"*Èrund had the only right idea,*" I thought to myself. I had to get to the top of a tree and strike down on it. I ran to a cluster of trees and stayed at the base of them. The giant punched at the trees, trying to rip them apart to find me.

I tried to run to another tree, but the giant caught on and ripped the tree out of the ground and threw it, with a loud yell, spit flying everywhere, like raindrops splashing down.

The garmec began to thin out, their bodies lying across the field. Maybe if I could just hold out until Scahl and Èrund finished them all off, but what if they were thinking the same. They had to be getting tired. My element tingled through my body. I jumped out of the way of a falling fist, and then formed the most significant fireball I could and threw it at the giant's face. The giant swatted it away, his hand catching on fire.

I ran away as he tried putting the fire out by trying to squash me. I threw another much smaller fireball at him and without thinking, grabbed a knife and threw it right behind the fireball.

The giant swatted the fireball down again, but the knife kept flying at him colliding with his right eye. The giant grabbed his bleeding eye, and I made a run for it, right past the screaming giant.

I climbed up the nearest tree as fast as I could. Halfway up, the giant uncovered his eye and began looking for me. I kept rising but saw he spotted Scahl and Èrund and started stomping towards them with gritted teeth. I yelled at the top of my lungs when I finally reached the top to get its attention. The giant caught site of me and changed course. It came up to the tree and grabbed it trying to shake me down.

I held my balance as best as I could and jumped from 16 feet up in the air, my sword pointing down above my head. Watching the giant look up at me, I immediately felt like I made a mistake, not catching the giant off guard. He waited for me, as I fell, to grab me and tear me apart.

But then a noise, like a car hitting a brick wall, echoed throughout the air. The giant closed its eyes in pain and wobbled as I landed on its shoulders bringing my sword down to the top of its head.

The giant went immediately silent after a final half grunt. I could feel it falling; bringing me with it. I jumped, tucking and rolling, the air being ripped out of me as I hit the ground.

I looked around, my vision blurry and saw Farley, wobbling towards me; two small bloody horns were now coming out of his head.

"That was quite a hit," I said to him realizing that was the cause of the loud crashing noise. I stood up and saw the two horn holes in the calf of the giant, blood dripping out of a giant bruise forming.

I was grabbed by collar of my shirt, and yanked with force. I tried to compose myself, thinking for sure this was the end. And it was. Scahl was dragging me away from the battle. I looked back, the garmec closing in on the last two remaining stragglers, tearing them apart.

"What are you doing!" I screamed, "We have to keep fighting!"

"It's over, Finn," Scahl said struggling to keep me restrained, "We have a larger battle to worry about."

He threw me behind the dead giant, Farley diving next to me. "What happened to Érund?"

"I'm hoping he had the same idea as us; I told him we had no hope in this battle. We shouldn't have stuck around for it."

The clashing of swords stopped, the only noise I heard came from garmec at this point. They continued on their path, tearing into the city, searching out the people who stayed in hiding. It was their city now, and there was nothing we could do.

Scahl stood up, heading towards the battlefield, out of site. I grabbed Farley, and we followed. The remaining garmec and stragglers lied on the field together in silence. Scahl was the first to spot Érund.

We ran over, and I pulled him out from under a garmec. Èrund was still alive, but he had a knife in his stomach and blood dripping from his mouth. I dropped to my knees beside him. He opened his eyes and groaned, "You ok?" He said to me.

I could feel a lump growing in my throat, "Still a little shaken up from seeing you jump from that tree, but I'm fine." I laughed, attempting to not let it turn to tears.

A smile grew across Érund's face, however, he was too weak to laugh, as blood dripped from the corner of his mouth.

"Èrund." I was able to muster out as his face when an unusual shade of white.

"Yea, I know." He said forcing every word he could get out. He raised his bloody hand up to his neck and pulled out a chain with a pendant at the end. He groaned, and a teardrop rolled out of the corner of his eye. He put a shaking bloody finger on my chest, as a steady stream of tears were now running down my cheeks and falling off my chin.

He closed his eyes, breathing shallow, and pointed back at the pendant, "Take it." His eyes never opened again.

I laid my head against his unmoving chest. I'd never lost someone close to me before. I only knew him for 5 days, but for a reason I couldn't explain, I couldn't control myself.

\* \* \* \*

162

We stood at the foot of our ill made gravestone, freshly dried tears on my cheeks and a bloody pendant gripped in my hand. We had a moment of silence for him, but I couldn't be silent anymore, "I can't keep going Scahl. The Elements told me I was not meant to be the one. I have nothing special about me to make this quest make any sense."

"Whether or not you were "the one" the Element still chose you, that's what makes this quest make sense."

"But the Element can't carry me through it all. If that were the case, that city would've been protected, if it weren't for me, someone better would have found a way to hold the garmec off."

"You just defeated a 12-foot giant," Scahl barked at me getting irritated, "There was nobody else out there that could've done anymore. Maybe you weren't the first choice for the elements, but you were a choice. That's more than anyone else in past D'Hanin history can say."

I looked down at the pendant I took from Érund. It was a transparent purple scale with a hook wrapped around it.

"Do you know what that is?" Scahl asked.

I shook my head no.

"It's the Pendant of the Scalesmen. Only a small handful of people were chosen to protect the Scales, and when they were chosen, they were given the pendant. When all the Scales were well protected, it was a great honor to be able to wear that around your neck, but when the Scales were stolen --"

I interrupted, knowing, "They were shunned."

Scahl nodded, "I had a feeling he was a protector when he told us the Fade spoke to him before we arrived."

"Is that why you were hostile to him," I said hostilely.

Scahl nodded slowly, "He fought valiantly next to me in his final battle, and I regret not seeing that fight in him before."

"The title of protectors stood on only a small handful of people, but it was everyone in D'Hanin's duty to take care of the elements. That's where you all went wrong even before the Great Drought." I said feeling heated.

"You're right," he said softly, "but you're wrong about your quest not making sense, we're all behind you in this, willing to fight alongside you to do it right this time. Érund passed his pendant to you, the only Protector of the Scales to have not been buried with it, in a way it was his way of reaching the end of the quest with us."

I looked deeply at the pendant before putting it around my neck and knelt down, placing my hand on his stone, "We'll get there for you my friend," I stood back up, "Let's keep going then."

# 13

## TIME TO RIDE

Rain poured down on us as we walked. None of us seemed to care; it felt fitting to the situation. The skies were filled with gray clouds and cast a solemn feel over the landscape.

Scahl slowed down for me so I could catch up. "I'm sorry about Èrund," he said trying to cheer me up.

I nodded, and he continued walking at my pace.

"But he wouldn't want you to continue to mourn over him, he was a warrior and went out fighting. In a warrior's eyes, there's no better way to go."

I didn't know what to say, I still felt terrible that

he was gone, if only I could have defeated the giant faster, I could have helped them.

Scahl pointed at my chest, "He gave you that pendant because he saw a warrior in you, and I see it too. When a fellow warrior dies fighting for the greater good, you should rejoice in his life and what he's done, not grieve that he's gone. Èrund would have told you the same; I promise you that."

I thought about Èrund jumping out of nowhere to slow the giant down and taking on the garmec. It was the most surprising and heroic acts I had ever seen in real life. Without him there with us, fighting, this whole journey would be over.

"You're right," I said. Strangely, a considerable weight felt like it was being lifted off my chest. With those simple words, I was more empowered than ever to complete this journey.

I glanced down at Farley, who was walking alongside us looking prideful. I patted him on the head, and he looked up at me.

I looked back at Scahl, "I think if this guy can take down a giant with a headbutt, I think he's ready to ride."

"I would agree," Scahl said with a smirk, "Strength was never a question with him, now that he's almost full grown, I wouldn't doubt for a second he couldn't carry you."

"So is it just like a horse?" I asked.

"A horse?" He questioned back.

"I'm just gonna assume yes," I said with a laugh, I swung my leg over and got comfortable in the saddle. Farley snorted smoke out of his nose and tapped his foot on the ground, apparently not liking me just jumping on. I patted him around his neck and started regretting just jumping on.

"Don't worry; he'll get used to it, just stay on and try to stay still."

Scahl was taken aback by my eagerness, "Ok, first, make sure you never grab onto his horns or fur around his neck for support. His horns are like his weapons; you wouldn't want someone grabbing your sword from you and his fur, well you wouldn't want someone pulling your hair either. If you feel like falling off is imminent, just tuck and roll, it's not a long fall, so you'll be fine, he will notice the lost weight and come back for you."

I nodded, feeling more comfortable as Farley became more relaxed.

"To get him to walk just tap him on the sides with your legs, the harder you tap, the faster he'll go. To turn just pull the reigns in the direction you want to go."

"And he just knows all this by instinct?" I asked.

Scahl burst out laughing, "Animals don't know how to be directed by humans instinctively, it's going to take consistent training. It will help if you talk to him as you perform these actions. He's known your voice since he hatched so you will have an easier time training him."

"Ok," I waited for more instruction. Scahl stood there waiting for me to make a move.

"Well go on, that's all I know. I've never ridden a toradrac before."

I gave him an "oh great" look, but I had no choice to take his word for it, and with slight confidence, I tapped Farley on the sides lightly and said, "Go." He looked back at me; I imagined him thinking "*Go where?*"

"Tap harder, those scales are thick," Scahl said.

I tapped a little harder and once again said, "Go." Farley didn't move; I looked over at Scahl then looked forward again. I tapped Farley even harder and said, "Go!" He went forward catching me off guard. My head snapped back, and I lost my gripping.

Scahl noticed, and shouted, "Let go!" Terrified that I might try to grab on. I landed hard on my back, and Farley kept walking forward.

I sat up, "Will he come back?"

Scahl watched Farley walking away for a moment, "I don't think so."

I rolled my eyes, and we went chasing after Farley who now thought we were playing. He started running away like a dog, dodging our every attempt to grab him. He swung his tail around and threw Scahl off his feet, splashing into a giant puddle of mud.

He let me get as close as possible to him; then he would snort a puff of smoke and run away.

"He thinks we're playing," I said to Scahl as he got up holding his side.

"Can you tell him to play a little gentler," Scahl asked.

Farley ran around us in circles. "Just let him wear himself out."

"I've never heard of a toradrac with this much playful energy."

"Maybe he's happy?" I said with a smile.

Farley got just close enough to me, and I chased after him and jumped onto his back. I pulled back the reigns and shouted, "Ok! Slow down buddy!" He put on the brakes quickly, and I fell forward off of him again, face planting into the mud. "Stay here!" I yelled at him, and he did. "Fun time is over." He snorted almost like he was laughing.

The riding became simple and more natural the more we went. After falling off 4 times, straying off the path even more times, and Farley not wanting to move with me on his back, we finally got the hang of it. I slowly lost the need for voice commands, and he would know when to turn, when to stop, and when to go. He was an intelligent creature.

I rode for a few more hours, covering about as much distance as we would have in almost a day if I had been walking. Scahl kept up with a brisk walk alongside Farley who was trotting.

"Do you think I could fight on Farley?" I asked Scahl, feeling powerful, like a knight on Farley's back.

"I wouldn't; he's too good of a fighter on his own. You'd be making two targets into one."

"I guess that makes sense." I unsheathed my sword, and held it out above my head, "Charge!" I yelled, imagining in my head a herd of garmec running towards us. Farley charged forward as I swung my sword around at the imaginary garmec.

Farley ran much faster than I expected and Scahl chased after us. I pulled back on his reigns a little bit, and he slowed down, bucking his head again. I sliced my sword through the air, jabbing and swinging, imagining the grandest fight in the history of D'Hanin.

I directed Farley around in circles and turns, stopping and fighting two garmec at once. Farley bucked his head again and kicked his back legs out causing me to drop my sword and grab onto the saddle for support.

"Whoa, Whoa!" I laughed as Farley settled down and snorted smoke out of his nose. I patted him on the neck.

"You must be crazy," I heard Scahl say as he caught up to us.

"It's not as easy to fight while riding as they make it look in the movies," I laughed again, adrenaline rushing through my body. I hopped off Farley and grabbed my sword. I wiped the muddy blade off on my shirt, and with a beautiful gleam, I sheathed it.

"You're having too much fun with this," Scahl said.

"If I didn't, I'd lose my mind walking all day."

"So in other words, you'd be like me," Scahl grinned and continued walking."

"You can't've lost your mind already! We've just begun!" I hopped on Farley, and he trotted to catch up alongside Scahl.

"It beats being locked up in a chamber I guess. You better do well, I plan to stay out here as long as possible."

169

"If getting all the Scales back is doing well, then yeah, I'm going to do well."

"That's a confidence I've never seen from you before."

"Well didn't you see me take down that giant?" I laughed.

Scahl laughed, "All right, calm down, it wasn't that impressive."

The conversation changed quickly when we both noticed we had finally reached the next town.

"This doesn't look good," I said looking at the burnt buildings, dried up crops, and the overall ghost town feel to this city.

"It looks a lot worse than it appears," Scahl reassured me, "When the Scales were stolen, small towns like this weren't so resilient. The crops dried up, when a building would spark on fire, they didn't have the resources to fix them. If they were unfortunate enough to cross paths with a group of garmec, they didn't have the people to hold them off. Eventually, the inhabitants would have to move to another, bigger city. You can imagine the fate of the Vita Festus city here."

I couldn't help thinking I was glad Érund wasn't around to see the Vita Festus looking like this. Life would have to be brought back to it, with the Scales, but even then it wasn't going to be the Vita Festus that Érund loved.

As we got to the edge of the town, I could see the city was indeed small. A cluster of huts sat scattered around us; then a single road stretched further down with six or seven individual shops lining the street.

"I guess that's our luck, when we finally find a town on our own, it's abandoned."

"There will be shelter, and I'm sure beds at least. When the people left, they left in a hurry, so we will find value from this town."

"And food?" I asked, starting to get hungry.

"We'll have to hunt, any food left here is sure to be spoiled by now." Scahl noticed my disheartened look, "Don't be so disappointed; we're not kings yet." Scahl headed back into the woods, "Try to find a couple of beds for us, I'll bring back food."

"We're splitting up?" I asked skeptically, knowing what happens when we get split up.

He kept walking and looked back, "It's me, I'll be back in 10 minutes with a feast."

"Talk about confidence," I shouted back. I heard him faintly laugh as he went into the forest lining the back of the city.

I didn't like being alone in this world. I hopped off Farley, thinking he could probably use a break. I noticed a wooden sign on the ground covered in dust. I picked it up and held it in front of myself. It read *"SEMUL"* in roughly carved out letters. I grabbed the two pieces of rope hanging from the side of the plank and tied them back together. I reached as high as I could to hang it on what I assumed was the post it was on before, in remembrance of the town.

We continued walking along the dusty road; the sounds of our footsteps were echoing, and the long shadows from the setting sun gave me a chill. I looked at the buildings as we walked, looking for an inn. I imagined the town as it was before the Scales were stolen. Families shopping, kids playing, I passed a market and just imagined a nice hanging sign and people going in and out all day. It was heartbreaking to see, in the flesh, what war can do to a place, a home for many people.

We came to the front of a building that looked most like an inn to me, I walked up to the front door, and Farley followed, "Stay here, I'll be right back out," I patted him on the head and opened the creaky door.

The inside looked simple, there were still chairs and tables, and 4 doors lined the right side of the building. A warm gust of wind came in through the broken windows and door; it seemed every little crack in the wall was letting in the wind. I looked around the room, and before my eyes, a figure formed.

I knew right away it was an element. The transparent figure stepped up to me, much more urgent than my last meeting with an element. *"You must leave, do not follow your path,"* It said to me both hands grabbing onto my shoulders, its lips staying completely still as it spoke, *"There is danger coming, I tried to warn you sooner, but I couldn't focus your concentration."*

I stood there speechless, I didn't know what she meant by focussing my concentration, but danger was a word I understood all too well.

"What kind of danger?" I asked hectically.

*"What kind does not matter, just be prepared. Keep your mind open to us young one. You will not survive this quest without the elements; you know this."*

At that moment Scahl came bursting through the door, and I looked back, "A feast!" He held up two fistfuls of dead animals.

I looked back to the element, but it was gone, then ran to the nearest window and looked out.

"What's wrong?" Scahl became grave.

"I've been warned of danger coming."

"By who?" Scahl set the animals on the ground and came over by the window.

"An Element."

"An Element?" Scahl said looking confused, "How do you keep seeing them, most people never see an Element in their lifetime, not to mention seeing them twice.

"She said I need to keep my mind open to them; they're trying to help me get through this," I paced the room trying to think, "There was a panic in her voice."

"Well don't worry yet, I don't know what she told you, but danger could mean way down the road, which is pretty obvious I think."

"I don't think so, she said she tried to contact me sooner, but once again, my mind was elsewhere."

Scahl looked outside, "Well where did the element go? Can you call her back?"

I thought to myself; I didn't know how they showed up; I know she said to keep my mind open to them. *"Did I have to be alone for them to show themselves? Did I have to concentrate intensely?"* I didn't know.

"Ok, give me a minute, go stand outside with Farley." Scahl turned and went outside.

I tried concentrating on the elements calling for it like I do to use my element.

Scahl walked back in as quickly as he left, "Sorry to interrupt, but we've got trouble."

"What is it?"

"I don't know, but I've got a hunch. Let's just get Farley in here."

"What's your hunch?" I said as I hurried to the door and went back outside.

"Let's just get him in here."

I heard marching and grunting in the not so far distance as we pulled Farley up to the door. His horns were so long now that his head wouldn't fit through the doorframe.

We tried twisting his head to make them fit, but he resisted and grunted himself.

"You've got to stay quiet and get your head through this door," I said into his ear.

He grunted, then stood back on his hind legs and rammed his head forward breaking the door off the hinges and leaving a large chip in the doorframe. Scahl and I both grabbed onto him, holding him still, as the echo of the breaking wood faded away.

Suddenly all the noise in the area faded. We stood in the quiet.

"Let's get him in," Scahl commanded.

"Do you think they're still coming," I asked hoping that the noise faded because the marching was going away from us."

Scahl waited to answer, then the marching and grunting got louder, I knew then that we were in even more trouble.

We pushed Farley in and went into the furthest room along the side of the wall. It was cramped, Farley barely fit in there himself, and then you add Scahl and me, we almost couldn't fit. On the plus side, there was a bed in there.

I stood up onto the bed and peered through a small window almost at the ceiling that reminded me of a jail cell window. There was nothing in sight; I still couldn't resist watching for any sign of the garmec.

I looked back down at Scahl who had an arm around Farley, "I don't see anything."

Scahl remained calm and silently told me just to get comfortable. I sat down and just listened, trying to be as quiet as possible.

The marching finally reached the town. I had to use every ounce of my strength to not look out the window. It pained me not to know what they were doing. I could only paint a picture in my head; I knew there were a lot of them and they were carrying something heavy.

Farley shifted his feet making the slightest bit of noise, and the marching stopped. Scahl closed his eyes tightly, and I involuntarily stopped breathing. It was quiet. I soon found myself missing the sounds of marching.

"Burn it down," I heard a feminine, but commanding voice, say outside, "We'll have to rebuild it either way for the new world."

I looked at Scahl for answers. I mouthed, "Is it the garmec?"

Scahl shook his head, no. I looked at him for more answers, but he just shrugged his shoulders.

I heard the torches being lit and the buildings starting to burn. I still imagined the garmec running around and burning the buildings. I couldn't visualize who else would do it. I heard a window crash, and a flame erupting inside the building we were in.

"Just stay in here, you can protect us from the fire, right?" Scahl asked quietly, under the noise of the fire.

I nodded, "I think so."

"Then we've just got to hold on until they leave, anyone talking about a new world, is bound to be an enemy."

Smoke started leaking in through the closed door and sweat began to drip down my face. I concentrated on the fire, picturing it on the outside of the door.

The element coursed through my body. Pushing it out, I creating a barrier around the room. The loud crackling of the fire made it hard to concentrate, but I forced myself to block it out.

Inside my mind, I could see an invisible flame crawling up the walls and spreading out over the ceiling. It covered the cracks in the door, and smoke stopped billowing in. I sat there in concentration, my eyes closed not knowing if it was working or not, but with no screams from Scahl or panic from Farley, I believed I was doing it.

After what felt like hours of concentration for me, I heard Scahl, "I think we're ok now, just put the fire out around us."

I lost concentration, and the fire began burning through the walls. I quickly regained it, and the room temperature dropped rapidly and the chilly night breeze blew through the room almost making me feel sick. I opened my eyes, and Scahl was sweating. I wiped my forehead and sweat was covering me like someone dumped a bucket of water over my head. I leaned up against the wall a wave of exhaustion hit me harder than I've ever felt, "I don't feel so good."

"Just relax, we're safe now. Let's get you out of this room; the smoke smell is gonna make me sick too." Scahl lifted me up putting my arm around his shoulder. He unlatched the door and pushed Farley out. I could see rubble everywhere. All the tables and chairs were now just a memory, all the walls were burned down, and we were in the last remaining room of the city. Smoke rose from the ashes, and a few small flames burned, casting just enough light for us to be able to see.

We stepped entirely out of the room and found a large group of men and boys staring at us in silence. A woman decorated with jewels and dark purple hair sat in a chariot looking down upon us. We both apparently didn't think about how strange it must seem to see one room in the entire city not burning and still standing strong.

We stood in silence. The woman appeared just as in shock as we were. She stepped down off her chariot and walked forward to us, her soldiers now bracing themselves for anything we might do. She stopped a short distance away from us and looked us all over, even Farley with an extended interest.

We waited patiently for her to speak. She must've been a queen of sorts, and it was going to be best to not get on her wrong side if we had any hope of getting away from her.

"Which of you have the element?" She said standing tall but still even shorter than I was.

"I do," I said, still hanging onto Scahl. I did my best to bow my head in an effort to suck up.

She looked directly at me, "And what is your name?"

My stomach turned over; I looked up at Scahl to get a hint as to if I should make up a name. He looked at me blankly, and I had to think quickly, I needed a new name, my mind raced looking for a different name. Then I got it, "My name is Finn."

I bowed my head again, this time in shame. I completely blew my cover.

"Finn?" She questioned, "That's a strange name. Where are you two from?"

It didn't seem as if my name blew our cover; I was pretty sure we were ok for now. "We're drifters."

She turned to Scahl, "And your name?"

Scahl turned to me, "They call me Scahl."

"Finn and Scahl, a couple of drifters. Why were you hiding from us?"

We both paused, waiting for the other to speak. We weren't prepared to make up stories of our lives. "Well when you support a new world, you tend to have a lot of enemies."

"And why were you hiding from us then?"

"We didn't wait around to see who was coming; we just went into hiding."

Unbelievably, even with our terrible story, she looked as if she was buying it. I didn't want her to think about it too long for fear she would figure us out.

"And may I ask your name, Madame?" I could tell her thought was broken when I asked.

"You may. I am Queen Salya of the Kahana Nation, Fliagenrè."

"It is a pleasure to meet you, Queen Salya." I stood up on my own now to give her a proper bow, and Scahl followed my action and bowed with.

She nodded at us, "So you say you have an element, please perform it for me." She demanded.

"Of course," I held out a hand, a ball of fire formed, hovering slightly above my palm.

"That is truly brilliant, Finn, the Drifter. I must say your skills would greatly benefit our ranks," she looked us over again, "Hook the Toradrac to the carriage, we will bring these two back with us." She commanded her guards.

Two bulky guards came over and grabbed both of us by the arm and pulled us along, not in a threatening way but definitely in a forceful way. The Queen took her seat back, and we were seated right under her.

I looked back for Farley. Four guards approached him with caution, then all at once lunged forward, grabbing onto his horns and two jumping onto his body to hold him down. Farley cried out in a whine, I had never heard from him, as they tried to wrestle him into the reigns they had set up onto a carriage opposite the Queen's. I cringed at every whine.

A guard came forward with a spear and jabbed him in the backside to move him forward. Farley whined again, and Scahl grabbed onto my arm, holding me in my seat.

The guard jabbed again, drawing blood this time. I jumped out of my seat, shaking free of Scahl's grasp, I wielded my sword and moved to the guards. Scahl jumped up next to me with his axe.

"Stop it now!" I yelled at the guards, but as quickly as we jumped up, a dozen guards swarmed us, all with spears pointing at our throats.

"Put down your weapons." I heard Queen Salya command us from her throne calmly.

I looked back, and she was standing up. Scahl pulled my sword arm down slowly.

"We only ask that you treat the toradrac with respect, he will not hurt your guards if they do not hurt him," Scahl shouted to Queen Salya.

"And what kind of bond would a couple of drifters have with an animal?"

"When you spend months on end in the wilderness with only the company of an animal, it becomes part of the group, no matter what kind of animal it is."

"That is noble, of you. However, it is not the way of our people. Guards, take their weapons and put them away, we will be taking them for further questioning."

The guards grabbed both of us, this time in a threatening way, and stripped us of our weapons and

178

threw us into a cage on the back of the chariot carrying Queen Salya.

Farley was loaded up into another cage on the carriage they were initially going to make him pull. He jumped up and down on his hind legs blowing smoke from his nose in fear. I wanted to reach out to him and calm him down, but there was nothing I could do as the chariot started pulling away. The carriage followed behind us.

We left the town, and it's burning ashes behind us. I looked to Scahl for answers; we couldn't just let them take us. We had to escape somehow.

"Just sit back and relax, there's nothing we can do right now that wouldn't get us all killed," he said somberly. He sat back in the cage and looked out to the landscape as the sun disappeared behind the land leaving us in the dark.

# 14

## FLIAGENRÈ

$W$e traveled through the night as I did my best to get sleep, but the constant bumpiness of the chariot kept me up. It was torture just waiting, not knowing where this Fliagenré was or how far off the path we were going to go.

I looked over at Scahl, who was deep in thought but chose against bothering him. I had a million questions that were most likely the same ones that were churning in his head. I scanned all the guards trying to come up with a half-baked plan to escape but knew it was probably better to let this ride out for a little while. We weren't in danger yet, and if we kept to the story of who we were to a couple of drifters, we would be ok. I would just enjoy the free ride and hope we were going in the right direction.

* * * *

The night was almost passed as we finally approached a small budding town. Families walked around going in and out of shops, just like any other town, no walls or motes, only a few guards standing around the perimeter of the city.

As we inched closer, I could see the town was grungy. Moss climbed the sides of buildings, people dressed in dark cloaks covering their faces, I saw what I was almost positive was a witch hunched over a cauldron spilling over with a thick, chunky, bubbling yellow liquid.

As the townspeople saw us approaching and parting like the red sea for their queen, I was now confident we arrived at the infamous, Fliagenrè.

The townspeople were as stone-faced as the guards, only when we passed them, would they drop their stone-faced look and give us a rotted tooth snarl. Rotten food was thrown from within the crowds at us, and nasty remarks were dumped on us by bold townspeople when we passed them, one even hocked a loogie that dripped down the bar of the cage.

I did my best to block them out. It was a disgusting place to be and you could feel the humid stench of the town latching onto your skin. I gagged at the thought of it on my skin. They must have taken offense to it because uproar was sent throughout the townspeople, more nasty names I didn't understand were shouted at us and more snarling didn't make me feel any better.

Scahl leaned over to me, "That's the smell of dark magic, they'll have to burn this town to the ground if they ever hope to get rid of it. Even if they do, the darkness will always linger in the land," he said sounding like he was even trying not to breath through his nose.

I pulled my shirt up over my nose, holding my stomach until we reached the end of the town and made a U-turn to be parallel with what I assumed was the Queen's castle.

It wasn't much more significant than any other building; it actually looked older than all the others with moss covering the structure and even hanging off the roof. Two guards stood in the doorway. I couldn't be sure that they were human; they looked more like minotaurs, but just in the face. They had terrible under bites with saber tooth like teeth going down their faces and rhinoceros-like skin. I did my best not to make eye contact with them.

When we came to a full stop, the guards surrounded our cage and pulled us out, spears rose to our necks and pushed us like cattle towards the castle.

Queen Salya marched forward quickly and entered the castle, leaving us behind. I looked around frantically and noticed Farley was gone, "They took Farley," I said to Scahl.

"It'll be fine, just keep composure, the town isn't that big."

A guard poked me in the neck with his spear, and I felt a warm drop of blood fall onto my shoulder.

"Keep it quiet, Queen Salya has had a long night, and we expect you to honor her while you are a guest, you will remain silent until she calls on you."

"Is this how you treat your guests?" I said under my breath.

He jabbed his spear into my neck again, harder this time, I cringed and grabbed my neck. I held back anything else I had to say and just walked like a good "guest."

They pushed us into the castle, and we walked down a long dimly lit hallway. We turned to a door on the right side of the hall and walked through down a short staircase. A jail cell was at the end of the stairs lit only by two torches. A man who was already in the cell jumped up to greet us.

"I'm good now! Please, I wanna be with you fine gentlemen on the ground level!" He shouted at the guards.

"Pipe down you kenk! We brought you company," the guard yelled back at him.

As we reached the front of the cell, the man was barely clothed, just a pair of tattered shorts and that was it. He had dark bags under his eyes, and his ribs could be seen through his skin.

"What are they gonna do to me! What did I do to deserve this! Please! Please! I want to be alone!" He whimpered and ran into the corner.

The guard threw us into the cell, "If I hear any more from you, you're gonna be fed to the animals, you hear me!" Slamming it locked, he exited back into the hallway.

Scahl and I watched the whimpering man in the corner; we kept our space as not to alarm him. He peeked over his shoulder at us and looked up the stairs at the closed door. He immediately stopped whimpering and turned to us, "the Kenks, you gotta let them think they get to you, if anything, it's a good laugh for me." He sat on the bed and leaned back, "What are you fellas in for, nothing too bad I'm sure, cause if you were bad, you wouldn't be down here. You've got a bunch of loons running around up there."

Scahl and I weren't sure what to do; we just looked at him puzzled. Our entire first impression of this man was changed in an instant; we didn't know if he had multiple personality disorder or if he was just messing with the guards.

"Did I scare you or what? Did they cut out your tongues?"

"Sorry, what did you say your name was?" Scahl spoke up first.

"Ah, an introduction is what you needed," he stood up and held out a hand, "Saeban Torkan the Fourth, but you can call me Torkie."

Scahl shook his hand, "I'm Scahl, and this is Finn."

I nodded to him and shook his bony hand. "How long have you been down here?"

"A year, maybe more I think."

Scahl walked over to a small barred window, looking up into the town.

"It's best you stay away from the window, terrible smelly drafts come through," Torkie said, "I learned it's best to stay by the bed. Believe it or not, it smells much better in the dungeons than up there."

"I believe you, I haven't gagged since being down here," I said almost gagging thinking about the smell of the town.

Scahl turned away from the window; the smell didn't seem to bother him as much as it did the rest of us, "so what do we do now?"

"What do you mean what do we do now?" Torkie said, "Look at where you are, you do nothing until the guards tell you to do something."

"You see Torkie, doing nothing isn't an option for us, we have responsibilities to be taking care of," Scahl said hotly.

"I thought you said just to relax," I snapped back.

"How am I supposed to relax when I've got a man with half a brain talking my ear off and nowhere to get away from it!"

"I may have half a brain, but I've a full heart!" Torkie shouted back.

I stepped between them, Scahl towering over Torkie, "Scahl! You told me to relax, and you need to do the same! We need to figure out a way of escaping," I said in a hushed voice.

Scahl gritted his teeth and took the bed over his head and slammed it against the wall. A deafening echo rang out throughout the chamber. Torkie and I both covered our ears and backed away from Scahl. He stood in the corner taking fast, short breaths.

A guard swung the door open at the top of the stairs and ran down towards us, "If I hear another peep out of this cell I'll personally take all of you for a beheadin! Now shut it!"

We stood silently like a bunch of school kids who just got caught by their teacher.

The guard banged his club against the bars of our cell and turned to walk back upstairs. A piece of metal, broken off from the bed, flew past my head and hit the guard. I ducked and turned to look at Scahl who was just standing there looking ready to explode.

The guard turned around holding the back of his head. He stood up tall, "The big guy rather die than stay in a cell, should've just said so." The guard turned back to walk up the stairs and out the door, slamming it behind him.

Scahl grabbed me by the arm and pulled me over to him. I flinched, ready to get thrown against the wall like the bed. Instead, he was positively calm, "Ok, they're going to come back here to take me away to get beheaded, I just need you to stay calm and listen to whatever Queen Salya tells you."

I just listened in awe; I was still confused if he was still furious or not.

"They don't want me for anything, they were planning on killing me eventually anyway."

"You can't let them kill you!" I screamed back.

"Quiet, I'm not going to let them kill me, I'm saying I'm escaping now instead of waiting who knows how long until they let me out of here to kill me."

"Wait, what am I going to do!"

"Just let me talk! They're going to be back any minute, I will worry about getting Farley while the Queen is preoccupied with you and then you'll have a tiny bit of freedom with these people. That's when you distance yourself as much as you can without looking suspicious, and I will come to get you, and we'll get out of here."

Five guards came pummeling through the door.

"Do whatever the Queen says," he told me gritting his teeth. He threw me to the side and hovered over me like he was going to stomp my face in. The guards barreled through the cell door and grabbed him pulling him to the ground and chaining him up. I watched in terror, but as they lifted Scahl up, he looked calm and confident again. They led him up the stairs, chained up like an animal, and out the door.

I looked over at Torkie who I completely forgot was even there. He looked completely blank, not knowing what to say for once.

"I'm gonna need you to play along, and maybe we can get you out of here too."

"There's no way out, believe me, I've tried."

"You haven't tried with us before. If you don't rat us out, we'll all be able to get our freedom back."

"Your friend is dead! I don't want any part of this! We can't escape!"

"Calm down, if you don't want to be a part of this then that's fine, just please be a decent person and let us escape."

Torkie paced back and forth, "I just can't let this happen again!"

I grabbed Torkie by the shoulders and looked him in the eyes, "Be quiet, they're gonna come back down again, but this time they'll be taking you!"

His eyes grew wide and fear set in. He sat on the bed again and buried his face in his hands. He looked up at me, "Just believe me. This isn't the first time someone's tried escaping," he said sounding more anxious.

"We can get you out too; you don't have to live down here anymore. You can do whatever you like once you get --"

Torkie interrupted me, "Don't repeat it, I had hopes of it one day, but they'll find me then they'll kill me. I'm better off just minding my own, down here."

"So you're fine with just spending the rest of your days down here alone?"

Torkie couldn't look me in the eyes, "it's not so bad really, and you get new cellmates every once in a while. They come 'n go."

"If you want to give up that's fine, but I'm just begging you to not bring me down with you."

Torkie looked up at me, "That's all I am, my brother used to tell me the it too, he always said it, and now you're saying it." He paced the room again, as I slowly backed away from him, trying to not watch him have a nervous break down.

"He knew me better than anyone else, you see we were explorers, we set out to make the first complete map of D'Hanin. I begged him to take me with him, when he finally came of age, he was ready to leave in a hurry, and I begged and begged, I wanted to leave as much as he did but I was just a child." Torkie didn't stop to take a breath, he just kept pacing and letting his story spill out, "I finally broke him down though, and we set off; him and I was gonna be famous. We traveled for years, trekking through more land than you can imagine and really seeing the world. Then we reached Fliagenré and they took us prisoner! We didn't do nothing to deserve this, and then he tried to escape just like you're trying to do now."

He cringed his face in anger and hit his hand against the wall, "they took our maps and destroyed 'em. But he was so sure, he had 'em all up here," he tapped on his head with a finger, "and he was gonna start again. So he got the guards down here to open the cell, and he killed 'em with their own clubs and ran for freedom," he turned to me, "why'd he have to kill 'em? We're not killers; we never killed before," he looked away again, then I heard them," he cringed again, this time more in pain, trying to hold back tears, "I heard 'em killing him, he screamed for me, but I was scared. I just sat right here on the bed and covered my head."

Torkie sat on the bed and covered his head once again. I didn't know exactly what to say. He had been tortured with that memory for as long as he was down here. I leaned against the wall exhausted just from the emotional level in the room.

"I couldn't imagine a better reason to try and escape with us."

"And what's that?" He asked still covering his face.

"You haven't let your brother down yet, get out of here and continue making the map. If you don't escape you can at least see your brother in the afterlife and stand face to face with him as a warrior, someone who fought for what they believed in and not cringed at the site of adversity; someone who curled up into a ball and died a frightened man."

Torkie finally uncovered his face, "But I am a frightened man."

"So am I! Everyone is scared, but if you live in fear you will never be courageous, if you live courageously you will never be in fear."

He swung his legs off the side of the bed and finally looked me in the eyes. "Don't stop looking up to your brother just because he's gone now because his influence and memory will always be there for you whenever you need it."

He looked as if he was going to say something, but the door at the top of the stairs swung open, and the silhouette of two guards came walking down. I looked back at Torkie, and his legs were once again curled up against his chest, and his face turned to avoid any eye contact with the guards.

The guards unlocked the cell and swung the door open, "You can come with us now," they said to me.

I pushed myself off the wall, and they guided me out of the cell. I looked forward up the stairs, a rush of excitement flowing through my heart.

We walked out the door and down the hallway towards the entrance to the Queen's throne room at the end, which had two more guards blocking the way. The doors swung open for us, as we reached them. The throne room was by far the most elegant place I've seen in this town, which wasn't saying much, but at least I didn't feel dirty standing in there. Queen Salya sat before us in an elegant throne. It was plated in gold, and two toucan-looking birds with long colorful tails were perched above her on the throne.

The guards led me up to her and presented me.

"Finn, I'm glad you are willing to speak with me," she said, "I have potentially great plans for you."

"Of course Queen Salya," I said doing my best to remember the plan.

"I would like to first discuss the matter of your friend."

I nodded for her to keep going. My gut churned feeling like I was being led in for questioning if I had anything to do with his escape.

"You're well aware I'm sure, that he was taken away for beheading for misconduct."

I looked at the ground, "Yes, I'm aware."

"And you're aware that the same could very well happen to you?"

My gut churned again for a different reason; he may not have escaped. Surely she would've been notified if he had survived. "Yes, I am."

"Of course we would never wish that upon you, you have a great ability and I believe you would fit in along our ranks as long as you're willing to conform just a little bit."

"I looked back up at her, "What kind of ranks do you mean?"

"Well the royal ranks," she said in a matter of fact sort of way, "There is not one person in Fliagenrè who possesses an element, and we could use that in expanding for the new world."

"What do you mean by the new world?"

She rolled her eyes a bit and let out a sigh, "You must be a drifter, you don't know a thing about what's going on, do you?" She calmed herself, "Please tell me you know about the Scales."

I nodded, "Of course."

"There is a certain group of people, that would like to get the Scales back into the hands of "the good people," but here in Fliagenrè, we believe in Apaku's quest for the strongest world we can create. The Scales were believed to make us a weak nation, nobody worried about war, or having crops, or anything, and who knows where this nation would have been heading if that wretch of a man had been able to make the other elements! By Apaku's control of the Scales, we ultimately become insurmountable. Now doesn't that seem better to you?" She asked me rhetorically.

It sounded terrible to me, I pictured a world of animals ruling D'Hanin but I nodded and had to agree, "and it will create stronger generations for the future."

She sat back on her throne; I feared I might have gone too far with my last comment. She looked me over like she did when she first found us.

"Now that we have a little backstory, we'll get down to the reason we brought you here. So what's it going to be? Are you prepared to join our royal ranks?"

I pretended to think about it for a moment, and then looked back up at her, "I am."

She smiled deviously, "Perfect; then we will have you demonstrate your abilities for us at a later time, for now, guards you can take him back."

I must have looked shocked because she became grave with me, "you will be under careful watch until we can fully trust you, and you don't run a successful empire by trusting everyone. If you truly de-

190

sire to be amongst our royal ranks, you have nothing
to worry about."

Before I was out the doors of the throne room
she squeezed in one last remark, "Prepare yourself,
Finn, the Drifter."

I nodded and the guards led me back to the cell
were Torkie was waiting; he stood up from the bed
when the guard opened the door. We walked all the
way down the stairs, and Torkie didn't make a sound.

"For once the lunatic is quiet! It's a miracle!"
The guard exclaimed sarcastically, "A little bit of company straighten ya out, did it?" The guard threw me
back into the cell laughing, then left us alone.

"What happened? I thought we were getting
out?" Torkie said as soon as the door closed behind
the guard.

"So you're on board then?" I asked.

"Maybe... I don't know! I just don't want to die
down here!" He yelled in a panic once again.

"We will get out of here alive; the Queen wants
me under strict watch until she trusts me."

"How long is that gonna be? I'm not ready!"

"I don't know, we just need to act normal, they
can't know what we're doing so you need to go back to
your regular self when the guards are around, and I'm
going to act like I don't want anything to do with you."

"Ok, so what's the plan to get out? It doesn't
involve me does it? Please tell me it doesn't!"

"I don't know yet, just do what I told you and
calm down for right now. I hope Scahl has a better
idea to escape than I do."

I couldn't talk to Torkie anymore the rest of the
night. He wouldn't stop rocking back and forth and
staring at the wall. I worried about Scahl; everything
seemed too casual around here; it was hard to convince myself that he had made it out alive. Thoughts
raced through my head about what I would do if he
didn't make it out alive. It kept me from getting any

sleep that night, and I was awake before breakfast came the next morning.

The guards came in with two plates of bread and rice and a pitcher of water. After a good night's rest, Torkie was acting like his usual self, jumping off the bed and running up to the bars to meet the guards as if he were dying to have another meal.

"For tha love of Apaku! Rice and bread! Please let me have more, I'm just so hungry, and rice and bread is me favorite!"

The guard hit his club against the bars, and Torkie belted out laughing, I made sure to stay pushed up against the wall, trying to keep my distance from him.

The guard shifted his focus to me, "Well if you want any you better get over here, I'm not your servant."

I stood up and quietly went to get my plate. I held out a hand, and before I grabbed onto the plate, he dropped it in front of me, the food splattering across the floor, "You think you're special just because you got an element? Just walk right in and be amongst the Royal Ranks?"

Torkie jumped off the bed and started scarfing down the food on the floor.

"You're just scum like this pathetic sap." The guard turned and left. I didn't realize I was so unpopular around here already. If only they knew.

Torkie looked up at me when he heard the door close. He wiped his face off and scooped the remaining food onto the plate, "Take mine, this isn't the first time I've had to eat off the ground."

"Thanks, Torkie." I sat over on the bed and began eating; it was all flavorless mainly just content to fill our stomachs, so we don't wither away and die down here.

"Do you think they'll come down for you today?" Torkie asked.

I shrugged my shoulders, "Probably."

192

"He said you have an element? Is that true?"
I nodded, and Torkie's eyes lit up, "Which one?"

"Fire."

"Can I see?"

I presented my hand out from under my plate and threw a small fireball at Torkie, his hands shot up to block the flame, and he fell back batting at himself. I laughed, and he looked back at me and started laughing, "That was brilliant, maybe you could've toasted this bread for us though."

"I probably would've burnt it."

"When the Queen sees that there's no way she'll keep you down here for another day."

"Hopefully neither of us will have to spend too many more nights down here."

Torkie looked down at his plate, "But you know if you can't get back here for me I'll be ok. I've been down here so long it wouldn't matter anyway. If Scahl was so desperate to get you guys out of here, you must be doing something important."

I set my plate down, "we'll get you out of here Torkie, you've got something important to do too."

"Yea, I'm just saying, make sure you get yourselves out, if there's no way to get me out with you, then I'll be ok."

I just nodded, understanding what he was trying to say.

* * * *

After breakfast the day dragged on, I sat in the corner, Torkie daydreaming about freedom and letting out a long sigh every few minutes. I thought of different scenarios that could get us to that freedom he was fantasizing about but found it hard when he kept trying to get details of my plan out of me.

"What if you got someone from the inside to help you?" He asked, throwing ideas out there.

"I've already thought about that," I snapped back.

"Ok, so what?" Torkie asked, wanting to know my plan.

"I don't know; I just don't know, I can't concentrate on an escape plan when I don't know the area."

"I know the area pretty well, look." Torkie knelt onto the dusty floor and started drawing lines. In about 20 seconds he had a map of the area drawn out. I hovered over him as he explained it to me.

He pointed out a short path, "This is where we are, this is Fliagenrè, and specifically this square is the Queen's Castle, which we are living under." The map became less detailed as it extended from Fliagenrè.

"To the North East, there is a river flowing around an island less than three miles from us. The river stems from the Potens River." The line showing the Potens River faded. "I'm not exactly sure where it goes or how far it goes before it ends, but it's not far from us."

He moved to a section of poorly drawn trees south of Fliagenrè. "There's a forest here that covers miles, but the trees are spread out, and without the Emerald Scale most of the trees are either dead or have few leaves on them."

Torkie had left the West side of us blank, "What's on the west side of us?"

"You would know better than I do, isn't that the way you came in?"

"Yea," I said, realizing I didn't pay much attention to my surroundings while they were taking us. "I don't think it's much, just hills and trees."

"That's what I figured, they picked us up by the lake, and we never were able to explore past Fliagenrè or ask the townspeople the names of the rivers and such."

I immediately thought the best way to go was towards the Potens River. I remembered Scahl mentioning the Potens River when we initially started or journey and knew that must be where we needed to go.

I patted Torkie on the shoulder, "Thanks, this helps." A glowing smile grew on Torkie's face.

It was at least a small start, and it got my mind off being in a cramped, dingy room. I looked out our window at the darkening town, imagining myself running like hell trying to escape, where I could go, where I could hide. I could see the forest Torkie was talking about at the far end of the town. It made me wonder if he had time to explore it or if he was just assuming it went on for miles based on what he could see through this very window.

I started thinking about plans without Scahl, in case he didn't make it out, I hadn't heard from him at all or even talk amongst the guards. Without his help in the escape, my only option would be to stay here for possibly months gaining the trust of everyone and sneak out in the dark of the night, silently. But was there any hope in that? Could D'Hanin wait months to be saved? I didn't know, but that was the best plan I could come up with.

# 15

## ESCAPE IN TURMOIL

Light streamed in from our little window, across my face. My first thought before opening my eyes was the performance Queen Salya was expecting of me. I didn't want to have to stand up in front of everyone and play with fire. I'd almost rather spend my last days in D'Hanin in this cell than to go through with this.

Torkie rolled over shortly after I woke up. "Has she summoned you yet?" He asked rubbing the back of his neck.

I shook my head no, "I think she forgot about me." I sat up on the side of the bed and stretched.

196

"I hope not, you're my ticket out of here," he laughed.

I looked out the window for any sign of Scahl, but there was nothing. I had to convince myself that he was still alive and that I had to be prepared for any moment that he might choose to save Torkie and me.

I worried about Farley as well; I just hoped that he was able to rescue him, if not I can't imagine what they would have done to him by now.

At about that time the familiar creak of our door being swung open sounded. I looked back, and sure enough, two guards with their chests puffed out, walked down the stairs and stopped in front of our cell. With a quick twist of the key, our cell door flung open.

"Queen Salya has summoned you," the guard said with a stern look, "She is ready for you to perform your element. Gather your things and follow us."

I looked over at Torkie who was sitting in the shadows, "I don't really have any things."

"Then let's proceed, Queen Salya does not have all day to wait for you."

I took a few slow steps forward, and then a plan began to emerge. The guard looked ready to pull me along. "I forgot I had a special demonstration for Queen Salya; I would humbly ask that my cellmate comes along so that I can perform."

The guards looked at each other, then back at me. "Queen Salya has summoned you and you only, to remove another prisoner from their cell would be out of the question." The guard motioned for me to walk ahead, but I stayed put.

"But you see, I planned it out specifically to be done around him. Please, Queen Salya will be captivated with the performance, and will recognize you two as the guards, confident enough to allow this to happen."

The bigger guard who had done all the talking stepped into the cell to come face to face with me; he raised his spear at my throat, "What kind of game do you think you're playing at you little kenk. Queen Salya has summoned you, and she will get you and you alone."

"I'm not sure what a kenk is, but, will you be able to lend me a guard then? Simply to perform a trick that would be invaluable to the army."

The guard didn't lower his spear until the second guard touched him on the shoulder and motioned for him to talk in private. They stepped out of the cell and lowered their voices. I looked over at Torkie and nodded to him to play along. If I had a chance to be out of this cage I needed to bring Torkie along just in case.

The bigger guard slammed the butt of his spear on the ground, sending a loud echo through the cell, "All right, he comes along, but we will be taking extra measures of precaution."

Both guards stepped into the cell, the second guard held a spear to my throat and watched me as the more masculine guard grabbed shackles off the wall outside of the bars. Torkie stood up, but the guard pulled him over into the light, almost sending Torkie back to the ground. He strapped on the shackles around his ankles then around his wrists and finally grabbed a pole with a chain around the end, much like what a dogcatcher would use.

"He will not be released until you are ready to perform, that is if Queen Salya will approve of it, he may be sent straight back here. Understood?"

I nodded.

"Good, now let's move, Queen Salya will be sending guards after us if we don't get there soon."

The guards herded us out of the cell and back into the hallway, Torkie squinted his eyes and looked around in amazement. I gave him a subtle nod to let him know everything was going to be okay. He nodded back and squinted his eyes to get the tears out then took a deep breath.

We walked at a hurried pace until we reached the door, this time I thought it was strange, there wasn't any guards blocking the doors, until we walked in I had realized almost every guard in Fliagenrè was in the room.

3 guards on either side of the Queen, 5 guards on both sides of the walls, 2 guards perched high above the Queen, bow and arrows at the ready, and 3 more guards standing in the center of the room, which we met.

The trollish looking guard standing in the center kept his eyes on Torkie, "What's his business?" He demanded at the guard containing Torkie.

"The prisoner that was summoned insisted that we bring him along for a special performance, of course, we took the proper precautions in bringing him and would gladly take him back upon the request of Queen Salya."

The trollish guard stepped to the side revealing Queen Salya on her throne; she smiled and nodded at me.

"Make your case," the trollish guard said to me.

I wasn't prepared to speak and stumbled over my words, but pulled myself together finally, "Queen Salya, I have put a lot of thought into how I would demonstrate my element to show you the true power it holds for your nation." (That was the biggest lie of them all, I hadn't thought about it at all until the moment they came down to get me) "And I feel my biggest demonstration, one that could change the face of our army, would be most properly done on a prisoner, rather than a guard."

Queen Salya took a moment to process the appeal, and then finally spoke softly, "You have not done anything to alarm me thus far, Finn, until now."

My gut dropped and a lump formed in my throat as she paused for another moment, looking me over like she had done so many times before.

"I find it strange that there is no resistance with you. Most people will cooperate to an extent, but you have been submissive since we found you. I thought for sure there would be rebellion brewing inside you when you stepped through that door, and even more when I saw your cellmate behind you, but then you tell me you have been planning to impress me?"

I looked down at my feet and took a gulp, trying to get the lump out of my throat.

"You don't strike me as a submissive person, Finn. So tell me, what are your plans? What's really going on inside your head?"

I was trying not to panic as I scanned the room, all eyes intently on me. "I had no intentions of alarming you Queen Salya, but I didn't choose to become a drifter. For as long as I have had memories, I have moved from town to town, traveling all over D'Hanin, never fitting in anywhere I went. Never having any family." I looked down at my feet again, really trying to sell the story. "Then you came along and told me I could be a part of your royal ranks," I looked back up at her, "how could anyone let that opportunity, to fit in, to have a family, slip through their fingers?"

She looked at me once again, a grave look on her face, and finally nodded. "We would gladly take you in as family, but to be amongst the Royal Ranks will depend on what you do here today." A vast weight felt like it was being lifted off my shoulders.

"So you absolutely need him here with you?" She asked me.

"If you would allow it."

"Ok, I will allow it. Guards, please step to the side, take the prisoner with you and give Finn the floor."

At once all the guards moved in unison, dragging Torkie along.

I wasn't sure how to start. Queen Salya just stared, waiting for me to perform. I could feel my palms begin to get clammy, as they all waited for me.

"How would you like me to start, Queen Salya?" I asked timidly.

"I want to see your element, impress me."

I held out my hand, and within seconds a flame arose. I looked up at the Queen, and she watched for something more spectacular. I rolled the fire into a ball between my hands and threw it into the air, and it withered away after it reached its peak.

Queen Salya, shuffled in her throne, "Show me more, I already know you have the element, I want to know how well you can use it."

I nodded and regained my concentration. I created fire in both my hands. I laid both palms onto the ground and spread the fire out in front of me, and then I stood up quickly, lifting my hands above my head creating a wall of fire between the Queen and myself. I then grabbed the barricade and whipped it around like a wrecking ball. All the guards took a step back, a warm, wind blowing in their faces.

I put the fire out and stood for a moment thinking what else I could do. It felt at this point my imagination only limited my abilities.

I performed for a little while longer, feeling like a jester. I began to get scattered oohs and ahhs from the guards and even a small laugh from the Queen.

"Your performance has been quite satisfactory, Finn. We could definitely use you among our ranks, but first I would like to see what your finale is that you have been planning." She motioned for the guard to let Torkie come to the center of the room. The guard unhooked his noose pole from Torkie's neck and pushed him forward.

In the midst of the performance, I forgot about my promise to show something spectacular involving Torkie. I tried to think of an idea as he sauntered towards me, still in his shackles.

"Right," I said, "if you could hold out your arms and pull the chains tightly."

Torkie looked at me nervously, but he did as I said. I lined up my hand with the chain like I was about to perform a karate chop, then with a swift motion, I lit my hand on fire, as hot as I could muster, and chopped through the chain, my hand melting the metal, instead of breaking it.

I stood back, pleased with myself. I looked up at the Queen who didn't look as thrilled, "I hope that wasn't it."

The smile quickly fell off my face, "No, no, I simply needed to remove his shackles to perform properly."

"Please remove the rest of the shackles, before the rest are ruined," she motioned for the guard to step forward, and they immediately removed them from his wrists and ankles.

"Ok, now that he is free, I will be able to launch him into the air for an aerial attack on our opponents, while shielding him in a ball of fire."

Torkie whimpered as I took a couple of steps back, my hands trembled not sure if I could pull this off, but I had to do something. The longer I stood there, the less I wanted to attempt it, I knew I was putting Torkie in danger. I gave him thumbs up to make sure he was ready. He shrugged nervously and took a stronger stance.

I rubbed my hands together, creating as much fire as I could, then like I was laying out a carpet, I tossed the flame onto the ground towards Torkie's feet. When it reached him, he let out a terrible scream. I continued with the trick and lifted the fire and Torkie high into the air.

I retracted the fire when I realized it was burning him and he fell to the ground with a loud thud. The Queen stood up, and I ran to Torkie's assistance. His pants and legs were burned up to his knees, but he held onto his elbow in pain.

"What was the purpose of this, how did you see this playing out in battle?" The Queen shouted at me.

"I'm sorry. Obviously, I didn't see it playing out like this." I snapped back.

"Guards." The Queen ordered them to assess the situation without saying. A short, pudgy guard examined Torkie's elbow and burns before standing back up and facing the Queen. "The prisoner's legs are severely burned and will need immediate attention, as well as a broken elbow that will heal just fine in a couple of months with proper setting."

"Sounds like a lot of work." The Queen said stepping off her throne to be eye level with me. "Someone please remind me why he is still under our care. If you all don't remember his brother, his brother's blood runs through his veins just like the blood of our guards ran across the cell's floor. Is this Apaku's goal for the Scales? Taking care of the weak in hopes that they will join us?" She motioned to Torkie who was lying on the ground, the pain showing more the longer he laid there. "Is this what we're doing here?"

She paced the room, scanning the guards, waiting for just one to speak up but they all remained silent. She stared me in the eyes, waiting for me to speak before she spoke to the guards, "Send the prisoner to beheading."

"Queen Salya!" I accidentally blurted out. She smirked, pleased with the reaction she got out of me, "I was in the wrong here, please don't punish Torkie."

"Torkie?" She laughed, "Is that what you call him?"

"It's his name; I spent two days in a cell with him. I was bound to learn it."

"Do you care for this prisoner, Finn?"

I couldn't answer her; I hung my head to break her glaring eye contact.

"Does it bother you that I say he will be dead in by nightfall? That with one faithful swipe his head will be removed from his body and all life that is shown in his eyes will leak from his head as the blood does from his body?"

I could feel her breath only inches from the top of my head, and her cold fingers wrap around the back of my neck forcing me to look up.

"Take one last look at Torkie. It is who you don't want to be in Fliagenré, but do not think you will not have the same fate as him if you show your weakness."

Our plan wasn't ending well, I was prepared to take Torkie and run, but we weren't at that point yet, I could still find a way out of this. However, the only option I had right now was to stand firm and silent, and I did.

"I expect much more from you; you need extensive practice with your element to be ready for the Royal Ranks. You can stay in the barracks while you are training and the necessary accommodations will be prepared for you if you make it to the Royal Ranks."

"Thank you, Queen Salya."

She turned and headed back to her throne, "Krodo, please take Finn to the barracks and return his belongings." A trollish looking guard, with the fancier attire, grabbed me and before leading me out was stopped by Queen Salya.

"Krodo. Take special care with Finn. I still don't trust him wholly."

"Of course, Queen Salya," He said smirking, his grip tightening unnecessarily as he forcefully led me out of the Queen's throne room, Torkie being led out of another door, shackled once again.

The walk down the hallway seemed longer this time; I couldn't have handled that situation any worse for Torkie, if I hadn't injured him it could've been his step forward to freedom as well. I closed my eyes tightly as we walked passed the door to our old cell. I couldn't bear seeing it if I wasn't able to get Torkie or Scahl back, I completely screwed everything up if I was going to try to go the rest of the way on my own.

The front doors opened up revealing the mid-day sun. I reached the outside world once again, in which felt like months, the disgusting stench of this putrid town immediately clinging to my skin.

We walked down the road, the looks from the townspeople had changed, most people with much more welcoming glares, as word got around of my business of becoming an element bearer amongst the Royal Ranks. If only they knew I was ready to burn this whole town to the ground. Even more so when the entire city stopped what they were doing and cleared the road, standing on the sides, including the guard and him pushing me to hold on the side. He looked over at me and smiled; bacteria filled drool spilling out, as another guard strapped up to a gurney, pulled it through the town.

I didn't know what we were all stopping for; this was evidently a ritual done many times for Fliagenré. I could see someone strapped to the back and thought maybe Torkie was being taken to have his wounds attended to instead of a beheading. Perhaps the Queen was just trying to shake me up.

On the other hand, as the gurney came closer I could see the person's legs were nearly hanging off the edge; Torkie wasn't much taller than me so I knew his legs wouldn't be hanging off the end.

As it inched closer to us, I could see a dark liquid dripping with every step the guard took. I could see the tarp was strapped, tightly covering the entire individual's body. As it passed us, I dropped to my knees. The world was suddenly frozen in time as I stared at the wrapped up body, knowing that he didn't make it out.

Questions rang through my mind, my mind screaming at me, that I had failed. I couldn't help to break down in front of the entire town whether it would blow my cover or not, it didn't matter anymore. I wanted to know what happened and why what he was planning didn't work, I knew Scahl didn't make this kind of mistake, he wouldn't have risked so much if he thought we wouldn't get out alive.

The guard, Krodo, pulled me up off the ground and struggled to push me forward, yelling at me to pull it together, as we followed behind the trail of blood before I was thrown, falling onto the floor of an empty room that had beds lining the walls.

I forced myself to move to the edge of the bed nearest me, Scahl had parished, and Torkie had the same fate unless I could do something about it. I needed to find Farley. I wanted to know that he was at least okay; I couldn't make another move without him.

By that time Krodo came back in holding my sword and other items, he tossed them on the ground in front of me, before turning to leave.

"Wait," I stood up from the bed, "Where's Farley?"

Krodo stopped, "Who?"

"The toradrac that came here with me, I want to see him."

"What do you want to see him for?"

"I want to make sure he's being treated properly. I'm not a prisoner anymore; I shouldn't have to beg to see him. At least tell me where he is so I can go."

"I will take you, you may not be a prisoner anymore, but that doesn't make you anymore trustworthy." He motioned for me to follow him out of the barracks, "Don't know why you care so much about seeing a damn animal."

He led me away from the barracks as soldiers were staggering their way back, the top of the moon creeping up over the tree line, casting a gloomy, but fitting look to the town. I could see the stables just on the outskirts of the city. The guard kept looking back at me, with ugly stares; making it known this was a burden for him, but wanting to keep the Queen happy.

"Here, go find your toradrac, I'm going to alert the Stable Master."

I browsed the stables, looking at the different toradracs, each one looking more miserable and poorly treated than the last. Until I saw a dark brown mane, and a slight glimmer of gold reflected from the moon's rays. I ran over to the stable, Farley hunched down and backed into the corner. "Farley," I said excitedly.

He looked up at me and immediately relaxed and walked towards me. I examined a chip off his left horn and more than a few minor cuts and bruises down his back. "Are you okay, buddy?" I asked gently touching his horn; he pulled away but snorted kindly letting me know he was all right.

"We have to get out of here, Scahl is gone, and I can't stand to look these people in the eye anymore. We're going to try and save a new friend I met in the cells, but if we can't, it's just going to be you and me, buddy. I'm glad they didn't do any worse to you." I stroked his mane, seeing the ropes were unbearably tight around his neck. I didn't know how he could even breathe. "Let's get this rope off you, it can't be comfortable."

Struggling with the tight knot, I was eventually able to get it loosened, slipping the noose off of his neck, revealing ligature marks all the way around.

"HEY!" I heard a deep, weathered voice scream from the entrance of the stable. I looked up, and the Stable Master along with Krodo was charging towards me.

I held my hands up, "I was just --." Farley started to puff smoke out of his nose and jump onto his back legs so I turned around to calm him before a fist crashed into my jaw, from behind. I fell back into the stable, Krodo and the Stable Master still charging me. They both got a few more punches before I was able to kick Krodo off of me, but the Stable Master was about the size of Scahl.

I recomposed myself in the midst of the pummeling and sent a flame shooting down the Stable

Master's arm. He finally jumped off me and started rolling around in the hay.

"It's the end of the road fire boy." Krodo lunged at me this time wielding his sword. I unsheathed mine, blocking his moves. The Stable Master in the midst of trying to put the fire out on his arm had the place bursting in flames, the dried out hay might as well have been gasoline.

I counter struck Krodo's moves easily knocking him to the ground. The Stable Master lunged at me, "Put it out! Put it out!" He screamed for help as he dove passed me, eventually landing in the hay again falling unconscious. I tried to put the fire out, but it was growing faster than I could contain it.

Krodo was coughing on all fours when he looked up at me, "For the hope of the new world, believe I will end --," unable to finish due to Farley donkey kicking him straight across the jaw, he immediately fell silent and dropped to the ground.

I grabbed my saddle hanging on the wall behind Farley and pulled him as quickly as possible out of the stable, which was in complete flame now. I could hear the cries of the other toradracs and couldn't leave them like this.

I concentrated as hard as I could on putting the fire out. Attempting to hold off sections at a time to keep the fire away from the toradracs inside. Desperately, I tried even to remove the fire from the building to put it somewhere else, but nothing was working. Cries from the toradracs pierced my ears; I couldn't be the reason for any more deaths even if they were animals, they were still innocent.

I concentrated one last time, and cried out for help inside me, to the elements. I closed my eyes and suddenly felt like a weight was lifted off me. I looked down at my body, and a wisp of smoke was coming out of my chest like a chimney. The smoke went to the stable, pillars of fire took form blocking the fire from the toradrac. Then the smoke took an appearance of a man, "Go on," he said to me in the same familiar voice that ran through my mind.

I hesitantly backed off, toradracs began to find their way out, and I knew I had to go. The sun still kept a light on the town, but the burning building shone bright like a warning sign.

Once the saddle was strapped to Farley, I jumped on and we took off towards the town. "We have to check on Torkie."

Farley grunted at me smoke spitting out of his nostrils.

"I know, I know, but I promised, and I promise you that I won't let them take you back."

He continued to the town at full speed until I pulled on the reigns for him to slow down. The city was still quiet, everyone settling in for the night must not have noticed the burning stable yet. I hopped off Farley, and we walked side by side towards the Queen's Castle. I thought I would have the best chance of finding the guillotine near there.

As we walked passed, I checked in our small barred window, in hopes they might have sent him back to the cells but the room was empty, just a plate and crumbs left on the floor from breakfast. I stood up and looked around the town; nothing much changed except for a few candles were now lit in windows.

"Come on," I pulled Farley along, but he resisted and began snorting. His eyes were fixated on something down the street and for a good cause. The Executioner stomped towards us, hood entirely covering his face, with a mace dragging on the ground, and on the other side, a body slung over his shoulder, his rear-facing us.

It was Torkie; I could see his hands tied up and looked for blood trailing. Before I could spot any, guards began swarming the street from the Queen's Castle. The Executioner raised his mace just off the ground to break into a hurried jog towards me.

I unsheathed my sword, prepared to fight him off; the word must have gotten to the castle of the stable fire. The Executioner stopped in his tracks as the guards began to catch up with him. Torkie was lunged off the Executioner's shoulder, head still attached.

To my surprise, Torkie rolled on the ground before jumping to his feet, hands still tied, he ran towards me for help.

The Executioner turned to face the guards, swinging his mace around, with power, fighting them off one by one. I acted quickly and jumped onto Farley's back, kicking his sides, we took towards Torkie. He jumped belly first onto Farley's back.

Torkie looked up at me, "It was Scahl! He saved me!"

I had no choice, I charged the guards on Farley's back, knocking a few of them to their backs. Scahl ripped the hood off his head, finally revealing himself, "I guess they found out it was me!" He yelled. "I could almost feel the blade on the back of my neck," Scahl said with a smile.

I still couldn't find the words to say, Scahl was alive.

"Come on, let's go, we can't fight them all off!" He commanded.

"Towards the river," Torkie chimed in quietly.

I jumped on Farley, and we took off as guards came sprinting around the corner sending the town into a panic, people emerged from their houses, a majority taking immediate cover as they saw Farley pummeling through the city. Other's now noticed the stable as the fire inched closer to them, continuing to become out of control.

The guards chased us out; throwing knives whizzing past our ears. I looked back and could see the building burning bright, and I could faintly see guards and townspeople failing to put it out.

The guards watched us run farther away, yelling at each other for letting us get away.

Scahl looked exhausted, so I pulled back on Farley to slow down. We were in the clear now.

Torkie jumped off Farley, laughing out of pure joy. He fell to the ground and smelled the grass then rolled over and looked up at the clear blue sky. "Freedom!"

I hopped off Farley and Scahl walked up to me. I gave him a hug, "What the hell happened," I exclaimed, I saw your body being wheeled away."

"Well, I guess we can say I had a little help from the executioner, I can thank him in the afterlife."

"What happened," I laughed.

"Well I'm not great with stories but they stripped me down to almost nothing and covered my head with a bag, I couldn't really see anything. But I listened closely. Every step someone took I heard it until I realized I was alone with the Executioner. So I knocked him out, switched clothes with him and chopped his head off. They never took the bag off his head, and I played executioner for awhile until I could find out more about your position."

"Did you have to cut anyone else's head off?" I asked in disgust.

"Almost," he pointed at Torkie, who still had his arm tucked tightly into his body, but laid on the grass, smelling the fresh air. "It was a bit trickier with him because a couple of the guards that had grown to hate him wanted to stick around for the show."

"So how did you get him out?"

"I said I had to play executioner for a while, didn't I? A guillotine isn't our only weapon." He smiled. "That's when I was able to talk to Torkie, and he told me they sent you to the barracks, and that's where I was heading when I found you."

"The kenks never stood a chance with you two," Torkie closing out the story, "I have no way of repaying you, for what you have done for me."

"Don't think anything from me, I would've left you in there if it wasn't for Finn," Scahl laughed, but I kind of knew he wasn't joking.

"That's what friends do for each other," I said to Torkie, "How's your arm?"

"It's sore, but not broken, the guards aren't the brightest bunch to diagnose anything."

"Hopefully we don't run into any immediate trouble once we reach the river, at least until your arm heals up."

His eyes got big, and his face glowed, "You're allowing me to come with you?"

"Of course, we could use the extra help," I looked at Scahl, and to my surprise, he nodded in agreement.

Torkie hugged me, "Thank you so much; I must admit I was nervous about going out into the world by myself, I don't have any more family to go home to now."

"You won't have to Torkie, but we better keep moving," I said hopping onto Farley, "and remind me to get you your own ride," I said to him as I pulled him onto the back of Farley.

"Yes sir, I promise not to be more of a burden than a helping hand."

Scahl laughed, "We just need to see how well you fight. Then we'll decide that."

I kicked the sides of Farley, and he started moving forward, "So are you gonna tell me how you got Farley out with you?" Scahl asked, "I'm guessing that had something to do with the fire?"

"I can't even really tell you what happened, I wanted to let Farley stretch his legs and the Stable Master and a guard, named Krodo, attacked me like I was trying to break him free. I didn't even plan on the fire."

At that point, I remembered the form of the man, and although they didn't deserve it, I hoped he was able to control the fire, "If it weren't for the Stable

Master rolling around in the hay, it wouldn't have started."

"But you set him on fire then?" Scahl laughed.

"Just a little bit on his arm, he was pounding my face in, what was I suppose to do."

"Scahl laughed, "Your mug has seen better days.

"Look, there's the river!" Torkie said pointing to a thin line of water streaming towards us, "I knew it! We're heading the right way!"

Scahl looked at him, missing out on our conversations in the cell.

"He's a map maker; he's setting out to create the first map of D'Hanin."

"Oh, well I guess you will be of greater use after all," Scahl said to Torkie.

"Well, I'll try to remember as much as I can."

Scahl looked to me for answers, "They took all his works when they found him."

As we neared the river, Torkie jumped off Farley and ran over to it. He stuck his hands in the water then took off his burnt shoes and dipped his feet in. "This feels amazing, you've got to come feel it." He said looking like he was in heaven.

We all found comfort on the riverbank, Farley taking gulps of water as I splashed water on my face and through my hair, the slight chill of the water running down my back was satisfying. It really made you feel renewed after being in a stink hole town.

Torkie fully submerged himself in the water, fully clothed. Scahl and I just laughed; this was the exact feeling of freedom right before us.

Torkie resurfaced and laid on his back, sighing and letting the current take him a few feet, then he swam back to shore and laid out under the stars.

"I hate to burst your bubble Torkie, but we should keep moving until we reach an area with more coverage," I said to him.

"I know, I know, I just needed that." He sat up and shook himself dry, then we all kept moving forward along the river, the fish would occasionally jump out of the water to catch a meal and birds would dive into the water to find theirs.

# 16

## A NIGHT BY THE RIVER

An hour later, still walking along the river, we finally reached a new town. It would have been reasonable for us to take a bit of caution, but from a distance, it looked the complete opposite of Fliagenré.

Brightly colored buildings lined the dirt street, the setting sun and the rising moon reflected off the water that surrounded the town casting enough light to see where you were going at almost midnight.

The town was nestled, where the river we were walking along and what I assumed was the Potens River, stretching hundreds of yards to the other side, forked into two separate streams.

"I think I remember this town now. If I could only remember the name of it." Torkie said gripping his head in deep remembrance, "I need to get a journal here, this can be the first entry of the new map! I can't wait to start interviewing the locals!"

"Let's make sure we're welcome here before you start running around and getting into someone's business," Scahl said firmly, clearly getting annoyed with Torkie's eccentric personality.

"I remember this is a really nice town though!"

"A lot has changed since you were locked up," Scahl said raising his voice slightly.

"Well excuse me, I seem to remember you two taking my advice to go towards the river, and that worked out splendidly, so I wouldn't throw my knowledge away about this world so quickly just because you think you're the boss." Torkie retaliated.

I could see an argument arising in Scahl, and decided to interject, "Look, we're here, let's just make a good first impression on these people and get a good night sleep."

Scahl bit his tongue and nodded, shrugging it off.

"I agree, I'm sorry," Torkie said, more to me than to Scahl.

With that aside we pulled into the town slowly, making sure to keep on our friendliest faces. People waved and smiled as we passed them. A portion of them were utterly indifferent to us, but there were no mean people in this town, or so it seemed on the surface.

Just about all the shops were closing down for the night, so we pulled up to a building with the word "*SLEEP*" lit up with bright candles above the door.

Scahl slowly made his way up the front steps as we tied Farley to the hitching post. We all went in together, peering around the door, as it swung open. A prim and proper older man, in formal attire and a perfectly groomed white mustache, greeted us before the door was even open.

"Hello, how can I help you, gentlemen?" The Concierge said sincerely.

"We were looking for a room for the night, it doesn't have to be much, it doesn't even need three beds, we'd just like to sleep inside tonight," Scahl said, more confidently walking up to the desk now.

"Why I could've guessed that, I don't know many people who enjoy sleeping outside," the Concierge exhaled, slightly less welcoming, "Let me see what we have available."

He put on a pair of gold-rimmed glasses and looked down at a chart on his desk, "Here we are, we do have a two bedroom available, with a view at the standard 75 denicks per night."

"Ok, that sounds great, but we came across trouble in Fliagenrè, and they took everything we had. Including our money. Is there anything we can work out?"

"Ahh, I see," the Concierge said expectantly as he put away the chart and set his glasses on the table, "Why that is a reasonable story, we often get it a lot. I'm not saying you're lying to me, but we have gone against lending rooms for free," he looked at all of us, "I'm sorry."

"We all have had a rough few days, and we hate to ask for anything for free, but we just escaped their clutches, and we would like to find peace of mind. If we sleep out in the open where anyone could see us or our fire, we worry that they will catch us again." Scahl pleaded.

"I understand your worry, but there's no need for it. There is a treaty amongst Fliagenrè and Tumin. They cannot come within a mile of us nor can we of them. After our first battle, both of our cities were almost wiped out with no victory for either of us. Our cities are so close in size, in population and army, that we must respect each other's boundaries or face both cities being wiped out, completely. So nobody, not even a 3-year-old child, will be able to cross our treaty line." The Concierge paused making sure that we were keeping up, "You will be safe, there isn't much to worry about in Tumin."

"All right, we've slept outside before, and we'll do it again," Scahl turned and stormed out the door as we followed.

We untied Farley, and we walked back out of the town.

"We're going to have to find shelter somewhere," I said to Scahl.

"We're just going to have to take shelter tonight, it's not ideal, especially when we're in a town, but we're going to have to earn a bit of denick tomorrow, there's not much use going too much further without any supplies."

"Well if it makes anyone feel better, I don't mind staying in town for a little while, I'd like to gather information about the town. For the map, you know." Torkie said timidly, preparing to be yelled at.

Scahl looked over at him, "We're going to need your help making money for supplies though, don't forget that."

"Yes sir," Torkie gave him a salute and a smile.

We walked only a little way outside of the town, along the river, when Scahl spoke up, "I guess this is as good as spot as any. Torkie, I will need you to dig holes for us to lie down in. They don't have to be real deep, just enough to keep the breeze off us." He turned to me, "I guess, work on making us a fire, I'm going to try and find us something to eat."

Torkie already began digging holes in the ground with his bare hands. Scahl walked off towards a wooded area, and I gathered up a few branches and leaves and threw them in a pile, then knelt down next to it. I tried warming my hands up, but I didn't feel that warm tingly sensation I usually do.

I closed my eyes and concentrated as best I could to block out the sound of Torkie digging. I imagined the fire coming out but nothing.

"Hey Torkie," he looked up like a dog does when you call its name, "Can you stop digging for a minute, I need to concentrate."

He nodded and crossed his legs on the ground.

I closed my eyes again, this time just trying to feel the element, but once again, there was nothing. I opened my eyes once more and looked at Torkie.

"What's wrong?" He asked.

"I don't know, I just, I'm trying to make something happen, but there's nothing there." Torkie just looked at me blankly. "Just keep digging I guess, maybe Scahl will know what's going on."

"Maybe you're just getting sick or something," he said, trying his best to help.

"Yea, I don't know, we'll see." I left it at that. Torkie went back to his digging, and as we waited for Scahl to return, I tried my best just to feel the element, and maybe resolve the issue before Scahl even got back.

But I had no luck, Scahl came back with 4 small animals in his grips, Torkie had our beds dug and was by the river washing off, and I was sitting in front of a pile of branches and leaves.

"Alright," he laughed, "I know there's not much to eat out there but you've gotta remember who you're dealing with. I would think you'd trust that I would bring back something to cook on a fire." He said as he approached, noticing the fire was not started yet.

I stood up and dusted off my pants, "It's gone."

"What do you mean it's gone?"

"My element, I can't use it anymore, I've tried, and I've concentrated as hard as possible, but there's nothing."

Scahl set the dead animals down, unsure of what to say but was undoubtedly disappointed.

"So you think I'll get it back?"

"I don't know, I know a little bit about elements, but I don't know of anybody just randomly losing it." He paced back and forth, pulling on his beard,

"There had to of been a moment when you didn't feel it anymore, right?"

"I don't remember not feeling it anymore, but I think it left my body at one point when I was trying to stop the fire back in Fliagenré. I know it did."

Scahl looked at me like I was crazy, "And you just left it there?"

"I didn't think it would completely leave my body. It must be stuck back in Fliagenré."

"And you think we should just stroll back there and get it back?"

"We have to! I can't keep going on without it; I won't last two days!"

Scahl grabbed me by the shoulders and came eye to eye with me, "Listen, there is no going back, we will not escape twice. You are a great swordsman. Your element may have helped us through everything, but I can tell you it's not the only reason we are still here."

My heart was beating faster than usual, almost in a panic.

"We will get this fire lit, and we will keep moving forward tomorrow, we're almost there."

"I can't do it. There's no way I can fight Abanyu without an element, that's the only thing that gave me confidence before. I had an upper hand on 1 thing, but I don't anymore."

"You have me, and Torkie now, and Farley. We will do anything to get you through this. We would die for you because we know you are brave enough to die for us. Do not lose it now, Finn."

We heard Torkie approaching us, timidly he said, "I can start a fire for us, my brother taught me when we were traveling." He held up a couple of pieces of wood, "I found this by the river."

"Please, go ahead Torkie, thank you," Scahl motioned for him to start making a fire. "We're going to get something to eat, maybe you'll feel better after that, but I'll never lose faith in you, remember that."

After Torkie started the fire, Scahl began cooking the animals one by one. They played through the rest of the night as if nothing was wrong. I watched everyone fall asleep, Farley curled up behind my head like a pillow, but I couldn't fall asleep. How could I when my mind was running a million thoughts per second? I sat up and looked up into the sky wondering if anyone was out there looking over this world. I needed to talk to someone, someone who could understand.

I left the campsite and headed for the river; I needed to be alone. I put my feet in the flowing water, sitting close enough that I was able to brush my hand over the water as well. Out of the corner of my eye, I saw a figure of a woman, standing knee deep in the water, watching me.

I kept eye contact with her, not feeling threatened before she slowly fell backward into the rushing water without a splash. I looked down at my hand in the water; I needed to talk to the elements. They want to talk to me and help me; I just had to be open to them, if it was still possible without an element.

I stood up and walked towards where the figure was. "I need your help, if you're out there, please present yourself." I closed my eyes and fell to my knees, the water splashing around me, trying to feel the water flow over my skin before it started rising against my chest. The current came crashing against my back, completely submerging me, underneath the water. I held my breath and opened my eyes seeing the bright-lit moon through the surface of the water, before the figure came back, submerging me in total darkness.

A force pulled me through the water before landing on the damp grass, the water being pulled off of me back into the river until not a single drop of water was still on me.

"Will you talk to me? I need to talk to you."

The woman emerged from the water walking up to me on dry land. "What do you need from the Water Elements? Do you not have your own to talk to?"

"I did."

"If you did not still have the element, I would not have presented myself."

"But I can't use it, a form much like you, was released from me back in Fliagenré and since then I can't use it. Can you please help me get it back? I can't continue to Abanyu without it."

The Water Element stepped back into the water, "So you are the child from another land? The one meant to save the elements of D'Hanin."

"Yes, if I succeed, the elements can strengthen once again."

"Look at my water flowing in the river, do you not feel the rain on your head or the harshest winter this world has yet to experience, finally subsiding. We are not all apart of this battle; we are not all so foolish."

"This doesn't have to be your war; I just need your help getting my element back."

"If you know where your element is, you need not do anything other than return and get it."

"I can't," I erupted at the stubbornness of this element, "It is in Fliagenré, I set fire to their stables, I'm not exactly welcomed back."

The river rose and flowed more fiercely; the Water Element stood in thought before responding, "If your element has not returned to you yet, it is not finished burning yet, or it is not able to control itself."

"Then what am I suppose to do?"

"There's nothing you can do," a large rain cloud formed above us; thunder followed closely behind, "You should know, with the Scales in evil hands, those elements cannot be trusted on their own, take caution with them all." The Water Element absorbed once again into the river without a splash, and I was alone. Lightning struck in the distance, and I looked up at the forming rain clouds, which quickly moved down the river, a single raindrop hitting against my face.

I couldn't say that it raised my spirits, but there was no use hanging around the river anymore, the Water Element was gone with the rain.

I went back and nestled up next to Farley and watched the fire crackle, my mind's thoughts still racing but finally, exhaustion overpowering it and forcing me to fall asleep.

Strangely enough, when I awoke the next morning, I was more rested than I had been since sleeping on the bed in the cell. I think Torkie felt the same way, waking up shortly after I did, with a big smile on his face and stretching.

Scahl was off by the river splashing his face with water. When he saw that we were both awake, he made his way back over.

"Are you guys ready to hit the town and make some loot?" He asked us.

"And how are we gonna do that?" I asked skeptically.

"The people in this town seem nice enough, besides that innkeeper not letting us stay the night, I bet we could find odd jobs around the town. At least enough to get us a few supplies."

"All right, let's get to it," Torkie jumped up, "Where should we start?"

"I saw a farm at the end of the road last night, I'm gonna go there, unfortunately for you two, your size won't help you in finding work on a farm, we'll just split up and find where you think you'll fit in best."

I looked at Scahl, feeling a lot less confident in asking random strangers for work, "What about me? I don't know how my skill sets transfer to this world."

"Knowing you for only a couple months, I can already tell your world isn't that much different than ours." He said as he started walking towards the town.

He was right though, change a few names in this world and this might as well be Scotland for all I know.

We gathered up the few supplies that we had, and we all headed into town. Scahl pointed out a tavern, "Let's meet up here at sundown. We'll plan our next move then."

Torkie and I nodded, taking in the surroundings to make sure we'd know how to get back.

Scahl turned to me, "If you don't mind I would like to take Farley along with me, I think he could be great help at the farm."

"Yea, that's fine."

Scahl nodded and grabbed Farley's reigns, "I'll see you at sundown then." He turned, and they both went off into the distance.

I turned to Torkie, "Alright, well I guess you take that side of town, and I'll take this side."

"Alrighty," he said, "I'll see you at sundown."

# 17

## A TREATY BROKEN

I decided to explore the town a little bit. Other than Kautun, I hadn't had much time to explore the villages in D'Hanin.

The buildings, which I thought were painted

bold colors, were just covered with various shades of flowers. The pinks, blues, greens, reds, yellows, all made this town jubilant and colorful. A flowery scent flew with each breeze that I didn't notice before.

I noticed a sizeable storefront with families going in and out carrying bags of goods down the street and immediately recognized it as a grocery store. My mother was a grocery store legend; I was guaranteed to have bagging skills running through my blood. I headed that way to see what I could find out, but was stopped by an old, but healthy looking man, looking down on me, "I don't think I've seen you around these parts."

I stepped back, tripping over my own feet.

"Calm down boy," he said helping me back up, "That's a mighty fine sword you have there." And with a blink of my eyes, he had my sword in his hands.

"Hey, what do you think you're doing?"

He stared intently at the blade, focusing in on Tor'oos' logo, "Don't need to worry," he handed the sword back to me with a smile, I instantly felt more in power.

"Next time you want to see something of mine, I suggest you ask."

"I'm sorry, it was terribly rude of me." He gave me a slight bow, "And what's your name young sir?"

I paused, feeling uneasy about this guy. Before I even had time to think, he interrupted me, "It's ok, we can talk in my studio." He moved in a little closer and put his hand up to the side of his mouth like he was going to whisper, "I can understand your fear of releasing your identity." He smiled and motioned me across the street to a building identical to the Fade's, with large windows all across the building.

I followed behind him, "May I ask your name?"

He turned back, "I am the Swift. You don't have to worry, the Fade is a close friend of mine, as well, all the trainers are."

"Did the Fade tell you I was coming?" I asked, feeling a little less on guard.

"We'll talk in the studio, don't worry." The inside of the studio was again, similar to the Fade's, except it looked much less used. The dummies hanging from the ceiling were almost in perfect shape, and the training weapons hanging off the walls only had minor dents and scratches.

He pulled up a couple of chairs for himself and motioned for me to take a seat, "So what is your name, again?"

"It's Finn," I said feeling less threatened than when he approached me in the street.

The Swift nodded, "Very well, just as the Fade told me. He sent me a letter about a month or so ago, telling me there would be a possibility you would be passing through and that I should report back to him on how you were doing."

"Well, I've made it this far."

The Swift laughed, "It appears so, but he told me you were traveling with another?"

"Yea, Scahl. He's out at the farm doing work; we ran into a little trouble and lost all our supplies so we thought we could do odd jobs around the town to make a bit of money and buy more supplies. We've got another partner who joined us not too long ago, who is out working as well."

"What kind of supplies did you need? I might be able to help you a little bit, although business has been terrible around here for me. With the treaty, not many people are worried about training, they just leave it up to the soldiers."

"Well, we need tents, blankets, spare clothes, maybe matches if you have them."

The Swift gave me a curious look, "Matches?"

I broke eye contact with him, ashamed.

"Matches to start a fire you mean?" He asked.

I wasn't sure if he knew I had an element, so I just went along with it, "Yea."

"The Fade told me you were equipped with the Fire Element."

Apparently, he knew. "I did, unfortunately along with the supplies, I lost the element as well."

"I've never heard of someone losing an element, that's not common, but I suppose it would be possible. I never was blessed with an element, so I don't think I can help you on that front, but I can introduce you to our Mayor. If you didn't guess with all the lively flowers on our buildings, she is a Plantation Element Bearer."

I nodded, "I guess that would make sense." My spirits were lifted, knowing I'd be able to talk to another person with an element, but the Swift could see my despair.

"You mustn't worry about it so much, while it is a significant loss, it isn't your only attribute that makes you, you."

"I'm not meant to be here though, the element was the only thing that gave me the ability to get this far, and I know it was."

The Swift looked taken aback, "What do you mean you weren't meant to be here?"

"The elements were talking about it; I was a desperation pick."

"I can't say I know what you mean. The Fade seemed to talk highly of you, and he is not one that I've known to be often mistaken. Either way, one person to the next, we are not more chosen than another to help protect the world, having the Fade or the elements or anyone else backing you, is just a nice perk. A boost for the ego if you will, nothing more."

I heard what he was saying, I still wanted my element back, but I would have to wait until I could get answers from the Mayor before I could move on from it.

"Let's get back to getting you supplies," the Swift said, standing up, "You were working to acquire money then? To buy supplies?"

I stood up feeling uncomfortable sitting down now, "Yea."

"How much have you made so far?"

"I didn't have a chance to work; I was going to check out the grocery store for a job before I ran into you. I don't even have a clue what I should be trying to make."

He walked behind a counter and pulled out a safe box and set it on top. I walked over as he was opening it. After he reached in, he pulled out a wooden coin with a dragon on it.

"Ok, what you have here, is a drègin, worth 5 denicks," he set it down in front of me, then pulled out a silver coin with a bird carved on it and set it to the left of the drègin, "That is a flègin, worth 10 denicks,"

He then pulled out a larger gold coin with a mountain on it that was coming off the coin, like it was 3D, and set it to the right of the drègin, "this is a kégula, worth 25 denicks," and finally he set down a shiny, platinum coin, almost twice as large as the kégula, with a mole like creature on it, "and this is an ikéka, worth 100 denicks. The four of these coins depict the illustrious Makalihi Mountains with its three mightiest creatures.

Many people would like to see the coin designs changed since Apaku has overtaken the mountain range, using it to protect his residence, Gensrobore. But with hope they have refused to do so, having faith that someone will come along and reclaim the mountain range." He looked at me, as to say I'm the one they're counting on.

After a moment he pulled back his coins and placed them back into the safe and put it away. "Is there anything I could do for you around the studio?" I asked.

"I could probably find many chores for you to do but you have more important matters to attend to. Let your friends worry about making money; we will see the Mayor about your element. That will prove to be more valuable than any amount of tents or blankets."

So with the hopes of getting my element back, we were on our way to see the Mayor. We walked through the town, farther passed the farm, and finally, right on the river a lovely two-story building covered with green, white, and orange flowers.

A woman stood in front of the building on a nice patch of grass, admiring the house.

"Mayor Malani, I see you have redone your home, it's enticing." The Swift said to her.

She turned around to see us. She was a taller woman, with a long flowing dress and curly blonde hair, and spoke tenderly, "Thank you, it took me all morning to get it just right."

We walked up next to her, "I would like you to meet a friend of mine, this is Finn Anderson, the one the Fade told me about."

"Oh," She turned to me in surprise and held out a hand, her smile was infectious, "It's a pleasure to meet you, Mr. Anderson."

I shook her hand, "It's nice to meet you too."

"We're contrite to bother you, but we were wondering if you had a moment to talk about elements?" The Swift asked her.

"Of course," she looked up in the sky, "I believe I could spare a few moments, for Mr. Anderson, we all know he has spared his time for us." She smiled at me, "What questions could I answer for you, dear?"

I was silent for a moment and looked around not wanting anyone to hear me talking to her. I chose just to speak quietly, "Well, I don't know if you knew or not but when I first came to D'Hanin I was equipped with the Fire Element."

"Yes, from my conversations with the Swift, it was naturally something I was interested in."

"Ok, well you see in our last encounter with Fliagenrè, somehow in our escape, I felt -- Well, I actually saw the element leave my body, and since then I haven't been able to use it."

Her face went from joyful to petrified in an instant. I stepped back to give her space.

"What do you mean escaped from Fliagenrè?"

I looked at the Swift, confused then back at her, "Well they took us prisoner, and we had to escape from them to continue our journey."

"And you came here?" She took a step away from me, "There's no doubt they know you're here," She said more to herself, then looked back at me, "Did they try to chase you down?"

I nodded.

"And you came straight this direction after escaping?"

I nodded again, feeling worse and worse.

"We need to get you out of here, immediately."

"What about my friends?"

Her face went pale, "You mean there's more of you!" She shuffled me off of her lawn, "Please find your friends and bring them back here, we will give you transportation on the river, and I ask you do not say a word to anybody about your little detour here."

By that time a bell rang out over the entire town, like a church bell. The Mayor's eyes snapped closed, and she stopped pushing me. "Exactly what I feared, gather up your friends, plans have changed. Prepare them to fight." She turned to her house and quickly walked towards it her white dress flowing behind her.

I looked at the Swift, "What's going on now?"

"This is absolutely unfortunate, with you coming back here, they must have thought you were apart of Tumin, and in retaliating against them, on their own land, you have broken the treaty and started a war."

"Why didn't anyone else say anything sooner, we would've been on our way!"

"I suppose with Tumin being safe for so long, the majority of the population have forgotten the specifics of the treaty. Sadly to say, I even assumed that since you were not actually apart of Tumin, you were not held to the treaty, but then again, I suppose Fliagenrè doesn't know. They've been begging for a chance to attack us since that new Queen has taken over."

"Well I've got to find Scahl and Torkie, I've got to let them know." I took off towards the farm, leaving the Swift behind, but before I even ran ten feet, he was out of site, on to prepare himself.

I reached the farm and jumped the fence; I quickly found Scahl cleaning out the stables. "Scahl!" He looked back in a hurry, "We've got to find Torkie, Fliagenrè is coming to attack, they thought we were apart of Tumin, and they think we broke the treaty."

Scahl hung his rake up, "Let's find him, I'll be glad to get out of this mess."

Scahl and I ran out of the stable and into the streets, which had been cleared out. "I told him to cover this area of town, so he's got to be around here somewhere."

"Let's go back to the tavern, hopefully, he's smart enough to go there in an emergency." Scahl kept running forward, "If he's not, I just hope he's got enough sense on his own to help us fight."

I followed Scahl all the way to the tavern, and we ran in. A handful of people were in there, cowering in the back. The Bar Keep, a fat man, with an apron on, stopped us in our tracks by pointing a massive sword at our heads.

Scahl stopped an inch from the blade, "I don't mean to alarm; we're just looking for our friend."

"What's your friend's name?" He said without lowering his sword.

"It's Saeban Torkin the Fourth," Scahl said.

The Bar Keep lowered his sword, "I've never heard that name in these parts."

"Ok, that's all we wanted to know, we'll be on our way." Scahl and I backed out of the bar; Mayor Malani flew passed us gracefully, heading out of town. We looked to see where she was going and saw an army coming our way. Scahl pulled out his mace, and I unsheathed my sword.

"Please, to avoid many deaths, stop where you are!" We heard the Mayor yell at the oncoming Army. The Army stopped 100 yards short of Mayor Malani by the hand of the leading officer.

"What is your business coming onto our land?" She said to him.

"The same reason you sent troops to our land, for casualties!" the leading officer yelled back.

"I understand your confusion, we did not send anyone, the travelers you are referring to are not of Tumin, and we are sending them on their way."

"Lies! You lie to us while our town is nearly all in ashes! We will not take this as an accident!" And with a battle cry, the leading officer pointed forward, and a giant wave of arrows flew over his head towards the Mayor. The battle had begun.

The Mayor ducked down as trees sprouted up in front of her, creating a shield. The arrows collided and she retreated, the trees reversed back into the ground revealing the Fliagenrè army was rushing towards us. The Tumin Army came out of nowhere, running full speed through Tumin, swords held high.

"We'll have to find him later! As long as we keep them out of Tumin, he'll be safe."

And just then, screaming at the top of his lungs, Torkie was charging along with the rest of the Tumin Army, holding a Tumin Army sword high above his head.

"They won't take me again! I'd rather die than be in their grasp!" He yelled as he passed us.

"We better follow Torkie then," Scahl said with a smile, and we rushed along behind them. As we left the entrance of Tumin, trees began growing into a heavily wooded shield, blocking the access of Tumin, with the Mayor taking cover within it. She created roots crawling through the grass and branches swinging back and forth in the path of the Fliagenrè army, making them stumble and fall to the ground.

We were on them quickly taking them out one by one. I saw the Swift in the middle of it, moving at a fantastic speed, taking two soldiers out almost simultaneously with each move. I fought off soldiers as best as I could but I wasn't able to grab my shield during our escape, so I was mostly on the defense. I looked over at Torkie who was doing the opposite, swinging his sword like a madman and Scahl was using his mace as a shield as much as I was.

I cut down a soldier and jumped over a body to grab a shield of another fallen soldier from Tumin.

"Scahl!" I called out. He looked back in fear that I might be hurt.

I threw him the shield and immediately he was able to start battling more intensely

I dodged my way through the raining arrows and swinging swords to find another shield. I grabbed it and got it on my forearm, seconds before I saw a sword coming down on my head. I lifted the shield, the sword still knocking me to the ground from the force.

Once again the soldier jumped on top of me and brought his sword, point down, towards my face. I moved quickly, the sword plowing into the ground. The soldier went to pull it out, but it was stuck. A root climbed up the sword and grabbed the soldier by the waist and threw him off me. The root descended back into the ground, and the sword dropped next to me.

I looked up at the Mayor who was too busy fighting, to look back at me. So I jumped back up on my feet and went to help Torkie who wouldn't be able to survive much longer by being so reckless.

I jumped over more and more bodies and slid into more pools of blood. The casualty count was growing every second. I reached Torkie who was dripping with blood and sweat, ready to faint.

I helped him fight and guarded him at the same time. It was enough to relieve Torkie, but it was too late. He blocked a swing from a Fliagenrè soldier, and his sword fell to the ground. I jumped in between the two, cutting the soldiers' arm off then finishing him. I turned back to Torkie and quickly felt for a pulse. He was alive but passed out from exhaustion. I continued to fight around him as he lyed in the grass, making sure he was going to be ok. But I didn't know how much longer I could battle in one spot without archers targeting me.

I had to get Torkie to safety. He was so thin from being imprisoned that I was able to swing him over my shoulder and run towards town. I could leave him in the tavern and come back to fight.

An arrow whizzed passed my ear as I ran away from the battle, then another, before I heard the ground shaking behind me. I looked back, and trees were coming out of the field, blocking the arrows, they would recede and build back up when more arrows flew in.

I reached the cluster of trees were Mayor Malani was fighting and set Torkie down. I looked over the war and realized we were closer to an end than I thought.

"Your friend is safe; you must return to the field," I heard the Mayor yelling at me.

"Listen, I need my element back, how do I get it back!"

For the first time, Mayor Malani did not seem peaceful and collected, "We will discuss this if we both get out of this alive!" She shouted back.

"But if I have my element, they don't stand a chance!"

"There are no guarantees with the elements, the only guarantee I have for you is if you die worrying about it, you will never get it back." A root grabbed me by the ankle and pulled me back into the battlefield across the grass. I jumped up as soon as it released its grip, not appreciating the force from the Mayor, and kept fighting.

I remembered what the element in the abandoned city told me, *be open to us.* And it sounded like my element was just lost. By instinct I closed my eyes, *I'm in Tumin, come back to me, immediately, I need you.* I cried out inside my head, with all my heart, The message left my body.

I stood up from the ground and picked up my sword, trying to feel the element again, but still nothing. I knew I didn't have it; there wasn't something for me to sense.

In the midst of the battle I closed my eyes and in a panic, I could see where I was, I could look at my surroundings in a haze, I saw Scahl shouting at me, but I blocked the sound out.

"Get up and protect yourself, Finn!" I heard Scahl's yell finally breaking through my concentration.

I continued to ignore him, closing my eyes again and looking through the shadowy world.

I stayed in that mode but was able to fight. It was difficult; I kept falling in and out of it until I couldn't concentrate and fight anymore. I released the hazy world and opened my eyes, Scahl fighting right next to me.

"I thought I lost you!" Scahl yelled at me when I continued fighting.

"I was just trying to find help."

"Well maybe find cover next time!"

We continued to fight as our soldiers began to thin out as well as theirs. The trees surrounding the Mayor we're depleting, and the roots were being controlled less and less.

The paramount feat was that Scahl and I were still alive, but we both couldn't fight much longer.

The Swift was even moving at a regular pace now as he pushed his way back to us.

"I can't fight anymore, I'm too old for this," the Swift said looking ready to drop.

The Fliagenrè Army was pushing us back into town. They didn't have much more energy or soldiers left than us, but it was all they needed. The battle would soon be over, and we weren't on the winning side. I looked back and saw an open path into Tumin; Mayor Malani was retreating, directing a soldier to carry Torkie to safety.

A heavy rainfall closed in on us, eventually soaking the battlefield. It didn't make anything easier for us, soldiers now slipping through the mud, trying to defend themselves at this point. However, I saw more than rain approaching.

I tapped back in to see if I could find the elements. I could feel the rain subsiding on my skin, and as the last raindrop hit the river, I could see the Water Element I spoke with the night before appearing from the water. In the distance I could see a familiar form in the darkening day, coming from Fliagenrè. But it was still too far away, she would eventually get to me, but I didn't have that much time.

I fell to my knees in exhaustion, my last effort, I screamed from within, *"Atta-- Attack... Attack the Fliagenrè Army!"* I saw my element turn into a giant flame.

The element flew around the battlefield swooping up soldiers and dropping them, quickly enough for our soldiers to finish them off.

The flame circled the battlefield, finishing off the last of the Fliagenrè army, and then came back to me. I absorbed the Element back into myself through my pores, and I fell onto my back, I could feel myself taking on the exhaustion of the element as the world slowly dimmed to black.

\* \* \* \*

I slowly woke up, lying on the world's comfiest bed. I fought the urge just to go right back to sleep, but my desire to know what happened outweighed it and I sat up in the king size bed. I looked around the room; it appeared as an upscale hospital. I swung my feet off the bed and went to the window to see where I was.

When my eyes adjusted to the bright morning sun, I looked out over Tumin, but not with as much joy as I usually got from it. No more colors on the buildings, just dead flowers, and wood. It was a sad site, I worried about the Mayor, knowing she was the reason they had such beautiful buildings, I feared the worst for her.

"Good to see you're finally awake." I heard Scahl say from behind me. I turned around, and he was holding a glass, "Here, the Swift said it would be good for you."

I took it and swished it around; it was the all to familiar drink the Fade made me guzzle down after every session.

"What happened? How long was I asleep?" I asked eager to ask every question at once.

"You were only asleep throughout the night and morning," Scahl sat down in a chair, with his drink in his hand, "Mayor Malani believes you got your element back last night, at the end of the battle. I thought you were hallucinating, maybe from exhaustion, then out of the woods, a flame came flying out taking down the final 20 or so soldiers that were left, then it came back and hit you. I thought you might have been killed, but the Mayor knew otherwise."

"What happened to Torkie?" I asked.

Scahl gave a little chuckle, "He fought valiantly all right, but I hate to say, he's in bad shape. He'll live, but he got cut up pretty bad and lost a lot of blood so he will not be able to move on with us. Mayor Malani assured me that he would be taken care of until he was better and would be welcome to stay here in Tumin."

"I didn't realize how banged up he got, can we go see him?" I said feeling bad.

"No, I already tried to get into his room, the nurse wouldn't allow it. But when you see him again, he owes you another life debt. If you hadn't brought him back to the Mayor, he would have died right there on the field. She wishes you would have brought more of her soldiers back though."

I cringed at the thought of the fallen soldiers, "How'd we fare against them?"

Scahl looked off, "Well, we didn't leave Fliagenré any soldiers to come back with but sadly the battle between Fliagenré and Tumin is not over, they will find a way to come back. For Tumin, 280 deaths, 90 injured, and 12 uninjured, including myself."

The numbers made it worse; I had dwindled a cities entire army down to 11 uninjured soldiers; 11 soldiers to protect this beautiful city.

At about that time, Mayor Malani walked in solemnly, but in her usual airy voice, "I thought I heard you two talking."

I nodded to her and Scahl stood up from his chair. "It's good to see you're okay. I'm sorry for the trouble I have caused, if I had known more about the treaty, I wouldn't have stayed."

"I understand. It was a regrettable event, but as a city, we are planning our next step."

"If there's anything we can do to help, I'd be more than willing to." I offered.

"What you can do is continue your journey, you will be no good to us fighting battles while you need to be fighting the war. We have had plenty of volunteers to stand up as soldiers and the Swift is training them as we speak to take down Fliagenrè while they are at their weakest." She looked over at Scahl, "If you would give Mr. Anderson privacy to change into his regular clothes, I will send you all off."

"Of course," Scahl said. They both left the room, and I saw my clothes, sword, and the shield I picked up during the battle in the corner.

I changed slowly and left the room. The Mayor was waiting for me outside the door, and she guided me to the front lawn where I had first met her. I looked at all the dead flowers on the ground, leaving her home looking unspectacular.

"It's difficult to keep the flowers in this town alive without the Scale. I guess it goes the same; it's hard to keep war out of the town without the Amethyst Scale." She looked at me for the first time today not so solemnly, "I don't want you to worry about us or the events that occurred yesterday, do not blame yourself. You have done more than any of us have to get this

239

world back to the great place that it is. We just blocked it out and tried to create our own little utopia. We will be fighting from now on; we will be on guard." She smiled, and I couldn't help but smile back at her.

At that time we heard Scahl herding Farley over from the farm. I patted him on the head, really glad to see him again. I noticed his packs on his saddle were overflowing with supplies.

"The supplies are a gift from the Swift; he apologizes he was unable to be here to see you off and sends his best wishes. He is overloaded with the new soldiers," the Mayor explained.

"Tell him I said thank you, it means a lot to us."

Scahl nodded, "We better be off; these dead flowers are bringing me down, we should go do something about that."

The Mayor smiled at him, "To help you get there faster, the city is donating a raft for you as well, it's not the best but, I can show it to you, it's out back."

We followed her to the back and in the river sat what looked like a large sheet of wood with a couple of ores. "It doesn't look like much but, it'll definitely get you there." She said.

"Wait!"

We all turned around and saw Torkie limping his way over to us, with healing wounds and bruises covering his arms and face, cringing every step of the way.

"Where the hell do you think you're going without me?" He yelled.

"What are you doing out here, you need to get rest," I said back.

"Just because I need rest, doesn't mean I have to be in a bed," he said sounding like a senile old man, "I bought my journal for the map, I've had about a dozen of those shakes from the Swift, and I owe you two life debts. So, let's get a move on so I can have a bit of rest." He walked into the water and got onto the raft to lay down.

"We've got to get him back to his bed; there's no way he'll be able to survive with us out there," Scahl said.

"I don't think it's about surviving anymore for him, plus I may need to cash in on those life debts," I said with a smile pushing Farley into the water. He hopped up onto the raft; I let it even out a little bit then I jumped on myself, "Let's go," I said to Scahl.

Scahl rolled his eyes, but was over arguing, he shook the Mayor's hand gently and jumped on from the shore. We pushed off, and Mayor Malani waved us goodbye as we drifted farther and farther away.

# 18

## ALL THE WAY TO MT. B'TUUL

We rode the river, enjoying the peace and the rest we were going to need before we reached our next obstacle, which I could assume would be imminent and the river was going to take us there.

Torkie was still asleep, next to Farley, who was curled up in a ball. Scahl and I sat on the front of the raft, with our feet in the water, keeping us from going straight down the river. We looked out into the rolling hills and watched

the fish trying to nibble at our toes while we drifted, moving faster than we ever walked on land.

"So did you end up making any money?" Scahl leaned over and asked me.

"No," I held my head in shame, "I was feeling a little self-pity."

"I guess it's not a problem now, but I did earn 60 denicks, I got a little sidetracked from the job, technically protecting his farm, and he refused to pay me the whole 120 for not completing."

"It's nice to have a little something, in case we don't feel like your famous home cooking," I smirked, "It looks like Torkie used all his money on a journal."

"A day ago, I would've told you I was surprised to see he got that much." Scahl said looking back to make sure Torkie was still asleep, "That's good he got one, D'Hanin could use a map. It would make our journey a lot easier."

"I've gotten used to it though, what's an adventure without a little wandering anyway?"

"I'm glad you can see the fun in this." He smiled. He glanced back at Torkie, "You think we should wake him up? He hasn't moved since we pushed off."

"Yea, he probably wouldn't want to miss all this traveling for his map." I stood up and walked to the back then kneeled down over him. "Hey, Torkie." I shook his shoulder a little bit, and he scrunched his face up and rolled onto his back.

"Ugh," he groaned, "I don't think I've ever felt like this," he looked down at his feet then back up to me, "I don't think I can move."

"You're fine, just sore." I helped him to sit up, and he winced.

"How long have we been going?"

"About two hours, two and a half maybe."

"Is that it?" He said stretching out his arms carefully and checking out his wounds, "I feel like I've been knocked out for weeks."

"I think I saw a canteen in the pouches, he looks like he could use water," Scahl said from the front of the boat.

Torkie smacked his lips together, "Yea, I still have the taste of that shake in my mouth."

I stood up and shuffled through the pouches, finding a small army green canteen. I completely submerged it in the clear, rushing water, filling it entirely up. I sat back down, handing the container to Torkie.

He immediately chugged it, water spilling off his chin, "That feels good, that's much better. Thanks." He took another swig.

I nodded to him, "We figured you'd want to see the area, for your map."

"Oh yea," he looked around and picked up his dark leather journal, "I've got a long way to go," he said flipping through the blank pages."

"You remember portions of the previous maps though, don't you?" I asked.

"Yea, a bit, enough to get me started."

"Do you remember anything about this river? Or where we should be headed?" Scahl asked looking back.

"Well, I don't really know where you guys are headed."

"The Fade told me to follow the rising sun."

"Ok, then yea, we can ride this for a long time. I believe if we haven't already gone too far south, we'll reach Mt. B'Tuul. We can stop before it and walk around the Lake of Dragons, or get off at a mining town my brother and I stayed at, and then go over the mountain. I think if we took the river any farther, we'd be going too far south." Torkie looked down at his journal, "but I'm not gonna write that down just yet like I said it would be a lot easier if I knew exactly where we were."

"Well, we went east from Fliagenrè and then South from Tumin. If that helps at all," I said wanting to know just as much as anyone else what was lying ahead.

Torkie went deep in thought, trying to remember the map. "I can't even remember, ever being in Tumin when we were originally working on the map." He opened up the journal and started sketching, "Maybe if I drew what I remembered out. I can start with Fliagenrè."

I looked over at Scahl, who was looking up at the sun, trying to see what direction it was going so he could have a sense of course as well, but it was so hard while we were moving so quickly.

I peeked over at Torkie's scribblings and could see a rough map developing. His lips were moving while he was drawing as if he was talking to himself, and then he would stop and close his eyes, then continue again.

"Ok," he looked up from the journal, "If Fliagenrè is here and Tumin is directly East of it, I remember coming across the river and walking along the North side of the fork that goes around Tumin. But, we didn't even reach the fork until we were passed Tumin, I think." He paused and looked over the map again, "We started just South of Mt. B'Tuul about 100 miles away from the Lake of Dragons. That must mean, if we are still North of Mt. B'tuul, then our map was right. If not, we may have miscalculated how far North we went to get to Fliagenrè."

"So what do you think?" I asked not sure if he still knew where we were.

"Well, we were wrong before, making the map was a lot of walking and fixing as we went. Our best bet is to ride the river."

"For how long?" Scahl interjected.

Torkie gave him a blank look, "As long as it takes, I guess."

"As long as it takes?" Scahl bit his tongue for once, trying not to start a fight with Torkie, "Do you remember anything along the river that would indicate, we're North of Mt. B'Tuul?" He said, dialing it back, "we're going to hit a waterfall, or rapids, or something eventually. A peaceful river grows angry fast, and I don't want to be stuck in that, especially with a 300 pound Toradrac." Scahl said. Farley grunted, steam coming out of his nose, indicating he knew he was in the conversation now.

Torkie went into thought, "I don't know, maybe if I see something it will jog my memory, but for right now we're going to have to ride it out, and I'll keep my eyes open."

"We've been going at this blindly. The entire time, we've run into troubles beyond my wildest dreams, I think we'll be fine." I said remaining positive.

He looked back at me, "I can deal with troubles on land," he looked across the river, both ways, "But look at this river, if we hit rapids, there's no swimming to land with our load. We'll hit bottom before we even come close to the banks."

"Then we need to move closer to the edge and keep a keen eye out for any signs of danger. It'll be more preparation than we've ever had and we've made up so much time by traveling the river; I don't think we should overlook that."

"We need to land at night, I'm not risking traveling at night," he said looking straight ahead.

Part of me was hoping that we would be able to continually be moving on the river, even while we slept, with someone keeping guard at all times, but I knew I wasn't going to be able to win this argument.

"There's no way we'd be able to see oncoming danger soon enough in the dead of night," he said.

"All right, that will be fine for me," I said and looked at Torkie.

"I'm just here to give suggestions, take it or leave it, I'm following you guys."

"Then it's settled," I said closing out the conversation. Torkie looked over his sketched out map in his book, but it seemed like he had maxed out what he remembered. I could see the frustration in his expressions.

Scahl directed the raft closer to the East edge of the river and remained quiet.

* * * *

We traveled by river for about another hour, Scahl began to get anxious. He felt like impending danger was on the way, and the farther we went down the river the closer we got.

Torkie fell back asleep, still exhausted and trying to recover, as dark rain clouds began to cover the sky above us. Whether it would be because of pouring rains or nightfall, we were going to have to go to dry land before long. It would at least put Scahl at peace.

I sat at the front of the raft with Scahl, as lightning thundered down, "We should pull over and get shelter before it starts coming down too hard."

Scahl nodded and directed the raft as close to the bank as he could then jumped out of the boat into the water and pulled it in until it grounded. A loud bang of thunder shook us all, Torkie jumped awake, cringing at his sides.

"It's all right, Scahl will make the shelter for the night," I said before he panicked too much.

Rain showered us with large drops; Torkie didn't look any less panicked. He jumped off the boat into the water and limped onto shore, a loud bang of thunder sounded again, followed by the sound of a falling tree.

"We need to get to hiding!" Torkie yelled at us.

Scahl wasted no time; there was a fear in Torkie that gave us no time to ask questions.

Scahl jumped back onto the raft and pushed Farley who wouldn't budge, "Help me," he commanded.

I ran over and grabbed Farley, "Come on Farley!" By that time our questions were answered. A giant grey dragon jumped out of the trees and soared into the air, letting out a roar we mistook for thunder. It shook our insides and paralyzed us in fear as we watched the terrifying, yet majestic beast was soaring closer to us.

Scahl grabbed me and jumped off the boat.

"Wait," I yelled, "we need to get Farley," Scahl didn't bother responding. Torkie stood up as fast as he could and ran as best as he could for cover. I watched Farley as he stood on the raft in the open. I struggled with Scahl, "No, Farley," I yelled at him to get him to come with us. The dragon moved closer once it spotted us. My heart was beating as fast as possible, my stomach twisting in knots.

"We can't leave him," I begged Scahl, "Please." Scahl ignored my plea and kept struggling to pull me away. I watched Farley, standing like a statue. I couldn't get him to come with us; I didn't know what to do when Scahl finally pulled me away, dragging me behind a cluster of trees.

I watched through the branches as the dragon caught Farley in his sites and gave out another booming roar. I closed my eyes and covered my ears.

I opened them once again, only watching Farley, knowing he wouldn't come out alive for us, knowing this would be the last time I saw him.

The dragon landed before Farley sending a wave of water over the raft, coming eye to eye with Farley.

Farley faced the dragon, boldly, and let out a booming roar of his own, fire spitting out of his open jaws. I covered my ears again as the cry echoed through the trees.

"Farley!" I gave out one last cry. Farley took his battle stance and let out the booming roar again, louder than I could've ever imagined he could make.

I looked into the furious eyes of the dragon, staring at Farley, as they suddenly became less fearsome. The dragon let out a roar of its own, less booming than before.

Farley roared once again, smoke coming out of his nostrils, and the dragon gave one last look at us and jumped into the sky sending even more water pouring onto us, knocking us all to the ground.

Farley continued breathing heavily, smoke coming out of his nostrils, looking out farther down the river.

We stared from the ground in awe, "What just happened?" I asked, my voice still shaking.

"Either the most terrifying spectacle I've ever seen or the most spectacular," Scahl said without taking his eyes off Farley.

"I'll tell you what just happened," Torkie said to us, "we just reached the Lake of Dragons."

Scahl and I both took our eyes off Farley to look at Torkie, "So that means--" I said before Torkie finished my thought.

"We're going the right way."

"But how are we going to get through another scene like that?" Scahl asked.

"We've got Farley," Torkie said, "but let's hope we don't have to use him again."

"We're in the Lake of Dragons! How are we not," Scahl exclaimed.

"We're not *in* the Lake; the lake is probably 5 miles off the river," Torkie said.

We all looked back at Farley, still shaken, we knew our day of travel was over, and it was time to find shelter and go to sleep.

We would all sleep better knowing now that we were headed in the right direction.

\* \* \* \*

We awoke the next morning to clear blue skies, under our canopy made out of branches that Scahl hastily put together. We were all still soaked but didn't complain because of the events that happened the night before.

We took turns on watch throughout the night, continually having to move the raft in closer because of the rising water in the river.

We all packed up, Torkie feeling much better and Farley being treated like a hero, we headed to the edge of the river.

We could clearly see the peak of Mt. B'Tuul in the distance now that the clouds had cleared and the sun was rising, casting its light on it.

"There it is," Torkie said to us, feeling prideful that he was right about where we were going.

"How long will it be before we're there?" I asked.

"We can be in the mining town by tomorrow night, I believe. I don't think I remember any falls or rapids North of the town, so I think we'll be safe."

Scahl started pushing the raft into the water, "We better get a move on then, I don't want anymore close encounters with dragons today."

We helped Farley get onto the raft, then Torkie and I jumped on, and Scahl pushed us out and jumped on himself before we started drifting down the river, effortlessly taking us where we needed to go.

With the confirmation that we were North of Mt. B'Tuul, Torkie began scribbling notes and drawings into his journal, as Scahl and I talked.

"What do you imagine will happen once we find Abanyu?" I asked knowing we were getting close.

"I don't know; we're going to have to be on our toes and come up with a plan when we get there."

"Isn't that getting old? Just coming up with plans as we go, not knowing where we were going?"

"Yea, but we're doing all we can to make sure no one ever has to wander again." He nodded towards Torkie who was still trying to figure out his map.

We floated along the river, passing more dragons in the distance, and reaching Mt. B'Tuul. We kept our eyes open for any site of the mining town Torkie told us about, not sure how far along the mountain it exactly was.

The mountain came all the way to the edge of the water. It was a great view being able to look directly up Mt. B'tuul, slowly fading into the white, puffy clouds. The opposite side of the river was nearly perfectly flat with strange animals roaming and flying.

Scahl watched them with as much wonder as I did. He had no idea what most of these animals were himself. Just like in my world, certain animals inhabited only certain parts of the world and even though Scahl knew what the average person in this world knew, they never traveled this far, there was no way they could know about these animals.

I turned to Torkie, "What kind of animals are those?"

He looked up from his journal and shrugged, "Why are you asking me?"

"I just thought since you were from around these parts, you would know."

He shrugged again, "I never really paid attention to the animals. That's a journey for someone else."

It dawned on me; I was a part of a world that was just beginning. It couldn't have been more than a few hundred years old.

"Do either of you know how old D'Hanin is?" I asked catching them both off guard.

They looked at each other, puzzled, "Probably at least five, maybe six hundred years old?" Scahl questioned.

Torkie nodded in agreement, "I left my village when I was pretty young, those questions never dawned on me to ask."

"It just seems like there's a lot to be discovered about this world. I know you guys live in it, but where I'm from, people only dream about this stuff."

"I guess there is a lot of spectacular parts to this world," Scahl said, "breaking out of our villages and seeing the world, the only other two people I know of doing anything like that is Keahi, and the Fade and even the Fade hasn't gone as far as we have."

"We should be taking notes like Torkie," I said to Scahl, "We need to take back the information we gathered and share it with everyone."

"We are," Scahl said, and he pointed to his head, "Up here. That's the best we can do for everyone right now. We have too many other duties to be worried about."

He was right, I hated to admit it, but the beauty of traveling down this river had gotten the best of me, "I know, maybe I get bored when we're just traveling."

Scahl laughed, "Well I enjoy it, I haven't had to worry whether or not I would die today."

I laughed, "Don't speak too soon, that's the one worry I don't miss."

And so we traveled farther and farther down the river, trying to convince myself I wasn't bored, we watched our surroundings for the next couple of days and took in more and more views.

Well before nightfall on the second day, as Torkie had predicted, we could finally see buildings, lining the river and boats floating in place. The town nestled in a flat, human-made area, within the mountain. I stood up on the raft to get a better view, "Torkie, is this it?"

Torkie looked up from his journal and finally noticed the town. "I think so." He looked down at his journal and studied it, I guess it was closer than I remembered," he paused, "or maybe it's a new town?"

Scahl paddled us closer to the shore, "Well, either way, we're getting off here, it seems nice enough, and there's no smell of dark magic."

"I agree, I need to stretch my legs anyway, and it would be nice to talk to the townsfolk, maybe they know of Abanyu's lair."

Torkie stood up next to me, "It all looks so different to me, it's amazing what a cell can do to a man's mind."

"Don't start questioning yourself now; you've gotten us this far," I said to him.

"I'm not; it's just--" Torkie drifted off into thought. I did my best not to worry and just assume it was something to do with the map location and nothing more.

Scahl wasn't as convinced as I was, "Torkie, what's wrong," he asked firmly, snapping Torkie out of his trance.

"Nothing, this was just the first town that we reached, and there's someone I need to visit."

Scahl looked at me suspiciously, "Who do you want to find?" He asked Torkie.

"Just a friend," Torkie mumbled, deep in thought.

"Ok, but let's not lose sight of where we're going," Scahl said.

"I know, I won't." Torkie started gathering our stuff up. I helped him get Farley up so we could load up the packs.

The sun was three or four hours from setting as we pulled up to the shore. The town was pretty quiet except for one building that looked like it was budding. No one came to greet us as we all stepped off the raft and onto land.

"Not much protection," Scahl said.

"I'll take that as a good sign. I'm guessing we should go there first," as I pointed at the budding building.

# 19

## LONG FORGOTTEN MEMORIES

We walked through the doors, and a burst of applause and excitement filled the bar, the three of us standing frozen with all the patrons cheering us on. Then it became quiet.

"'Oo da 'ell er you's," the drunk patron closest to the tap said as he fell off his chair and stayed face first on the ground. The bartender, a short man with dark make up and piercings all over his face, came around as the bar once again bursting out in laughter, loud talking, and beer guzzling.

"Sorry about my friend," the Bartender apologized. He limped over to us, and we then realized, he had a peg leg.

"Although, I am curious who you are," he said as he got to us.

Scahl introduced us all by name, and then the Bartender spoke again, "Well I know your names, now I want to know who you are. We only get a visitor about once a year, if that, and they're usually up to something."

"We mean no harm to you," Scahl assured him, "we're just looking for a place to stay for the night, then we'll be off up the mountain at daybreak."

"What's up the mountain that you need to get to?" The Bartender asked skeptically.

Scahl lowered his voice and inched closer, "We're on a journey to bring the Scales back to D'Hanin."

"What happened to the other guy? What was his name? Grayble? Grenble? Gre-something?" The Bartender scrunched his forehead trying to remember.

"I believe he did not complete the journey, which is why we're here."

The Bartender nodded, "Ok, just be on your best behavior, and we won't have any trouble. The name's Batty if you need anything."

Batty turned to walk away, but Torkie caught his eye, and he stopped, "What did you say your name was, son?" He said to Torkie.

Scahl stepped to the side giving Batty a better look.

"You look familiar."

"It's Torkie," he said, not making eye contact with him.

Batty's eyes got wide then he burst out laughing, "Well what're you doing standing behind this big fellow, How have you been? It must've been three years since we last saw you!"

"About," Torkie said, oddly looking uncomfortable.

"I hardly recognized you without the belly," Batty pulled Torkie along, "Come on, the big fella looks like he can drink, so we better get started!" Batty sat us down at a table, and he called over a woman with three drinks in her hands. She threw them on the table and ran over to help the other people.

"Stop being so shy lad, how's the map going, where's your brother? What's his name again?"

"It was Saeran; he's dead."

Batty became somber, "Sorry to hear that, Saeran was a good man. If it's not a problem, what happened?"

"We were captured by a horde of Apaku's followers. They killed him; I only managed to escape because of these two."

"Well let's have a drink to Saeran, he was a nobleman." Batty lifted his glass, and we all drank. I cringed at the taste; I never had any alcohol and imagined this is what it was. Scahl drank it as if he was drinking water. I set my glass down, only taking a sip out of it.

"Was your brother's passing recent, then?" Batty asked.

"A little over a year has passed, they saved me about a couple of weeks ago."

"So there's no asking where the weight went, you being locked up and all." Batty gave a small chuckle, trying to lighten the conversation.

A fight broke out, sending a few glasses to the floor.

"I better take care of this, not so much worried about the fighting; it's the glasses I can't afford to lose!" Batty stood up, "It was good seeing you Torkie."

Torkie nodded, and Scahl was already motioning for the woman to bring him another drink.

"Well boys, let's not look at the past or the future.  Let's have one last night of fun so we can be fully charged for the trip ahead."  Scahl said as the new glass was set in front of him.  He held it up and tipped it back, guzzling it down.  I pushed mine over to him and took his empty glass, slamming it down as he came back to earth for a breath.  "Wow, didn't know you could handle the drink that well, and look at this service," he held up my full glass I pushed over to him, "already got me ready for another drink!"

* * * *

Scahl eventually drank himself to a point where he was comfortable with all the townsfolk, laughing and joking with all of them as Torkie and I kept to ourselves at the table.

"It's funny how our senses can trigger memories," Torkie said lightly, keeping his voice below all the noise so that only I could hear, "the simplest smell or sight can bring back the deepest, most forgotten memories we have."  He paused for a moment, "come with me; I don't think Scahl will even know we're gone."

We left in a hurry; I followed Torkie because he seemed to know where he was going.

The crisp, wet air hit my face, as the door behind us closed, the noise of the patrons was silenced just enough to hear the river flowing and the animals in the mountains stirring.  It looked like what I imagine a pirate city would look like.

"I remember everything that happened in this town," Torkie began reminiscing, "but when I saw it earlier today, it looked so much different, but I don't think anything changed."

I just let him talk, I didn't know what to say, or if I was even supposed to say anything at all.

"I'm a murderer, Finn."  He said to me heavy heartedly.

I took caution, "What?" I asked him.

"Don't make me repeat it." He said his face buried in his hands.

"Well tell me what you mean?" I said firmly, feeling like I had no idea who he was anymore.

"My brother was a bad man, no matter what anyone thinks," he looked back up at me, "he even fooled me, he took me away from my home and my family. He was one of them."

"One of who?"

"The Apaku Worshippers. He was on a journey to find more people like him, and he had me believing the same."

"What about the map, and your brother being killed? What happened to him then?" I asked.

"I was just a child; I made the map because I was afraid I'd never get home. And they did kill him; that part was true, but it was my fault. As I grew on our travels I began to think for myself, and when the people of Fliagenrè found us I rebelled, and they killed him and threw me in jail. He tried to save me and convince them I didn't mean any harm, but they killed him before he could get it out."

"So because they killed your brother, you think you're a murderer?" I asked him, still confused.

"No," he said frustrated.

"Then just start at the beginning, who are you and who did you kill?" I said to him.

"Please, keep it down. I'll tell you my story." He stopped at the edge of the river, a way down from where we landed. He removed his shoes and stepped into the ankle deep water approaching a large boulder. He ran his fingers over words that were carved into the boulder. When the moonlight cast across it just perfectly, I could see that this was a memorial. Without looking back at me, Torkie began his story.

"We lived not far from here, where Abanyu's lair is visible from the highest peak of the town. When Saeran learned about the Scales and Apaku's plans, he was immediately on board. But to his surprise, no one else was.

He lived in silence for many years; except for one person he shared all his thoughts. The youngest, and most vulnerable villager." Torkie lowered his head in remembrance, "Unfortunately, that happened to be me. He told me all the plans, and I saw his excitement, which in turn, made me believe.

A couple more years passed and he couldn't hold his tongue anymore, he needed to be around people with his same views. So in the dead of night, he packed me up, and we left our family and friends."

Torkie looked up at me to quickly try and see what I was thinking, but I still didn't know what to think.

He looked back down and continued, "the next morning I was in a panic, I loved my brother, but I didn't want to leave my parents and my friends behind forever. No child would, but I had no choice, I had no way of finding my way back.

That's when I started drawing the map; my brother was all for it, it kept me quiet. I thought if I ever wanted to go back to visit my family, I would be able to retrace my steps, but now, I understand that I probably wouldn't have been welcomed back.

So, we strolled along the river, and through the mountains for months until we finally found this town. They welcomed us as strangers just as they did to us now. My brother drank with them just as we do now. But I was young and didn't like all the screaming and throwing drinks around; I let myself outside to sit by the river until Saeran would tell me what to do next.

After a little while, a man spotted me on his way to the tavern. He was amicable at first, just seeing what a young boy was doing by the river all by himself but then I talked to him and told him our business. I didn't realize what outcasts we were or how fiercely people were against us."

259

Torkie paused; I could tell the story was getting harder for him to explain, which meant there was only one outcome.

"The man became angry and was yelling at me and told me he was going to expose Saeran and I. The man grabbed me, so I grabbed a rock near the river in a panic and hit him in the head. The man fell, pulling me into the river. Blood pooled around us as we started drifting. I screamed for help and desperately swam and kicked for my life.

I freed myself from the man but still struggled to fight the flow of the river until I was able to grab onto a branch hanging close enough to the water. I looked back down the river, the man never resurfacing, just his blood fading into the water. I knew he was never coming back. I panicked, realizing what I had done. I knew in my heart that I was just trying to make him let go of me, but I screamed for help, at the top of my lungs as I struggled to get back to shore.

After a short stint, Saeran came running out and pulled me out of the water. I tried to explain what happened to him but he covered my mouth and told me to be quiet, as more of the townspeople came rushing out. He lied to everyone, said a man tried to save me but was knocked out on a nearby boulder.

Saeran feared if we ran off right away, the town would become suspicious, so we stayed for his memorial service. Every single person in the city was present, but it was his family that stood next to us as people spoke highly of his character. He was the peacekeeper of the city, a local hero, and by the constant flowing tears of his daughters, a hero to his family. Something I had ended with one fatal swing.

However, shortly after the memorial service, Saeran wasted no more time getting us out of the town. He made me believe his story; he made me forget what I had done because he knew it would break me. After a while I became his story, it all came back to me when we got here."

260

I stared at him for a moment; he wouldn't make eye contact with me.

"I don't even know what to say; I think the worst choice you made was continue with your brother. I don't know whether to feel sorry for you or mad at you."

"I owe you my life; I would've rotted away in that cell if it hadn't been for you. I just ask for another chance." He pleaded.

I thought to myself, processing all the information. "You're not a murderer, Torkie. Well technically you are, but you couldn't have meant to do it, right?"

"Of course not." I helped him out of the river, he sat down in the grass and began putting his shoes back on, "I was scared back then, every day of my life was scarier than the last since the moment my brother took me away."

"I know Torkie, it's just a lot of information to take in," I said trying my best to be empathetic.

"I'll catch up with you and Scahl later; I just need to be alone."

I didn't want to argue, in fact, I preferred it. I left Torkie alone on the riverside to dwell. I decided to get a room ready at the Inn for Scahl, which had a large sign that read *Rooms As Dark As Coal.* I figured any morning sun to Scahl would only make him more on edge.

\* \* \* \*

Scahl and I woke up the next morning and found Torkie already sitting at a table in the tavern of the Inn with plates for all three of us.

"Morning," Scahl said to him.

"Morning, I got you guys something to eat, then I figured we'd be on our way. I got Farley ready to go and everything." Torkie replied enthusiastically.

Scahl took a seat, looking at him strangely, "Where'd you sleep last night, I don't even remember you two leaving the bar."

"I just got a room by myself," Torkie said.

"I guess a good night sleep in a bed got you going," Scahl said still unaware of Torkie's real story.

I had a terrible time looking at Torkie or Scahl now. I didn't know if it would make any difference to tell Scahl or not, but I thought it would explode out of me if I couldn't tell someone.

Torkie sat and ate breakfast with us for a while, tapping his foot and not making direct eye contact with me until he realized what I was thinking. He finally stood up with the journal in his hand, "If you guys don't mind, I'd really like to ask the people around here about the area, so I can have a bit of history to go along with the map."

Torkie rushed out of the diner trying to get an escape so I could talk to Scahl, but I still wasn't ready. "That's fine, just don't disappear too long," I said to him before he was all the way out of the door.

Breakfast from there on was silent; I made sure to keep my mouth full of food so I wouldn't have to talk. Scahl finally broke the tension.

"So I figure, when we get to the top of the mountain, we'll be able to see where his lair is, and we'll have a better idea of how long it will take us to get there."

I nodded, "And let me guess, there's not a nice little path that leads up the mountainside all the way to the top?"

Scahl laughed, "I don't know, but have we been that lucky so far?"

By then an old man, who looked ready to keel over, joined in on our conversation from across the room, "Did ya'll say you were going up the mountain?" He made his way slowly over to us.

"That's the plan," Scahl said.

The old man took a deep breath; the walking must have gotten to him. "Are you going to the top?"

"Yea," Scahl said.

The old man took another deep breath and coughed violently into his arm, "My friend is up there, please will you give him a message for me?"

"Why don't you take a seat," I said to the old man as he started to sway back and forth.

"I don't need a seat," he said, "I just need you to tell him --"

An elderly lady, however, much younger than him came over an interrupted him, "Come on, they don't have time for your trouble," she said to him then looked towards us, "I'm sorry, I take my eyes off him for a second and he runs around terrorizing anyone he can."

"It's no problem," I told her, feeling bad for the man.

"No," he said, "His name is Adipm, the Fat. Tell him --"

"I'm sorry he's a decrepit old man and has a million stories to tell."

"It's ok," Scahl said, "Maybe it would just be easier to let him tell us."

The older lady was silent, "Ok then."

The old man took a couple of deep breaths and finally brought himself together, "when, I was a young lad, just like the two of you, mining the mountains every single day," he took another couple deep breaths, "I mined straight into the home of Adipm, the Fat."

The old man gave a short laugh, ended with a cough, "you should have seen the look on his face; it was already uglier than an ogre's bottom. But the way he jumped," the old man struggled to laugh again, "he wasn't used to having his prey waltz straight into his home like that."

"Come on, you're not gonna finish the story at this pace," the older woman interjected.

He nodded, "Anyways, I didn't let him scare me, and believe me he tried, but I tried right back." He took a deep breath, "Turns to find out, he had a loot of gems and gold and every other type of precious jewels and metals you can think of stashed away in his cave."

The old man's eye's glistened as if he was looking at the stash once again.

"He didn't mean no harm to anyone; he was just protecting his loot." The old man wobbled, and the older lady pulled out a chair and forced him to sit in it.

He took one final deep breath, "So, anyway, if you come across a fat, ogre's bottom looking man, recite this to him," the old man closed his eyes and recited in a melodic tune:

> If you're the one they call Adipm,
> I ask you not to fright.
> You should know we're of your kin,
> that's why we wouldn't fight.
> For we don't want your treasure,
> You should know we all were warned.
> You ask us how you can be sure?
> Why, we heard your tale from Kelendred,
> That's why we're prepped before.

The old man cleared his throat, and let out a laugh, "I haven't told that story in years, thank you, boys. You shouldn't run into any troubles on your journey up the mountain now."

Scahl and I both smiled, "Thank you, we appreciate it," I said to him.

The old man nodded with a smile; the older woman whispered to me as she pulled the old man away, "Don't worry, he tells everyone going up the mountain that, we all try to humor him."

"All right," I smiled and nodded, "Either way it was a good story."

"Have a good journey," she said as a final good-bye. We left the tavern shortly afterward.

We got Farley ready for the journey, we both knew in the back of our minds traveling up the mountain was going to be the hardest on him.

We found Torkie a few minutes later talking to a man in a rocking chair smoking a long pipe. Torkie thanked him, with a big smile and he caught back up with us, filling us in on what he found out.

"Ok, so the town's name is Durbshin, known to the surrounding cities as the mining city. The surrounding cities being, Perubumare, by the lake of dragons, River End, which is across the river, and Latet, which is separated from the river by the mountains."

"You learned all that, from just that one guy?" Scahl asked as we walked towards the mountains.

"Yea and more, he didn't have much information on the other cities, but at least we have a good idea what's around us."

"Did he have an idea what's on the other side of the mountain?" Scahl asked looking for more information about our journey and not for the map.

"Not really, just of Perubumare, but that's more to the North East. He had some interesting history of the city though."

"Well write this down in your notes, Adipm the Fat," and Scahl recited the song to Torkie, but without the melodic tune. Torkie scribbled it down.

"You think we're actually going to need that?" I asked Scahl, "I thought it was just a little town legend."

"It seems like a lot of energy for the old man to be wasting if it wasn't true."

"Yea, but what else does he have to be spending his energy on?"

"That might be true as well but as the song says, *"That's why we're prepped before."* We might as well prepare for something." Scahl said, making his point.

"It's kind of cool to have on the map too," Torkie said, putting his two cents in.

We reached the back of the town and could see miners walking along paths up Mt. B'tuul and tracks coming down and up into the mountain.

"I guess we can start on these paths, take them up as far as we can." I said, "Did that man tell you anything about where the paths go, Torkie?"

"No, I didn't have a lot of time to ask him much," Torkie paused, looking embarrassed.

"Ok, Torkie," Scahl said, "From now on you know, you're a part of this journey and if you're going to be working on the map and asking questions, you need to figure this kind of stuff out."

"Got it," Torkie replied.

"It looks like this one goes the farthest up the mountain, "Scahl pointed to a path farther on the right side of the town, "We might as well take that one."

# 20

## THE VIEW FROM THE TOP

$W$e were finally above the town, being able to see over it, the villagers looking like ants running through town. We passed many of the miners, most of who ignored us and minded their own business. Carts full of rocks and gems whizzed passed us going to the bottom of Mt. B'tuul where the other miners were waiting. This high up the mountain was just as busy, or possibly busier than the actual town.

We moved up the mountain a lot faster than I thought we would. By mid-

day, we were beyond the busiest part of the mining tracks and had a forest that got thicker as it climbed up the mountain, in sight.

"It looks like we're getting to the end of the paths," I said, seeing it slowly fade into the mountain.

"That's fine; we'll rest for the night once we have shade in the forest," Scahl replied.

\* \* \* \*

Another hour or so passed and we reached a plateau in the mountain, a small canyon, about forty feet across, before us, and only a rope bridge to get us across.

"Are you sure this isn't a video game?" I asked Scahl, after seeing the moss covered bridge.

"Pretty sure," he questioned, not sure what I was talking about. He continued up to the bridge and put his foot on the first board, "It's well made, let's go." He stepped forward.

"Is it going to hold all off us though, even Farley?" Torkie asked, "I don't even think the bridge is going to be wide enough for him."

Scahl looked back, already on the bridge, "It'll be fine, just spread out," and he continued walking.

I looked down both sides of the canyon, it seeming to stretch miles down into a death filled oblivion, I wanted to run as quickly as I possibly could across the bridge, but I knew I had the responsibility of getting Farley across safely as well.

"Good luck," I motioned to Torkie to begin across. He went reluctantly, placing one foot out, looking straight ahead. He stopped shortly after taking a couple of steps onto the bridge, after hearing a loud creak. Still looking forward he yelled back to me, "You're not going to be able to get that toradrac across, Finn!"

Scahl jumped off the bridge to the other side and yelled back, "Torkie, just get across the bridge, I'm 200 pounds heavier than you and look where I am."

"Really? 200 pounds," Torkie yelled back, "I'm not that scrawny." Torkie continued walking forward, both hands on the rope handrails.

"You ready, Farley?"

Farley snorted smoke out of his nose, and I pushed him forward. The bridge creaked as soon as he stepped on, but it seemed to be holding up. I let Farley create a bit of distance ahead of me before I stepped on.

I looked down, through the cracks of the bridge. I got a lump in my throat and thought it would be best to keep my mouth shut and continue walking.

My heart skipped a beat with every creak of the bridge. Torkie was a little farther than halfway, feeling more confident with every step, but I had a long way to go ahead of me, and it was about to get longer as I heard little gusts of winds. Torkie looked back at me.

"Just keep going," I called to him as I heard the same roar we heard on our way down the river.

Scahl's eye's got wide as ten dragons came sweeping out of the sky towards us. Torkie began to run, the bridge shaking beneath my feet, causing me to grab the railings. Farley seemed uninterested in the dragons, but I couldn't say the same for myself. I pushed Farley to move faster, only causing planks from the bridge to snap in half.

Scahl and Torkie watched in terror, knowing they couldn't do anything now but wait. I pushed Farley trying not to watch the oncoming Dragons.

I heard the gusts of wind from the giant wings closing in on us. I hunkered down and closed my eyes. The bridge started swinging back and forth, Farley began to grunt as the dragons passed us. I looked up at them as they flew over, the bridge swaying violently back and forth with every flap of their wings. I clutched the railings as one came loose on Scahl's side.

The bridge began to lean. I jumped up and pushed Farley forward; I knew we couldn't just sit there.

Scahl grabbed the hanging railing and lifted up the leaning side as best as he could so we could at least keep our balance.

I kept going forward the last of the dragons passing over us, the bridge being clipped by a giant claw, causing me to fall to my hands and knees and the railing being ripped out of Scahl's hands. He grabbed onto the edge of the cliff and hung there. I waited for the bridge to stop swinging before I jumped up, the bridge now hanging violently to one side.

Torkie dove for Scahl, trying desperately to pull him up. It didn't look like Torkie would be able to pull Scahl up without our help, but we were moving as fast as we could.

Scahl slipped a little out of Torkie's hands, "Come on, Torkie, I'm not that much heavier than you!"

Torkie eyes dilated and whimpered as Scahl kept slipping.

"Come on Torkie, just hold tight until Finn gets here, don't let me fall!" Scahl said, loudly but calm.

Torkie looked up at me trailing behind Farley, "Finn," Torkie wailed, terrified as Scahl slipped a little more.

"Just hold on," I cried back and pushed Farley a little stronger until we got to the edge of the bridge and I leaped over and grabbed Scahl by the back of his shirt. Torkie readjusted his grip, and we were able to pull him up over the edge of the cliff. He crawled over and fell on his back.

"Who would've thought, you'd save my life," Scahl said to Torkie, "I kind of thought you'd let me go down," he said with a smile, avoiding looking down the cliff. Scahl stood up, "let's get away from this cliff, it's about time for us to rest for the night."

Scahl left us on the groundkeepoing to himself, he knew, out of the entire journey, that was the closest, and hopefully closest he'll ever be, to death.

Torkie, as well as I, didn't hide our fear as well as Scahl. He almost looked petrified, if it wasn't for his chest rising and falling rapidly.

"Come on Farley," I said. He looked up from sniffing around an animal hole; seemingly unaware of the danger we just faced and trotted over to us. I helped Torkie up onto his back, and we followed Scahl up the mountain even farther finally reaching the forest about an hour before sunset.

After cooling down from the previous events, Torkie spotted an area where a tree's roots hung out of the side of the mountain, creating a cave-like shelter, and with a little sprucing up from Scahl, it was a perfect accommodation for the situation.

Of course, we all knew our roles, and I started making a fire, while Scahl hunted, and Torkie found firewood.

I had the fire going by the time Scahl returned. The night brought a brisk wintery chill, and I began to feel the effects of the high altitude.

Torkie sat across from me, almost sitting in the fire, shivering.

"Are you going to be all right, Torkie?" I asked.

"Yea, I'm warming up, thanks," he said, "I mean, I know we're up a mountain, but come on, you'd think to be in the middle of summer, the mountain would warm up too."

Scahl didn't have much to say about the cold; he just prepared our dinner. I thought this would be the right time to bring up Torkie's past to Scahl. I looked at Torkie, and he understood as well. He put his head down, embarrassed.

I opened my mouth to speak, but something inside me stopped any words from coming out. I thought Torkie hadn't done anything for me to worry about his past, and his heroics earlier showed me he was with us.  There was no point in bringing up his checkered history in a time when he's finally left it behind him.  It would only cause problems for everyone, so I kept it to myself.

Torkie looked back up at me, and I nodded to him, hoping he understood his past was erased from my mind.

He reassured me with a smirk; there was no need for him to worry about his past anymore.  It was completely gone for both of us, and we could finally move on to do great things.

We ate our expertly prepared dinner and went straight to sleep under the forest's shuffling leaves.

* * * *

The next morning brought warmth once again, Torkie and Scahl both were able to shed the many layers they slept in.

We continued up the mountain and across hoping to get to the other side of the mountain faster.  The trees gave us shade, making it hard to tell the time of day.  We had to make use of the small openings in the trees to see the sun and make sure we were moving in the right direction.

Torkie noticed a rock formation that jutted out of the mountain, clear of any trees. He directed Farley over to the rock formation and jumped off, knowing Farley would not be able to climb up.  He struggled himself to climb up, almost falling twice.

"Be careful," Scahl yelled at him, why are you so worried about getting up that rock?"

"I just want to see the sun, make sure we're going in the right direction." He shouted back, continuing to climb.

"Just trust me, I know where we're going," Scahl said impatiently.

272

Torkie reached the top of the rock and looked down at us with a smile then looked out over the tree-tops at the world and became speechless.

"What is it?" I yelled up to him.

He still couldn't produce any words; he just stepped forward, closer to the edge of the rock.

"Watch where you're going," Scahl barked at him.

Without taking his eyes off of what he saw, he finally spoke, "This is it guys, it's beautiful. I can see towns, and forests, and rivers. I can see the edge of the world." We could see his eyes watering up, "It's like looking at a giant map, this is what I want everyone to be able to look at."

Scahl looked over at me, "I guess we should go see what all the fuss is about." He began climbing up the rock, and I followed him, wanting to see now as much as Torkie did.

Scahl reached the top of the rock, and I heard him say, "Wow." I knew it must have been something special if it impressed Scahl, and it was. I reached the top of the rock and stood next to them, all three of us gazing out over the beautiful world of D'Hanin.

We stood in silence, being able to see where we had gone the past few months for the first time. We could even see the moon setting on the horizon, bringing the night to that side of the world.

"I'm sure we could stand here for days, taking in the view but we've got to keep moving," Scahl said.

I nodded, agreeing, although Torkie was hypnotized, "Just give me a moment, I need to record this. I couldn't miss this kind of opportunity to see the world while I'm drawing the map."

Scahl paused for a moment but eventually gave him what he wanted. He headed back down the rock as I followed to provide Torkie with his concentration.

\* \* \* \*

An hour had passed, Torkie jumped down from the rock with a smile on his face, feeling a sense of pride.

"Finally, let's get a move on," Scahl said.

"Wait, look what I've gotten so far," Torkie said, and flipped to a page in his journal, then held it out for us to see. A detailed map filled the entire page, "It's only about a quarter of D'Hanin, but I could see a few cities I didn't know the names of," he pointed out a couple of areas with question marks on them, "but I'll know where to go to find them, it'll save me from wandering."

"It's great," I said.

"Yea, it's great, it'll help a lot of travelers one day, but right now we've got to keep going," Scahl said.

I pulled Farley along, and we kept heading around the mountain. The walk became much more relaxed, and we were moving around the mountain a lot faster than when we were scaling up. It always seemed though, when we were journeying more quickly, or in a good place, problems would arise. It gave me anxiety to think danger was lurking, but all around us, there was nothing more than a few strange animals and birds flying from bare tree to bare tree.

However, as Scahl pointed out in the distance, storm clouds were looming. It wasn't actually a danger, but with the limited coverage we had, it was going to be a long, cold night.

"When do you think they'll reach us?" Torkie asked.

"I'd give it an hour, start looking for any shelter," Scahl said.

The wind picked up, giving us chills much like the night before.

"Do you think we should head down the mountain, it might be warmer below?" I said, throwing any ideas I had out there.

"It might help a little," Scahl replied.

"In temperatures like this, and rain looming, that little bit might be the reason we survive," I said.

"Yes, but we have the top of the mountain, there's security knowing we're above many creatures."

"How do you know for sure though? We don't know what kind of creatures could be flying above or living at the peak of the mountain. It might be best to move away from them." Torkie interjected.

"How do we know anything for sure? The rain clouds might get swept away and miss us entirely," Scahl replied, "And then we would only have wasted an hour going down instead of taking the fastest route to where we're going."

I thought of our options, wanting to help make a decision that was right for the group.

"I'm not sure about you two, but I'm anxious to finally be able to see where we're going," Scahl said.

We were all anxious, and we all had handled more danger than a rainstorm could cause us.

"Let's just keep going forward until we know for certain the clouds are going to rain on us. Even if they do, we will still have time before complete nightfall to trek down the mountain for warmth."

"Ok, I guess that's a reasonable request," Torkie said, although he was not ashamed in showing he was the most terrified to see where we would potentially meet our doom.

As the hour passed the clouds and thunder grew closer and closer. It was now imminent that rain would cover us within a half hour.

A single drop of rain hit the top of my head, sending a chill down my spine. The water droplets were as icy as could be without us being struck with hail.

"Do you think we should start going down now?" I asked Scahl.

A drop of water landed on his face and dripped down his nose. He tried to look as far as he could through the trees.

"We're not going to get there before the rain, Scahl."

"Let's just keep pushing forward a little longer."

"That's time that could be spent moving towards warmth." I snapped back.

Scahl ground his teeth, "Ok, let's go." He moved down the hill faster than the rest of us, but we didn't trail too far behind. Rain kept falling harder and harder, our hair starting to feel damp and our ears starting to feel numb.

We all looked desperately for shelter, but, unless we wanted to stand all night, we weren't finding anything. Rain continued to pour harder and harder; thunder shook the trees.

"We're going to have to stop here and make a shelter," Scahl said.

"What about our tents?" Torkie yelled back over the pounding of the rain.

"They'll soak through in less than twenty minutes," Scahl explained, then pulled out his mace and hacked it against a tree with all his might. He chopped and chopped as we watched, the mace not correctly doing the job his axe used to. However, the tree finally fell, more from blunt force than axing. We jumped out of the way of the falling tree as it crashed to the ground.

Scahl instructed Torkie to find as many branches as we could as he put the fallen tree into position.

"Start a fire, Finn, dry the ground for us." He told me.

I went to an open patch of ground and laid down an armful of branches. They were already soaked from the rain. I worked at the fire, but the flame wasn't able to catch on the firewood and stay lit. I could only get a small ball of fire in my hands. I stood up, "I'm going to need shelter before I can make any fire for us." I said to Scahl as a loud crack of thunder rang through the trees, bringing even more rain with it.

I could see Scahl was trying to yell something at me, but the noise of the rain was drowning him out. I took a step forward to get closer to him, but the ground was slick and found myself on the ground, sliding down the mountain, banging my arm against a sharp rock.

I cringed in pain, but my biggest worry was stopping myself from sliding down. I grabbed onto a small tree but could feel it giving way to my weight. The tree came out of the muddy ground with me, and we continued to slide until I was able to dig my feet and hands into the ground and hold myself in place.

I could faintly hear Scahl and Torkie shouting my name. I didn't want to move because I could feel if I let go of the mountain I would keep sliding. So I laid there, the cold rain slapping against my back. I called back out to them, to let them know I was ok, but I wasn't sure if it did anything.

An enormous hand grabbed the back of my shirt and lifted me up under the arm of a morbidly obese man. The man moved up the slope of the mountain that I had just slid down as quickly as walking on a plain.

I could see Scahl stop in his tracks at the site of this man, then recite:

If you're the one they call Adipm,
I ask you not to fright.
You should know we're of your kin,
That's why we wouldn't fight.
For we don't want your treasure,
You should know we all were warned.
You ask us how you can be sure?
Why, we heard your tale from Kelendred,
That's why we're prepped before.

"Come with me!" The man shouted over the rain, which I now could be sure must have actually been Adipm, from the story.

Scahl, Torkie, and Farley left the fallen tree behind and followed Adipm back up the mountain, with me under his arm.

We walked passed the height we were at, Adipm, not saying a word. We had to trust he was taking us to safety because he was our only hope in getting out of the rain.

I was soaked to the bone, we all were, when he finally set me on my feet, and said, "In there." He pointed to a small opening in the side of the mountain. I crawled through, and every one followed behind.

We were finally out of the rain, and the loud noise of the rain dimmed to a soft pitter-patter. The cave was simple, there was a bed in the far corner, and fresh animal hides hanging from the walls.

"Sorry, I don't get much company." He said breaking the silence, finally revealing his face in the light of a small crackling fire. Kelendred was right; it did look like an ogre's bottom.

"It's fine; we're just glad we're out of the rain." Scahl said, "So you're Adipm?"

The man laughed, "Not the original, no, but you can call me Adipm if you want."

"What do you mean?" I asked.

"Adipm the Fat is an old legend, the people of Durbshin, have always believed in the legend, but truth be told we're all Adipm. There's probably ten of us living in the mountains just trying to get away from those people and whenever a miner catches a glimpse of one of us he expects it to be Adipm."

"Why did you help us if you were trying to get away from people of Durbshin?" Torkie asked.

"You three aren't from Durbshin, I can tell by the way you slid down the mountain, you lot aren't miners." He said laughing.

We couldn't take any offense. He was spot on. "Well thank you for bringing us back here, we really appreciate it," I said.

"You're welcome, I know how rough it can be out there, I've lived here for 50 years, I've seen the best and the worst of it. I was around when those troll people started taking over the bottom of the mountain. They don't come up this high, so they haven't bothered me. You three were getting close in on their territory though."

"You mean the garmec?" Scahl asked for all of us.

"Right, I guess so; the ones causing all the problems."

Scahl looked at me, knowing we almost walked right into their hands.

"I can show you guys tomorrow when the rain clears up; there's a spot on the mountain you can look down at them all."

"We would appreciate that," I said.

"But if you lot were thinking about going through, you better find a way around."

"It's actually right where we need to be," Scahl said, "We're going after the Scales."

Adipm didn't look surprised, "I s'pose it makes sense, why else would you be all the way up the mountain. Surely it wasn't to visit me," he chuckled, making his entire belly jiggle.

"It couldn't have been any luckier that you did find us," Scahl said graciously, "As much as we would like to socialize, we should probably get on a dry pair of clothes and rest."

"Of course, of course, I'll leave the bed for either of you, the rest of us will have to sleep on the floor. Like I said I wasn't prepared for company."

"It's ok; it's nothing we're not used to."

We dressed in new clothes and Adipm took down his animal hides so we would be able to hang our wet ones. Scahl picked me to sleep in the bed, so I

crawled in and fell asleep to the thought of the impending war that would begin tomorrow.

* * * *

The night couldn't have gone any faster. It
seemed as soon as I fell asleep, I was opening my eyes,
feeling rested. Scahl was sitting up, talking to Adipm
and polishing his mace, and Torkie was still fast
asleep, in what looked like the most uncomfortable
position he could have been in.

I sat up on the bed. Scahl and Adipm looked
over but continued to talk.

"So you know of a way to get to the bottom of
the mountain?" Scahl asked, letting Adipm continue
to tell him what I had interrupted.

"Yes, it's an easy trail, but I can't guarantee that
you won't be ambushed once you make your presence
known."

"Then we'll have to go in unseen," Scahl replied.

"As if a nearly full grown toradrac and three
men are masters of sneaking," I interjected.

"The path won't allow the toradrac to assist
you. Toradracs are great in open field battle but will
be a burden in this situation." Adipm said, "I have already discussed this with Scahl, I will watch the toradrac while you take care of your business."

I didn't like leaving Farley behind, but I knew
that would be for the best, so I nodded and agreed to
it, "That's more than what we could've asked from you
Adipm, thank you."

Adipm accepted my thank you, "I think we
should wake your friend and see what lies ahead for all
of you." Adipm stood up as we woke Torkie from his
coma. Farley shuffled and looked at us, but went right
back to sleep. Torkie instantly knew where we were
going, and stretched out then followed us, Adipm leading, out of the cave and into the bright morning sun.

The day left any traces of a thunderstorm behind, the trees and the ground were dry, and the clouds had passed, leaving us with clear blue skies.

Adipm led us through the trees and to a rock much like the one overlooking D'Hanin, but in front of us, mountains still stood tall. In this one particular spot, the mountain went flat for only a few hundred yards and shot back up, creating walls that the garmec lined fighting with one another, trees being ripped out of the ground for no purpose, flames burning out of control, and a sickening smell rising to meet us. We all stood silently looking down on pandemonium.

At the foot of the mountain, tunnels were being created or had been established. Garmec were running in and out of them, carrying animal carcasses in, bones coming out.

We were going to have to go into the mountains to find Abanyu and the Emerald Scale. What we were going to do when we got down there was still a mystery.

"I will be able to take you to the foot of the mountain, without being noticed, but getting into the tunnels and finding what you're after will be up to you," Adipm told us, breaking the silence after a few minutes of letting us take it in.

"Let's get going then; we'll have the Emerald Scale back in our hands by day's end if we move now," Scahl said.

Adipm nodded and led us to his secluded path, filled with dead, overgrown plants and trees; we hiked our way down the mountain.

# 21

## THE EMERALD SCALE

"Any ideas on how we're going to get to Aba-nyu?" I asked Scahl quietly.

"Yea, but involves cutting off a garmec's heads and wearing it as a disguise, and I don't think any of us would want to do that."

"It's more than what I've got," I replied.

"Let's use that as a last resort; I can't imagine it would work that well anyway." Scahl laughed.

We continued to hang back a little ways from Adipm and Torkie; I walked a little closer to Scahl to make sure Torkie couldn't hear.

"I think Torkie should stay with Adipm when we go in. He's a decent fighter, but I don't see a situation where he'll get out of this alive."

"I don't really see that great of a chance that we will either," Scahl said as a matter of fact.

"But it's our duty. He's got the map. That's his duty, and he shouldn't risk losing that for us."

Scahl thought about it for a moment, "You're probably right, but knowing him now, he's not going to allow that. He's as much invested in this as we are."

"But we have to take a stand, this is still what we were sent to do, he was sent into this world to make a map, and even though I want him to help us, it would be selfish to take him away from what he is supposed to do."

"We already lost Farley, and now you want to lose more help? Let's go back to the garmec head one."

I watched Torkie walk ahead of us; he looked ready for battle at any moment, his hand on the hilt of his blade and standing tall.

"We'll just see when we get to where Adipm is taking us," Scahl said.

"No, there's no more just seeing when we get there. We're here, and we need to figure out how we're going to get in and out of there as fast as possible. We need a plan A, B, and C."

"Ok, plan C, garmec head, let's start figuring out plan B then," Scahl said defensively.

I thought and thought, trying to figure something out without knowing what was lying ahead.

"Ok plan B," I said, "Flush them out with fire. There can't be that many tunnels, I could create a wall of fire, and we could run behind it until the tunnels are cleared.

"Perfect, now how would we get into the tunnels? There's already uncontrolled fires around this place; a little bit extra won't be enough to distract them."

"Well, I'm planning to be in the tunnels by then anyway. Like you said, a distraction. Plan A, we could set up a distraction, get as many of the garmec away from the tunnels and then run in and take care of Abanyu and any of the garmec that are left, grab the Emerald Scale and get out."

"Who's going to cause the distraction then?" Scahl said looking at Torkie.

"It will have to be you, Torkie is out of the picture, and I have to be the one to go in after the Scale."

"Why does it have to be you?"

"Because that's what I was brought here to do."

"I don't think anyone cares how you get the Scale back, whether it's you or me, they just want it back."

"Well in the worst case scenario, I have the elements at my side, you'll be going in with no back up other than your mace."

"Fine, I'll be the distraction, but you have to promise if Torkie refuses to let us go in by ourselves, he becomes the distraction and I get to go in with you."

"What do you mean refuses to let you guys go in alone?" Torkie said turning around, overhearing us, "Why would I let you guys go in alone?"

I looked at Scahl and knew this wouldn't be a conversation that would be easy to have, but I knew it had to be done.

"Listen, Torkie, we've decided it would be best if you stayed back while we take on Abanyu."

"I didn't come all this way with you guys to sit out at the end."

"He's right, "Adipm interjected, "He'll go in alone and you two we'll come with me."

"Do you have a plan, Adipm?" I asked feeling strange he would suggest anything, being that he didn't want anything to do with fighting.

Adipm stopped and looked through the trees at the foot of the mountain. I heard plants rustling and an all too familiar grunting. I looked up at Scahl who had his eyes locked on Adipm.

A garmec jumped out of the trees, Adipm stood utterly still, but Scahl swung his mace and knocked the garmec's head clean off. Four more followed and grabbed Torkie then as fast as the first 5 attacked, 10 more bombarded Scahl and me, holding us captive.

"Sorry everybody, but this is what must be done. Adipm said turning around, then pointing at me, "Take him to Abanyu, the rest of you follow me with the other two."

"They've locked us up before; you can't keep us prisoners!" Torkie yelled at Adipm.

"We're not planning on keeping any of you as prisoners," Adipm said then turned and started across the mountain, the garmec following, taking Scahl and Torkie with them.

The garmec pulled me down the mountain with them; I had no other choice but to watch them take my friends, and let them take me to Abanyu.

We emerged out of the heavily wooded area into the view of hundreds of garmec, all of them turning to see who it was. An eruption of yells and grunts shook my insides; it was terrifying to see all of them watching me.

The entire way down the mountain was like this, a couple of garmec nearby couldn't control their rage and would bound after me to kill me. The garmec taking me wouldn't allow it and would, in turn, kill the other garmec.

We reached the foot of the mountain, and they dragged me into the tunnels. I strained my neck to get a last glimpse of daylight before being thrown into the narrow tunnels.

Inside, I could see plan B could have worked, but I didn't have an escape plan. My best bet right now was to memorize where we went in the tunnels, but it was hopeless, they were much more intricate than I could have imagined.

They continued to shove me in the direction of Abanyu's lair. I would have to figure out an escape plan when I met face to face with Abanyu. I imagined the room would be similar to Queen Salya's and tried to figure out other escape plans I could have used in there.

The tunnels became darker and darker the deeper we went. The torches lining the walls grew more distant as we went and I began tripping over rocks and running into walls. The garmec would hit me across the back of the head and roughly pull me to the feet every time I fell, but the last time, I involuntarily reacted and hit the garmec across the face.

The other's immediately struck me with a club and kicked me until I stopped resisting. I was tempted to grab my sword and chop their heads off, but they were leading me to Abanyu, and I needed to save that energy for him.

The garmec I hit, pushed the others out of the way and struck me with his club one last time before grabbing me by the hair and pulling me to my feet, then pushed me to keep going.

At points, I was walking in pitch darkness; I did my best not to stumble so I wouldn't get hit anymore. I could see the flames dancing against the walls in the distance and used my element to brighten them just slightly when I couldn't see at all. I didn't want to alarm the garmec, but they were too stupid to realize a slight growth in the flames.

I heard a growl, louder and more profound than any of the garmecs I had heard, that echoed through the tunnels. We were getting closer to Abanyu. Another roar echoed through the tunnels and another, all of them getting louder the closer we got.

His growls sounded angry and made my bones tremble; I just wish we could've gotten here when he was in a good mood, maybe I'd have a better chance.

We turned a corner, and I could hear the growls of garmec and the familiar sound of wood smashing against bars.

We reached a small opening, where a group of garmec stood. A smell of raw meat and blood filled my nose and made me gag, bringing another fist plummeting into the side of my head.

I winced and composed myself, trying not to breathe through my nose. The garmec noticed us and parted, giving us a front-row view of Abanyu.

He was locked away in a small cell within a larger cell, about 40 feet in diameter, his fists tightly wrapped around the bars, staring at all of us, teeth bared.

His feet were like raptors, his arms almost three times as large as Scahls but his rib cage jutted out of his body from malnourishment. Blood and scars covered his body and face. But with a closer look, he looked like the rest of the garmec that were standing by my side, torturing him. He was just overgrown.

I heard the unlocking of the outer gate and the creaking swing. A stone-like hand grabbed me by my arm and pulled me into the cell. I didn't have much time to think, I was obviously food for Abanyu, and I still needed a way to escape and find the Emerald Scale.

The gate slammed behind, and I jumped. The garmec that led me in let go of my arm and walked to the center cell where Abanyu drooled profusely and chopped his fangs together, his eyes locked on me. The garmec turned to the other once he reached the gate. Abanyu growling in his ear, he slammed his hammer against Abanyu's fingers, he immediately fell back.

The garmec had a large smile through gritted teeth. Abanyu made his way to the gate and rattled the door, "That is last strike, it's no pain as to what will come to you," Abanyu said foam building around his mouth.

I backed myself clear across the cell, waiting for something to happen. The garmec turned to the others, who were peering in intently, and bowed before releasing Abanyu.

He stormed out, almost ripping the gate off the hinges and grabbed the garmec, one hand piercing the rock like skin, thick blood oozing as the garmec screamed. Abanyu slammed the garmec into the ground twice before throwing him at the guards watching and then turned to me.

My heart dropped as the demonic eyes of Abanyu locked onto me. I acted quickly and sent a wave of fire through the bars of the cell, engulfing every garmec that stayed to watch the massacre. They let out loud growls that I hoped sounded as if they were cheering the slaughter on, as not to alert any of the other garmec.

The garmec burned brightly and made Abanyu cower for just a moment. Out of the corner of my eye, I saw a green gleam the size of a half dollar on Abanyu's chest. The green mist sparkled from the light of the fire, almost mesmerizing me, that the thing I traveled for so long for was right in front of me. But I still had Abanyu to deal with and would be able to admire its beauty when I was free.

Abanyu regained himself, and took towards me with caution, "I like nice fire."

I created another wave of fire, in an attempt to faze him again, but it did nothing. The initial shock of my abilities wore off, and Abanyu pursued me, charging like a raging bull.

I dove for my life, my face planting into the dirt floor. I jumped to my feet wielding my sword and Abanyu faced me. He charged again, and I ran for my life, bouncing off the walls and letting him plow head-first into them. Dirt would fall from the ceilings with every blow. I feared the tunnels would start collapsing. Maybe that would be the final way to get out of here, but I couldn't afford that right now.

I stood battle ready, with my sword in the air. Abanyu faced me and walked forward, breathing heavy, saliva spitting out with every exhale, "Apaku wanted you here. I am a fool for ever trusting him," he swung an open hand at me, his claws coming inches away from me; I brought my sword down, making a small cut on his rock-like skin.

He didn't seem to pay any attention to it, "You are no more a pawn than I was. It was his fire element. He found you." He began clawing viciously at me backing me up against a wall. I sliced at him with my sword to counter his attacks. The cuts made him cower and back off slightly, but I wasn't doing any kind of damage he wasn't already used to.

"I'm here aren't I? You won't be able to beat me; I'll let you live if you just let me get the Scale," I said to him to try and sound mightier than I actually was.

"Live for what? I was promised kingdom, I was promised love, all I became was a snare."

I backed straight into the wall, as he pounced towards me, seeming angrier. I was able to dodge a couple of his attacks, but his hand hit the whole side of my body and sent me flying 10 feet across the room. I landed and slid in the dirt, holding onto my sword for dear life.

He didn't waste any time; he leaped from where we were, to where I was laying. I sent up a ball of fire as he landed, hovering over me. He brushed it off at first but I continued the attacks, and he eventually fell to the ground engulfed in flames. I stood up and watched him burn, desperately trying to rip the fire off of himself.

I ran to his cell and heard a loud growl. I looked back over my shoulder, small flames still burning on him, but the majority was put out on his burnt skin. I faced him again as he charged. I sent more fire at him, but he knocked it away with his arms.

His arms engulfed more and more with every fireball, but he was determined. He plowed into me like a battering ram and sent me flying again. I landed on my back, the room spinning. In a matter of seconds I was lifted off the ground and thrown across the room. I flew through the air, thinking I was never going to land, but then collided with a wall.

I rolled around trying to see where Abanyu was before he pounced on me. When I spotted him, I attempted to build myself a wall of fire, but nothing happened. I was too discombobulated to make it work. I looked around for my sword, but I must have dropped it.

I heard garmec storming in the cage. I looked back to see my imminent demise, but they didn't even pay attention to me, they began attacking Abanyu, punching him and battering him mercilessly. I just laid there, playing dead in hopes they wouldn't see me.

They slung a chain around Abanyu's neck pulling him back towards his little cell. The most surprising part being he would not fight back.

I couldn't stand to watch it, it felt acceptable to try to kill him if he was trying to kill me, but they were just tearing him apart. I got up on one knee and swung a ring of fire around the two closest to me, throwing the garmec off of Abanyu.

The chain kept choking Abanyu while a couple of others spotted me. I did my best to throw fireballs, but nothing big enough to do any real damage. Before they were able to come after me, Abanyu snapped, crushing both of them, and throwing the one with the chain across the room, before jumping on top of him and taking an enormous bite out of its neck.

I saw Abanyu rubbing his arms in the dirt, putting out the last bit of fire. I tried to stand up but my legs gave out, and I fell back to the ground. Abanyu stomped towards me, picking up my sword on all fours.

I sat up and watched him closing in on me quickly. I looked for a way out. My limbs were like Jell-O, and my mind was lost. The garmecs outside the cell still burned lightly.

I thought if I could summon just enough concentration I could use the pre-existing fire to consume Abanyu. But it was too late. Abanyu stood tall over me, sword still in hand.

"There will always be more pain for me even if I kill you here. I was here to give you a direction to death. You are in Apaku's hands now."

"What do you mean?" I was able to choke out.

"Apaku brought you here, he sent the fire to find you."

"Why did he want the fire element to find me?"

Abanyu paused for a moment, letting out a few small breaths, "It's not my fight anymore." Bruised and bloodied, with the last bit of energy he had, he lifted the sword to his neck, "You know not what you've gotten yourself into," and sliced into it.

Blood squirted across the room as he fell onto his back. Blood pooled up for only a few more moments until there wasn't a single breath of life left.

I sat confused, not sure what happened. The victory was in my grasp, but it wasn't what I expected. Abanyu's scarred and bloody corpse was in front of me; however, no questions of my being there were answered.

I heard chaos in the tunnels and had to continue without thinking anymore. I loosened Abanyu's grip on my sword and put it back in its sheath. I knelt down next to Abanyu's lifeless body, examining the sparkling green scale, made up of jagged edges and a swirling green mist, the color of a brightly shined emerald. I wedged my fingers underneath the Scale, peeling it back until it released its grip onto Abanyu.

The tunnels began to shake and creak; dirt fell from the ceiling and walls. I feared that I might have taken a booby trap. The tunnels were going to collapse.

I ran out of the cell and could see garmec running for their lives as well. I hung back as long as I could so I could follow them out. The tunnels shook more and more violently; a sound rang through the tunnels as if there was something tunneling all throughout the mountains.

The first time through the tunnels was hard enough just not being able to see, but with the violent shakes and shifts of the walls and floors I could barely stay on my feet for more than a few steps.

I took my chance and started following the garmec. I was able again to shield myself with fire and plan B came into effect, except I was blocking the trailing garmec from getting out, for one I didn't want them catching up to me and two I was going to have enough garmec to deal with if I got out of the tunnels.

I lagged as far back as I could from the garmec leading me out, in hopes they wouldn't see me.

They led me straight to the opening of the tunnel, I could see daylight again, and the closer I got I could hear the commotion outside was just as violent as it was inside. I had no choice but to get out of the tunnels before they collapsed though.

When I emerged out of the tunnel the light cast a white shade over the entire world until I could readjust my eyesight to beautiful, blossoming trees. The mountains covered in green and the ground beneath my feet covered in pristine green grass. I stood drowning out the commotion and taking in the beauty.

I looked down at the Scale in my hand; it was the actual Emerald Scale. The victory was starting to set in until a loud thud landed right before me. I looked up to see Adipm, eyeing the Scale. I unsheathed my sword and held it up high, prepared to strike Adipm down.

"You mustn't fight with the Emerald Scale!" He yelled at me. Scahl landed just behind him and grabbed onto his shoulder.

"Keep him safe!" Scahl yelled at Adipm, then turned and ran into what I now noticed was a battle before me.

"Don't worry, I will get you out of here," he told me.

I gave him a blank look and took a closer look at the battle happening before us. I could see an army of men and women who must have been fighting the entire time I was in there.

Garmec were falling in high numbers, but I still had to help them finish the battle.

"We have to help them," I yelled to Adipm, still struggling to regain trust with him.

He grabbed onto me, "I'll explain as soon as we are in safety. Please just follow me, we need to protect the Scale."

He dragged me along his old path, which was now full of green bushes and lively trees; we scaled back up the mountain as fast as we could.

"Is Abanyu --?" I cut him off knowing what he wanted to know.

"Yes, the tunnels are collapsing and will bury him," I said.

"The tunnels won't collapse, the garmec are well known as tunnellers."

"I heard them collapsing though," I said offensively.

"You heard the roots of a thousand trees coming back to life." Adipm just smiled and continued to push me up the mountain until we reached the overlook where we first found the garmec.

I watched as they fought, the battle coming to a close. The view from here was completely different now.

"Where's Farley?" I asked Adipm when I remember I had left him behind.

"Down there," he said nodding to the battle, "don't worry he will be fine. He's quite the fighter."

"I know," I smiled, "he's gotten me out of trouble more than once."

I relaxed, finally being able to say that I made it through, the Emerald Scale still clutched in my hand. The victory did not feel as great as I had hoped though. My final encounter with Abanyu felt like anything but a noble victory.

I didn't know what to think, I still questioned Adipm's loyalty, I went in believing he was the enemy and came out to an ally. "So you're an ally?" I asked him, "Can you explain why you gave us up to the garmec?"

He nodded, "The Fade placed me in these mountains many years ago. I was instructed to wait and gain the trust of the garmec, until the right warrior would show up to slay Abanyu. It was my duty to find a way to get you into the tunnels, face to face with him."

"You couldn't have filled us in on the plan?" I asked.

"Your duty was not to be a part of the act, but live it. You would have never gotten through the tunnels without the garmec leading you."

I looked out over the battlefield from safety, "What about everyone else? How did they get here?"

"They were waiting as well, in nearby towns, posing as villagers, there were other "Adipms," scattered throughout the mountains. Every once in a while the villagers in Durbshin would catch sight of us. Even the miners from Durbshin that found us had to become convinced to become part of the plan and keep us secret."

"It worked though, after all these years. It worked." I asked.

"It won't work again though. The only reason it worked this time was because we fell off Apaku's radar."

"What do you mean?"

"We were the calm before the storm. Apaku knows that you have the Emerald Scale by now, there will be no more calm in D'Hanin."

"How could he possibly know that I have the Emerald Scale?"

"Apaku will know about you and Abanyu's death, just by the green in the trees; everyone will. This was the easiest part of your journey. Death and despair will continue to flood D'Hanin until Apaku is dead," he looked down at me sullenly, "this is a moment to be shared in joy, but let us not forget that the war has officially begun. Nothing will be kept in secret, and trust will be only had between your closest allies."

In my mind, I didn't believe there ever was a secret to my being there. Apaku sent for me. He controlled the fire element that brought me here, the one that clung to my heart.

Apaku had much more control than what people knew; Abanyu took more secrets to the grave than what anyone was prepared for.

An eruption of voices rang out and the same chant I had heard at the end of my first battle, I heard again faintly in the distance. "To Apaku! We send the ashes of your warriors into the sky to show you; we will not fall to a dark summoner! And though you have taken some of our own with yours, we pray that they know they have not gone in vain and will forever be remembered throughout D'Hanin for the rest of history!" They had finished the last of the garmec on the mountains.

Adipm stood up and let out a cry of his own, thrusting his fist in the air. I stood up alongside him and held the Emerald Scale into the air under the setting sun. I only hoped that they could see what they had just fought for, however it didn't bring me any peace.

# 22

## THE HAND THAT GUIDES ME

Adipm and I returned back down the mountain to Durbshin. I enjoyed the peace that Mt. B'tuul had brought after the war, the loudest of the noise being the rustling of the trees as they flaunted their branches filled with bright green leaves for the first time in a long time. This was not the same mountain I initially traveled; nothing was remotely recognizable in the best of ways.

On the way down I had a moment that I believe was a Plantation Element reaching out to me. A strong wind blew, rustling the leaves and tilting the trees, the ground creaking beneath me, creating a voice that Adipm did not hear like I heard, *"The Plantations will never forget you.*

We traveled through

the lush forest for hours, searching for a break in the leaves so we could see how far away we were. But, before we had a chance to find the break we saw lights of the small town through the trees, and eventually small noises until we finally found our clearing and could see the whole city less than 50 yards away.

"It's much quieter than I would expect after the events that just took place, maybe word hasn't gotten around yet."

I looked up at Adipm, "How many miners from Durbshin did you say went to fight?"

Adipm looked down on me, "There was at least 30 of them." He looked back over the still city, "Don't assume the worst just yet, we've killed an entire army of garmec and scared the rest off for miles, there's no trouble here," he said precariously.

Adipm continued down, a small knot formed in my stomach, but I shook it off. We've been through enough trouble to get to this point and succeeded; I had to have high hopes at this point.

The moon towered over the town as we reached it, the streets lit only by signs and the little light that showed through the windows of buildings and houses. We approached the bar, the unusual silence still cautioning us. Adipm grabbed onto the handle and slowly peaked in as he opened the door. It was business as usual inside, a few people sat in groups, a bartender manning the drinks, and the Fade seemingly out of nowhere occupied the back table in the darkest part of the room.

A smile quickly grew on my face, and a sense of relief washed over me, as he stood up before us with his arms outstretched. "Fade," I exclaimed as I crossed the room, and hugged him, feeling proud. He pushed me back with both hands on my shoulders, "When did you get here? Nobody told me I'd see you again so soon," I said.

"I told you I'd see you on the other side, didn't I," he smiled. "You and Scahl made quite the commotion on your way here," he smiled naturally, just as happy to see me.

"Well we could've used your help on more than one occasion. Why didn't you just come with us?"

"My name is too well known throughout D'Hanin. If word that I was traveling through D'Hanin had gotten back to Apaku, there would've been unnecessary complications for you."

Knowing what I knew now, I didn't think it would've mattered to Apaku that the Fade was traveling with us, my mood quckly declined as I was obligated to tell the Fade what I knew.

"Apaku already knew about me. Abanyu was not what we thought."

The Fade rarely looked surprised, he always took a look of interest over surprise.

"Abanyu was not amongst Apaku's faithful followers, he was simply just a prisoner, burdened with the Emerald Scale. I did nothing to get the Scale back."

"Finn, please don't worry. Whatever happened in the tunnels does not matter. What matters is that you have the Emerald Scale now."

"You don't understand, Abanyu told me Apaku was the one that sent the Fire Element. I would not be here if Apaku didn't want me here. He knows I will fail."

"Do you have the Emerald Scale?" The Fade asked, reaching out his hand I pulled it from my pocket and placed it in his palm.

I looked confused for a moment, looking down at the Scale I could see the emerald color fading. The Fade pushed my sleeve up, placing the Scale on my upper forearm. It pinched but eventually felt natural.

I could feel a presence within me flow to that spot, the emerald mist swirling faster and brighter than what I saw when it was on Abanyu's chest.

"Your first portion of the journey is now complete. You have taken the role that Keahi had put on himself and with the Emerald Scale a part of you the element will flourish." He rolled my sleeve back down, covering the Emerald Scale before looking back up to me, "You have not failed, Finn."

"Not yet." I said sullenly.

"What Abanyu is claiming, that Apaku somehow harnessed his own element to find you, is not possible. Keahi is, and will always be, the only man to ever harness an element."

"I believe Abanyu, there was something about it all that we need to move forward cautiously on."

"Of course," the Fade said, "It has always been the plan to move forward cautiously, whatever Abanyu says you need to put in the back of your mind and just relax for a moment," the Fade leaned back, "Now listen, we just got the Emerald Scale back, and we are overjoyed, but there are Apaku Worshippers who will now be entering your life under the radar, wanting to stop you in the worst of ways. Like the man speaking to the bartender right now." The Fade motioned for me to look.

I slowly looked over my shoulder, and a man sat at the bar, covered in dirt and scars all over his face and hands. His hair flowed down his back in every direction, darkened by the mines. He spoke softly and slowly to Batty, who looked hostile.

The Fade grabbed me by the arm, bringing my gaze back to our table.

"As I said, tonight, ignore him. I do not believe he will bring harm to you. He knows who I am and he knows I know who he is."

"Who is he?" I questioned.

"That man is the Arcane, the former trainer in the Northern Curve. He formerly trained alongside the rest of us to find potential Keahi's Warriors."

"What do you mean the rest of us?" I asked.

"There are a total of 5 trainers, each one assigned a main curve to train Keahi's Warriors to protect each curve."

"So why is he here?"

"After Keahi's death, as you know, I made the decision to freeze the warriors. It did not come without help of the other trainers, including the Arcane, who outwardly hated the idea. He gave up his curve and fell right into the palm of Apaku."

"Why is he here then?" I asked again.

"He is here because of Adipm, most likely to send a message. You have unleashed so much good in this world, Finn, but with that came so much darkness, much worse than what you have experienced at this point. You are no longer able to go into this journey alone, we will be by your side, but it will be up to you to protect yourself, pushing yourself to greater lengths than what I was able to train you in."

I nodded, "I'll be fine Fade; I had plenty of training of my own in the past months, I've been through and seen a lot of bad things, I will go forward with whatever this world gives me."

The Fade turned his focus to Adipm, "The others should be here soon, are you ready, my old friend, to continue this journey. You'll have been amongst the few to have stood amongst the Arcane as an ally and word will spread like wildfire of your stance."

Adipm just smiled, "They'll want to kill me as much as any of the rest of us, I'm ready to return to this world, I'm done watching over it in silence."

"We'll be glad to have you back," the Fade said as he lifted his glass to Adipm, "and so a night of rejoice shall begin," and he finished off his drink as the silence of the small town finally broke by the footsteps and chatter of a dozen people entering the city. I turned in my chair, hoping to see Torkie and Scahl and all the other soldiers. Batty prepared the drinks as he expected it too. The sense of hostility on his face wholly transformed into excitement, due in part, of the absence of the Arcane.

I turned back to the Fade to see if he noticed too.

"He won't be back tonight, enjoy it this one time."

The door swung open, and they all were back. The bar erupted, louder and louder as they all piled in ready to celebrate.

Even a man from the mines had already begun drinking with Scahl as they journeyed back to the bar after the battle but sobered up enough to stumble over to see me. I started to stand up, but he slammed a large hand on my shoulder bringing me back to my seat and got down to eye level with me, "I knew ya could do it, from the moment I saw ya's three stumbling in that night." He said, "Ya've given all o' us hope again, and it's just tha beginnin'!" He roared back to the crowd splashing his drink on the floor.

Then without being able to contain his excitement, Farley came bursting through the doors.

"Ay, get that animal out of 'ere!" Batty yelled as he watched his glasses falling off the tables onto the floor.

Farley ran up to me, digging his head into my chest so I would wrap my arms around him. I tried my best to calm him down, but shared in his excitement to see him back safe. Scahl and Torkie made their way over to help me as they dragged him out of the bar, "It's alright big guy, you did good, but there's no place for a toradrac in a bar," Scahl said to him, patting his back side as he walked back out the doors.

Scahl and Torkie came back to greet me and join in celebrating, however I was still bothered. I showed off the Emerald Scale, and told them of the valiant battle between Abanyu and I, leaving out Abanyu's idea of Apaku harnessing the fire element to find me, someone he knew for sure would fail. I wanted them to be happy and enjoy the victory, no matter how it came to me. I wanted them to continue having hope; we couldn't afford any negativity in pursuing the rest of the Scales.

However, as quickly as the party started, it became dark. The Fade approached me calmly but urgently, "Finn."

I suddenly leaned down on the table grabbing my chest, my heart feeling as though someone was squeezing it. I could barely catch my breath. I looked up at the Fade while I held onto my chest, "What's going on? I think I'm having a heart attack."

"I was wrong, Apaku had more followers in the mountains, they are trekking off the mountain as we speak. The battle is not over." He whispered in my ear, "Take the river south and exit at the falls. Take Torkie and Farley with you."

Another burning sensation pumped through my heart, crippling me at the table. "Fade!" I yelled as I grabbed my chest. The bar became quiet as they stared at me.

"Everyone! Prepare for battle!" The Fade yelled over my cries for help. The bar erupted, swords being wielded, Scahl and Torkie jumping over the table. The Fade turned back to me, "Finn!" I could see him yelling but no sound leaving his mouth. The bar got quite as I struggled to get a clear vision.

My veins burned as the fire coursed through them. For a moment the noise came rushing back and I regained my vision.

At that moment the doors of the bar were ripped off, the noise in the bar turned to panic immediately. "Avoid the Arcane wherever you go, he will be watching you, just stay safe," the Fade yelled at me, as he prepared to fight, a group of people rushed us, similar to the kind of people we encountered in Fliagenré.

Swords were unsheathed, Batty dove from behind the bar tackling a man that was as dirty as the

302

Arcane, and Scahl threw tables out of the way. I backed myself into a wall as everyone began fighting.

I scanned the bar for Torkie, still clutching my chest; my heart burned as I thought about Abanyu saying, *"Apaku's element found me."* The burning sensation in my heart was released through my body, my vision faltered again, nearing a blackout, however, before I closed my eyes a glimpse of wings and fire came towards me again. I closed my eyes before it hit me and the world went quiet again.

I was in the same nothingness I was when I entered D'Hanin. I was no longer in the bar. Everything was black, but I could feel the wind blowing past me, nothing was holding me up, and I wasn't holding onto anything. I couldn't even tell if I had a body anymore, it was as if it was just my soul flying through the unknown. However, this time someone pulled me away and when I opened my eyes again, I saw Alina. I couldn't concentrate on the surroundings and couldn't figure out where I was. I could only see Alina as she held a beautifully blossomed flower up to her nose before handing it to me, "I thought you might like to see the beauty this world actually has to offer," she said.

"I saw it long before I even left Kautun," I said looking into her eyes. There was nothing else, just her and I, no other noise, no other sights, nothing else to feel.

She blushed and gave me a long intimate hug. "I wish I could say this whole war was over with this, it almost feels like it, but I know we've got a long road from here." She stepped back, with her hands still on my shoulder and looked into my eyes."

I caught myself gazing at her and didn't know what to say, and just let something out as to avoid the awkwardness now that I realized what I was doing. "I won't let you guys down; I'll keep fighting until I have all the Scales."

Of course, it sounded more heroic in my head, I travel this entire world, fight countless garmec, and I capture a protected Scale, but I still can't seem heroic in front of a pretty girl. A kid who just won capture the flag could probably sound more heroic than me. But either way, it still made her smile.

"It's not just about you getting the Scales back anymore, it's all of us, and if we can't do it, you're still remembered as the one who gave us hope to go into it. It's right now or never again will we see a good D'Hanin."

I held up the flower; I almost forgot she gave it to me. I slid the stem of it into a tear in my shirt, like a boutonniere. "There's no going back for me either; I'm all in, to the very end."

I looked into her eyes one last time, but something was different, a light came from her eyes as she stood there. It was dim at first but slowly kept coming into view until it consumed her entire eyes.

She began to fade; it was all just an illusion. Before she was completely gone she grabbed me by the hand; however, as I looked down to it something had changed. It was a familiar hand, but it was not the same one that guided mine along the back of a unicorn. I was finally able to open my eyes again, and when I did, I looked up along her arm all the way to her face; it was my mother's. I was home.

# DOMINICK RUSSO

BEGINS HIS WRITING JOURNEY
WITH KEAHI'S LEGACY, A SERIES
THAT TAKES PLACE IN THE FANTASY
WORLD OF D'HANIN. AN IDEA THAT
WAS INITIALLY SPARKED OVER 15
YEARS AGO HAS BEEN IN DEVELOP-
MENT FOR THE PAST 6 YEARS WHILE
HE ATTEMPTED TO FIND TIME
AROUND HIS DAY JOB OF SELLING
ICE CREAM TO THE MASSES.

YOU CAN FOLLOW THE DEVELOP-
MENT OF THE STORIES AND
DOMINICK'S WRITING JOURNEY AT
UNICORNSNEST.COM.

www.ingramcontent.com/pod-product-compliance
Lightning Source LLC
Chambersburg PA
CBHW030246030726
47493CB00023B/612